No Good Lie

A psychological thriller

Claire Stibbe

Bookpreneur

Claire Stibbe's Publications
The Detective Temeke Crime Series
The 9th Hour, Night Eyes, Past Rites
Easy Prey, Dead Cold, Silent Admirer

Psychological Thrillers
Into The Silent Sea
No Good Lie
Play Him, Play Her

To Jeff,
for every thing
and
Jamie, my miracle

1

FREYA

IF I HADN'T MET him, everything would have been different.

A thick head of dark hair, an infectious grin. Now I can't shake the feeling that someone might have seen us.

I have a routine before I leave the house at 7.00 am: keys and phone in yoga pants, torch in backpack. I check the street from the kitchen window, and again from the front door. Always focusing on personal safety, always on the lookout. It's worth getting up before dawn, because it's my own chunk of quiet time where I can run through the streets unseen. Some people sleep in, squint at the alarm clock and rush for the bus and I'll bet they're berating themselves for missing the best part of the day.

A salt wind blows in from the open door and an owl screeches, sending a rhythm of warning hoots. Jack says I rarely smile unless I'm running, otherwise my features are blank and unreachable, and he can never tell what I'm thinking.

There's the tree with the sign that says HAVE YOU SEEN

ME? The poster is half lit by the lantern outside number 26. Elisabeth Sanders. Long black hair and a perfect smile. A daily reminder, as if she's saying, *I'm still lost. I'm still out there.*

A slash of light between the curtains of a neighbour's house. Gayle Daniels is frowning at me. Being the daughter of an MP you'd expect her to be a snob. But she's not. Like me, she keeps herself to herself. If we meet at the post box, we rarely talk which suits me just fine. People tolerate me, but they are genuinely fond of Jack. He's the extrovert, always stopping to say hi. While I wave a tight-lipped greeting and run along the pavement as fast as I can.

I pass the last house on the corner, every light on inside. Then come the glass fronted flats with the strong scent of juniper, the type that sticks. I run downhill to the promenade, lamplight slicing through a sea mist.

Exercise is good for the body and mind. An hour a day helps me to manage my stress. I handle incoming calls for the *Bournemouth Daily Echo*, which matches the reputation of larger newspapers although the pay may lag several notches behind. Given my lack of qualifications, I class myself as the lowest of the low. If we ever move out of this building and into smaller satellite offices, I'll probably lose the job altogether.

The ringing of my phone shatters the silence and stops me short. It could be Liv asking me to come in early. It could be Jack. The screen lights with a series of numbers. No name.

This is the calm before the storm.

Then a second text streaks across the screen.

Everything that happens now is entirely for your benefit. We both know it's the right thing to do.

Is it a wrong number? Or is someone messing with me? I'm guessing the first.

I ignore it and set off again. Today, despite the good weather, there's an air of grimness. The clouds are ruffled like a giant quilt above the rooftops and there's a creeping north-easterly wind that burns my cheeks. An ache shifts from the base of my throat to my stomach and I wonder if all this running takes me away from the memories and the guilt. There's been something in Jack's voice lately, a harsh burn of anger. I always remain silent. There is little I can say.

When I reach the pier, the silence disappears. Water slurps around the pillars, seaweed bobbing on the waves. There's nothing for miles, just sky and sea and a sliver of light between them. A tanker skulks on the horizon, too far out to tell if it's moving. I usually stay here for a minute or two before setting off through the cold October air, but I find myself looking for signs of danger, the snapping of a twig, a distant howl. It sends me running back towards the road that cuts between the dunes. Some knotted place inside me hates myself for being so weak.

Rounding the corner near the restaurant, I catch something in the corner of my eye. I wouldn't have noticed if the moon hadn't come out from behind a cloud. There it is, a pinprick of brightness against the dunes. Is someone there?

A clatter rings out and a rock bursts through a snarl of Marram grass, sending up a squabble of seagulls. Near a straggle of beach huts, there is a shift – someone crouching like an injured animal. My heart kicks out a rhythm and I see tiny puffs of my panicky breath. Shadows are fickle things. They'll get to me if I let them.

The seagulls are mobbing and diving now. Instead of the sappy green scent of nearby woods, it smells like there are a million dead and rotting things. I put my hand over my mouth and breathe hard into my palm. I can't help feeling the weight of hidden eyes as if someone has been creeping through the net-veined ferns. My skin itches with the urge to run – every muscle wants to, but I don't.

Under the street lamp, a tangle of netting flutters and I think it's a baby seal, one of those creamy ones with grey faces you see in Poole Harbour. Either that or a gleaming mass of bass and whiting. But it's something else, something I shouldn't be seeing, hideously translucent in the moonlight. Through the feathery brush of shock, I make out the trail of an arm, hair matted with sand. Every part of me wants to say, *hello, hello, are you OK?* but all I can scream is, *Oh my God, oh my God.* I want to run, I want to get the hell away from her, but I know I can't.

She needs my help. Even though terror writhes through me, I make myself touch her, two fingers on her throat above where a cord pinches her neck. No movement, no life. Her eyes don't blink in the morning sun. Every wisp of air has been torn from her lungs and the stench tells me how long she's been gone.

I shuffle backwards towards the beach, stumbling and gulping fresh air. This isn't happening. It can't be. But I know it is and what needs to be done. Fumbling with my phone, I dial 999. Relief spreads through me. A voice. Someone to help.

'Ambulance.' The words sting in my throat and my mind races. 'There's a woman. She's here... on the beach and she's not breathing. No, no, she's gone. Yes. Dead.'

They're asking for details; my name, where I am. Is anyone else with me? That's when I turn back to look at her again. The creeping dawn highlights every detail; her bare feet and the colour of her nail varnish. Scuff marks extend to the promenade, monstrous tracks she could not have brought on herself. There's a ribbon on her wrist, snapping in the wind, indecently red. It's this feature that catapults me to the past.

I imagine she's my Kate and I'm pleading with her to wake up. A play dead joke. A twitch. The flicker of an eyelid, the tremor of a smile at the corner of her mouth. I have a sudden pang of loss; the past tumbling into my head, that feeling that I can't go back in time and bring my daughter back. My thoughts are running into each other and making no sense.

Tears well hot in my eyes and it feels like ages before I'm roused by a far-away sound. Then it's loud and close and real. A bristle of figures runs towards me, hands lifting me out of that dark place.

'Are you OK?' the officer asks.

I consider this for a moment and nod. 'I'm Freya. Freya Thorne.'

'Was there anyone else about?' His eyes roam up and down my face and I'm briefly distracted by the woman they're trying to revive. 'When you're ready, Freya. Take your time.'

'No. I mean, that doesn't mean there wasn't anyone here. I just didn't see anyone. I'm sorry. I know that's not very helpful.'

I want to ask him if she's the woman in the papers, the face on every billboard. But this face is puffy and sad, and there's a lump in my throat as hard as a stone.

'I think I'm going to be...' I push him away, heaving and coughing until there's nothing left in my stomach

He takes my arm and we walk to his car, passing two men in white paper suits. While the officer takes down my address and telephone number, I notice a scar above his left eyebrow and flecks of rust in his eyes. He inspects my hands and stuffs my hoodie in an evidence bag, says it may have touched the victim and immediate scene. He hands me a baggy sweatshirt from the boot and a can of Coke.

'You should drink this.'

I take a sip and almost choke. Coughing, I clear my throat.

'It's Elisabeth Sanders, isn't it? I mean, it looks like her.'

'I couldn't say, love.'

The static of a radio tears my thoughts away – a hiccup of code. The officer turns his back, and I notice his overshoes as he walks away. For now, I lean against the car seat, squinting at a narrow line of dunes where two officers are keeping dog walkers and runners away. Crime scene investigators erect a tent and she's covered at last. There are no other sounds but flapping tape and the drag and thump of the sea.

Volunteers, police and coastguard have searched hundreds of miles and now this. I think of her mother and I think of the police officer. It will consume them as much as it's consuming me.

After Kate died, I barely got through the first week. I didn't know how I would get through life, knowing my daughter was never coming home. But the difference is, she had fallen from a boat. Air searchers had a position where she was last seen and calculated tide and wind to make an approximate trace. But here, the police are preserving a crime scene, a murder, where a young woman's body will go to a mortuary for a post-mortem.

The officer's voice crashes through my thoughts, his name tag says Petersen. 'You'll need to give a voluntary statement at the police station. Have you got someone to pick you up?'

'No. Actually, I live up there. So, not far.'

I want to write an account on my phone to keep it fresh in my mind and I want to call Jack. This is nothing like Kate. I *know* it's nothing like Kate. The police never said hers was a murder. No matter what I might think.

Flashes of light burst through the edge of my vision and my mind tracks back to the coroner's photographs; sand and seaweed and long black hair.

A group of fishermen found her on the beach. There was a bone-deep gash on her forehead and a red ribbon tied to her wrist.

past. I've watched you many times. Sometimes on the street, sometimes at the beach. Little chance meetings with your lover. He's the type to pick up on subtle messages and non-verbal cues. He picked up on yours. What's it worth to keep a secret like that?

I'm not a creep, if that's what you're thinking. Just because I've been close enough to smell your hair doesn't make me dangerous. I'm not here to make matters worse, but I'm asking you to back off the Sanders woman. A few more nudges will tell you how serious I am.

Edward.

'How long have you lived here?' she asks.

'Since I was a child.'

'And your husband?'

I take a few seconds to answer, knowing that if I lose the hostility, I'm more likely to gain her trust. 'He's retired now, flies model aeroplanes at Wimborne. It's the closest he gets to a runway.'

She moves the pen on her notepad, just so, constantly adjusting the angle as if she's shuffling files into neat piles.

It's hard to think of her throwing someone to the ground to the jangle of cuffs or questioning a suspect. Yet, here she is, talking to me. In a strange, loaded moment, neither one of us breathes. I want to mask the awkwardness, but I can't think of anything to say.

'Finding Elisabeth Sanders must have brought everything back,' she says. 'I'm sorry. I understand how terrible it must have been. I read Kate's file.'

'Then you'll agree there are similarities.'

Patti leans back and crosses her arms. The effect is vaguely imposing. 'I'm not following. Kate's death was an accident.'

'Well, yes, but... it's odd, that's all. They were both found on the beach. Both wearing red ribbons.'

'I wouldn't let it play with your imagination.'

But it does. It plays on it in the worst possible way, hiding behind every door and teasing me into thinking I'm next. I want Patti to find this man. Whether he's a pervert in a white van or the mayor, I don't care. She's read my statement. She has all the information she needs.

'There have been some thefts in the area,' she says, dropping the letter into a pouch.

'What kind of thefts? Or aren't I allowed to ask?'

'Cars mostly. Make sure you don't leave yours running outside the house. As far as this is concerned,' she says, tapping the pouch. 'I want you to keep a log of any malicious calls or texts. Don't answer them.'

When she leaves, everything goes quiet. The sequence of events of how I found Elisabeth is fading, and my memory has gaps of time where my imagination fills in the rest. It's as dangerous as it is confusing.

I call Jack. 'Do you know anyone called Edward?'

'Edward? Edward who?'

'So, no.'

'Listen, love, I'm nearly home. Remember, we're going to Liv's tonight.'

He hangs up before I can tell him we need to talk.

Silence, agonising at the best of times, feels exposing. Where before, the house was a place to breathe and relax, now it no longer feels like a sanctuary. I listen to a symphony of creaks and groans, as if the timbers expand every time the walls take a breath. I check my phone and there's a text from the same unknown number.

Think calling the police was a good idea?

his arrogance in the letter. The dread that we may come face-to-face when I least expect it.

'They say strangulation takes exceptional strength,' Theo says. 'Bastard has such terrible regard for people. Women in particular.'

'I think we've heard enough,' Jack says, swooping into the conversation. 'I hear you won another award, Liv. Here's to the loveliest lady ranter. What is it now? Feature Writer?'

'Women's Prize.' Liv lifts her glass. 'Actually, I've been writing a new series called, *A Business Affair: are office romances over?* Crushes on colleagues, conflicts of interest, that kind of thing. Have you read it, Freya?'

'I haven't.' The words tumble out of my mouth. 'I mean, I'd like to, but what with everything else—'

'It was in response to my trainee reporter and the reasons she left,' Liv says. 'People are still gossiping about it.'

Theo tops up Jack's wine glass. I put a hand over mine. More than once, I turn and catch Theo's gaze trained on me, only to quickly flit away.

The discussion turns to the new right-arm fast bowler in England's cricket team, his use of reverse-swing and yorkers, whatever that means. I can't help studying his vocal tone and body language, and mentally logging all this distances me from the subject of ropes and letters and office affairs.

The sour flavour of wine dances on my tongue and I try to swallow my way through it. As Liv and Jack go into the kitchen to fetch more wine, I feel a clamping sensation in my lungs as each breath brings me closer to the past, squeezing sideways through time, almost nearing a blackout.

'Penny for them?'

I feel Theo's hawkish gaze behind his glasses, his eyes darting from my neckline to my hemline. My chest tightens and I can't help wondering if his interest in me goes beyond the platonic. If it does, he's shit out of luck.

'I'm dreading Elisabeth's inquest,' I say. 'There's no way you can prepare for a thing like that.'

'I expect you're also thinking about Kate.'

'I always think about Kate.'

I feel the familiar plucking sensation deep in my chest. Theo knows the part of me that has died inside. My heart aches for her – my beautiful daughter with her endless laughter and sweet-smelling skin. The coroner's report identified her through dental records and stated blunt force trauma, which matched the boat's side where she fell. There was another wound, consistent with a propeller blade.

'Who was that man you were talking to in Sainsbury's?' he asks.

'I didn't go shopping this morning.'

'Not today. Yesterday. Rather striking.'

Theo tilts his head up, as if searching the skies for a non-existent star and sucks in his cheeks, the prelude to uncontrolled laughter. Somehow he thinks my answers are funny, or futile, or both.

It comes in waves – the twisting in my gut, a blush of shame.

on a rain-soaked street. A squeal of brakes and the car veered off the road and slammed into the barrier, headlights blazing. Glass shattered, and two dazed passengers stared out through the frame of an empty windscreen.

He staggered to her side of the car. The front bumper, impaled on the barrier, had lifted the car almost four feet off the ground and the tyres were still spinning. It took three powerful tugs before the door groaned and popped. Tiny yellow sparks flickered under the chassis, a slick of oil about to ignite.

He reached in and yanked the keys from the ignition. Freya and her husband were groaning and disorientated. He wanted to take her then; it was the perfect time. As he leant over and popped the seatbelt, he felt her hand on his shoulder briefly before it flopped to her knee. But a distant shout caused him to rethink his strategy.

He left her on the pavement and ran to his car. His bumper had caught on hers and, shifting into reverse, it took a few seconds before his car broke free. It wasn't until he got home that he found her bracelet had snagged on his sleeve.

It takes Edward a moment to transition to the present. As an anonymous source, he's in half a mind to submit raw video to the *Daily Echo* of Freya finding Elisabeth Sanders' body with the headline: *Front desk receptionist up to her neck in scandal.* Now, that would make a great story.

He listens to the wind pulsing off the sea, tousling an alcove of evergreens at the corner of the street. Through the branches of the tree above, he sees a full moon. It's insanely beautiful tonight.

The cottage appears out of the darkness, dormer windows jutting out of the sloping roof like two little dog kennels. The porch light casts a weak circle on the doormat. A cat cowers away from a spit of rain.

He moves down the alleyway between Freya's house and a neighbour's. Pressing his back against the wall where the shadows are the darkest, he inspects the planks in the back fence, two of which are cracked near the fasteners. Holding a small torch between his teeth, he crouches near the gravel boards and finds two protruding screws, which he removes with a pair of locking pliers. The third screw head has sheared off completely and taking a utility knife, he grinds away the wood. Clamping the pliers to the shaft, he twists anti-clockwise and works it loose. By separating the boards wide enough, he squeezes through, before levering them back together again.

A strong smell of rush matting greets him as he opens the back door. The fridge hums. The clock ticks. He passes a picture of Freya on the wall, loves it when she smiles. She doesn't have to be happy all the time, but she smiled the first time he saw her and it unlocked something in him, a feeling, a memory, and right then, he knew there was no going back.

Wind squeals around the eaves and a window rattles upstairs. He slots each creak into his memory and stalks towards her bedroom. Moonlight slinks through the window and slashes the opposite wall. It is bright enough to see the contents of the drawer he opens.

He detects jasmine with notes of freesia and rose. He opens a small leather box and finds emerald earrings, pear cut, antique, and a small photograph by the mirror; a woman with olive skin and a slash of eyeliner. She could be Nisha if he squinted hard enough. He rams both into the pouch of his hoodie, along with a tube of lipstick.

He peers through the open bathroom door, inhaling the scent of Icelandic moss soap. He imagines steam, skin, and Freya. Kidnapping a woman is reckless, especially if she is naked and slippery with soap. Yet he finds himself at a crossroads. He must sell his house and give notice to his lodger. How does he think that's going to go?

Downstairs, the blinds are closed and a small lamp glows on the kitchen shelf. He pours himself a glass of wine, returning to that ill-formed thought.

Did she recognise him?

Any injuries caused by ramming her car weren't serious, much less fatal. Nobody could bring a charge of grievous bodily harm or psychiatric GBH against him.

He smears his lips with Angel Matt lipstick and smokes a cigarette, tapping ash into the sink. After he's finished, he drops the butt in the bin and leaves the packet in a drawer. His eyes swim in and out of focus for a second and he marvels at the world Freya sees.

A redhead paces about in the flat opposite, unable to sleep.

He catches the sliver of her darting like a pale exotic snake in the window. He's seen her sitting in the tropical gardens, a wisp of smoke rising from a cigarette. It's the way she watches the street that bothers him, like she's watching now.

Edward knows the woman better than she remembers. A nightclub back alley, hooking him up when there's a drought. They don't share names. No one does. But she's a known treasure trove of 'roids and vallies and some new concoction she's been harping on about. He doesn't need a weather forecaster to know which way the weed blows in Westbourne.

He moves to the back door and surveys the garden. Pinching his fingers around a joint, he takes a few hits, studying the back fence for any signs of tampering. All planks in a neat row, nothing out of place. Flicking the joint into the wind, he watches it glow for a few seconds before it hisses in the grass.

Freya is always under his skin. He wants to be under hers.

8

FREYA

IN FORTY-THREE YEARS, I'VE lived nowhere other than Bournemouth. Layers of memories have been made here. Lives lived. Yet everything could shatter in an instant.

When I think of the beach, I see white sands and a pier that reaches out to sea. Windy shoreline walks and Kate complaining about how cold it was. I'd wrap a towel around my little girl, pulling her against me.

'It hurts, Mummy. It's prickly.'

Then I realised I was rubbing sand into that tiny little body. So I simply held her. Warm and safe. Jack would tell us stories of pirates who moored their ships at the centre point between Sandbanks Beach and Hengistbury Head. Sometimes, he'd take us out at night to hide in the dunes because those same pirates flashed their running lights at the smugglers on the beach. You could make out ghostly rigging through the binoculars on a cloudy evening. So he told us.

Liv drives me home to Burnham Road and tells me she will

deal with the towing company. No amount of arguing will change her mind.

'You're to take as much time off as you need,' she says.

What she means is there's no point turning up at work looking like a domestic violence victim. Our Editor, Drew Martin, has organised a photo day, which I'm glad to be missing.

I keep reminding myself I'm lucky to have a job. My background in hotel and catering, and occasionally playing the fiddle in a local pub, is not what you call relevant. Liv could have picked a Goldsmiths graduate, but sometimes it's the devil you know.

'I gave Theo Jack's keys. I thought it would be nice for you to come home to a clean house. He mentioned there was ash in the kitchen sink. Jack oughtn't to smoke in the house.'

While she rambles on about the dangers of smoking, I'm trying to grasp why Theo is cleaning our house. It's not dirty, nor is it Liv's idea of surgically clean. But we have each other's key's in the rare instance we lock ourselves out.

I gaze through the car window as we approach our cottage and the potted laurels beside a navy blue front door. Wind paws at the exuberant wisteria, whose territory has extended over the front facade. Here I am, living in the same home my parents once owned, formerly part of the Alum Chine coach house and stables, and a quick walk to the sea. Everyone knows everyone, which means everyone knows me.

'Thanks, Liv.'

'Call me if you need anything.'

The smell of exhaust and a car slowly receding down the street has always gutted me. After Kate died, and once I came through the initial darkness, I put precautions in place. When Jack went out, I never waved through the kitchen window like before. I turned my back as if it didn't matter. He was only going flying or to the shops. He'd be back.

'You look like you've been through a meat grinder.' Theo walks me into the kitchen. 'Bloody joy-rider. I hope they catch him.'

I smell furniture polish and bleach. 'Did she make you do all this?'

'Shit, no. I offered. Anyway, what else would I be doing? Moping?'

'You could beat it, you know.'

'Cancer? I wish,' he says, exhaling. 'Did she tell you there was ash in the sink?'

'She did.'

He flips open the bin with his foot and we're both looking down at the stub of a cigarette which is smeared with lipstick; a dusky pink, similar to the shade I wear. Theo gives me a sidelong smile as if he believes I'm hiding an addiction.

'Not mine,' I say. 'Jack only smokes cigars.'

'A workman?' Theo offers.

I shrug. It's been years since I smoked, yet the thought of an intruder soft-footing it around the house with a lighted cigarette makes me want to vomit.

'I'm going to see Jack this afternoon,' he says. 'Promise me you'll rest.'

'I promise.'

He hands me Jack's keys, and a shared glance tells me today is neutral and friendly. His interrogation last night forgotten under the weight of my bruises and his devastating illness.

Now that I'm alone, I feel like a child left at school on the first day of term and my gut clenches in the silence. I'm thankful there are no texts from Edward. My instinct has always been to fight not flee and I creep upstairs, crouching to look under the beds. After completing a systematic check of each room, I'm satisfied nothing's been moved.

I glance at Jack's shed through the back door, better known as his "hangar" where he keeps his remote control planes. But today, the door is closed. No aeroplane parts on the lawn or the intermittent shriek of a grinder. I take the key off the hook, kicking up a pile of wet leaves as I head towards it. On his workbench are the usual pins, screws and nuts, and between the glue caddy and his transmitter is an open file. Inside is a letter with the heading "disciplinary action." My eyes graze over the words Civil Aviation Authority and a statement from co-pilot George Morter about Jack's failure to stay awake. He'd already been verbally warned. I'm struggling between the retirement story he'd been cultivating to me and to our friends, and the more complex truth he'd been hiding. There had been no decline in Jack's capabilities, although he could have found a job in aviation or as a flight trainer. The question remains, he'd concealed this from me for no other purpose than to save his reputation. I have no guarantee that anything he says from now on is the truth. And he had the gall to talk to me about being a doubting Thomas.

I leave the letter where it is and return to the house. As I hang his keys on the peg, I notice what appears to be a spare house key, same make, same shape, but stained with some kind of black residue. Probably something Jack used as a tool. I try the front door. Definitely not a house key.

I rummage around in my handbag for my set and comfort myself with the notion that they must still be with our car. I walk outside to the patio. I say patio, but it's a gap between the houses with a wrought-iron bench, wide enough for the car we no longer have. A wall extends from our home to the next and two lanterns hang from the trellis.

I send Jack a text to ask him how he is. When he doesn't respond, I call him.

'So what's the damage, my darling?' His voice rushes me and I soak up every breath.

'A few cuts and bruises. The doctor said I might have problems with my memory. How about you?'

'My ears are ringing and I'm soaking in painkillers.'

'I'm so sorry, Jack.'

'It's my fault. I should have been the one driving.'

'It's not your fault. It's no one's fault. It was a hit and run.'

My mind spools into a different space, bright headlights and a car snorting clouds of steam like a bull waiting to charge.

Scenes from the accident are not as hazy as they once were. Contact with the steering wheel must have blown away the mist, and sharper images are forming.

'Theo was here when I got back. Cleaning. I suppose Liv thought it would be nice for us for when we got home. Thing is, he said there was ash in the kitchen sink. It wasn't you, I know it wasn't. I just wondered why the house smelt so bad.'

There's a long silence, as if increased wariness has attached itself to his reasoning. 'Could have been a blocked drain. Coming from his sterile home, anything smells bad.'

'I'm worried about my keys.'

I hear muffled sounds, as if Jack is talking to someone else and has put the phone to his chest.

'Are you there?' he says.

'Yes. I'm here.'

'You said keys. They're probably with the towing company. Look, I want you to rest. Watch a movie. Have an early night. No more worrying, all right?'

Before I can protest at the constant references to rest, he's telling me how much he loves me and that he'll see me tomorrow. I know he's trying to make me feel better, but somehow I feel lost.

As the phone fades into black, I feel the dull crush of misery as the walls close in. Scooping up my mug, I swing the front door with my foot, inching inside before it closes.

I sift through an article about the greens being set alight at the Bournemouth Golf Club and a fluff piece about Old

Christchurch Road in the 1920s with a boxout: 'Name that department store'. Then a page lead about county coroner, Rebecca Griffith, announcing Elisabeth Sanders death by homicide from manual strangulation, followed by the news story.

Search for Elisabeth Sanders' killer continues
By Andi Wynter
Senior Crime Reporter

County Coroner, Rebecca Griffith, confirmed that Bournemouth assistant librarian Elisabeth Sanders was strangled to death. The forty-year-old went missing on Tuesday 1 October and her body was discovered on Alum Chine beach during the early hours of Tuesday 15 October.

Dorset Police have revealed that a white car seen by a witness parked in front of the Alum Chine beach gate is the same Vauxhall Astra later recovered outside a house in Cassel Avenue.

So far, no suspects have been identified

and no arrests made, prompting growing
frustration from the family and the public.

The beach road is a pedestrian zone and only allows vehicles
with a permit. The witness had noticed the car parked in front
of the barrier gate because it was unusual. I google Vauxhall
Astras and the headlights are nothing like the car that rammed
us. I'm convinced it was a dark-coloured SUV, but how many
hundreds of SUVs are there on the roads? Even if the driver of
the car were to be apprehended, I wouldn't be able to identify
them.

There are cameras on every corner, and under constant
scrutiny by the authorities. The Cliffside Dene apartments,
for instance, perched between the road and the clifftop and
overlooking the scene where we had the accident, has two.
With a hit-and-run, what would the perpetrator do? In the
event he took his car to a local garage for repair, enquiring
police would easily identify him. There's only one explanation.
Hide it. With the efficiency of public transport, he could easily
go undetected for quite some time.

I rest my head on the back of the couch and close my eyes,
and soon I'm dreaming of a long road, yellow lamplight and
fog. A noise wakes me. I press my hand against the foam neck
brace, lifting my head slowly. It's only the wind beating against
the windows. Nothing to worry about.

It's gone 9.00 pm and I've had nothing to eat. After poking

about in the fridge, my stomach rebels against anything other than yoghurt. I turn on the TV and settle on *Primal Fear* – an altar boy, a brutal murder, an attorney who takes on high-profile clients. My mind worries away at a story of ego and emotions, and I try to assemble a list of suspects while Roy confesses to the archbishop's murder on TV. My phone pings.

Remember me? Just giving you a friendly nudge.

I feel as if I'm sealed in a vacuum, air tepid like bathwater. Being cocooned under a rug on the couch stops the far corners of my mind taking over, but the temptation to reply scuttles by. I hear a sound outside, a boot scraping against pavers.

Reaching for the remote, I turn down the volume and listen again. Wedging a hand between the blinds, I study the flats. Lights on, blinds drawn, the usual sights. I'm about to believe it's Chester, my neighbour's cat, pawing its way up a drainpipe, when I catch a spill of light in my peripheral view. The smudge of grey through the panes in the back door tells me I've got company.

I stagger through the hall and turn on the porch light. The beam illuminates a scrawl of shadows and there's a narrow ribbon of light between our house and the neighbour's. No sounds of pattering feet. Not even a swish of grass.

I feel certain there's no one there.

9

FREYA

CLOUDS BOIL OVERHEAD AND wind wheezes through an open window. My mind tap dances around whether or not I had opened it. I throw back the duvet and my phone thuds to the floor. I've overslept.

My thoughts slither off to Kate-dom. Swallowing a lump in my throat, I try to skim through the hours before she left the house for the last time. I would have clung to her if I'd known she'd never come back. I wish Aynur hadn't organised the booze cruise. The whole idea was foolish, teenagers on a boat, drinking until the early hours.

I miss Aynur's friendship. We used to sit on the reception at the *Daily Echo* and fantasise about becoming journos until my promotion to PA put mileage between us – one floor – as did my incessant wittering about Kate's accident. Accident? It wasn't an accident. The problem is, the police don't share my opinion, neither does Jack – nor the friends I once had.

I glance at my face in the mirror. Freckles hardly noticeable under a marbling of blues and reds. I use concealer to cover it, including the scar that pulls at the Cupid's bow of my upper lip and curls around the right nostril. I've had it since birth.

Jack sends a text asking if I'm on my way. I schedule an Uber – Ambrose Ibrahim. Red Toyota Corolla. One hour

I swipe through the *Daily Mail* and BBC headlines. Elisabeth's name is front-page news, regurgitating old ground and keeping it fresh in readers' minds but adding that her flatmate believed Elisabeth received a phone call in the pub that night and left soon after. There is a photo of the street, which leaves me to imagine the rest.

My phone rings. This time it's a DC Owen with a sing-song voice. He wants to take a brief statement over the phone and asks me to confirm the Hunters' address.

'Do you remember what time you left the party?' he asks.

'After midnight, I think.'

'Drinking, were you?'

Something in the tone runs a shiver across my heart and since neither Jack nor I had taken any kind of breath test for alcohol at the hospital, I can safely assume my one glass was within the driving limit, and that's what I tell him.

'And your husband?'

'Two or three.'

'See, the thing is, a neighbour confirmed hearing the crash outside their house around 1.00 a.m, which is a little odd if you left at 12.30. You live, what, two minutes away?'

'You said a neighbour? Do you have a name?'

'We don't give out names, Mrs Thorne.'

My mind goes blank, and I try to do the maths in my head. Where had those few minutes gone? I almost ignore the question, and then I remember. 'Jack wanted a smoke. So we parked down the street.'

'Then you pulled out and *wham*!'

'No... no, it wasn't like that.'

'Well, what was it like, Mrs Thorne? Because you and your husband ended up in the hospital.'

While I'm trying to construct and deconstruct every tiny detail, I realise my hands are shaking. If DC Owen thinks I failed to check my mirror before pulling out, I'm at fault. There's a thin line between impatience and carelessness.

'It was a hit and run,' I snap.

'So you say.'

'No, it was an accident. He slammed into me. Twice. I'd say it was deliberate.'

'How are you going to prove that, Mrs Thorne? There are no cameras in that area. We've already checked.'

'My husband and I are the victims here. I've already given a statement in hospital.'

Before I can get another word in, the line goes dead. Any confidence I once had in the police has diminished with this snappy little power display.

I cross the living room and stare at the back door. The porch light glares through the panes and I could have sworn I turned it off last night. Throwing open the door, I notice a jar of jam with a note attached.

A little goes a long way.

I'm locked in a nightmare, fear rising and swelling inside me. I walk outside, eyes glaring at the back fence. He climbed over... that was the sound I'd heard last night. Not the wind, but a clatter of wooden slats.

I slam the door and hurl the jar into the kitchen bin. The cloakroom door is ajar and something flickers between the gap and the doorframe. I stare at it, goosebumps rising on my arms. So many jarring things have happened and I'm tempted to call out. My feet sink into the hall carpet as I step further towards it. Reaching the knob, I fling open the door. The sudden motion stirs the curtains in the tiny window, which is open an inch. The rush of relief is so intense I almost sink to the floor.

I slam the window closed and lock it. Dragging myself upstairs, I study every angle of the garden and the street. Anxiety is like an elastic band, stretching on and on until it breaks. I rip off the spongy collar as I undress. Under all that concealer, my face is a stamp of freckles and bruises, and there are more under my breast and belly. I turn on the shower and a torrent of warm water hits my head. Every time I move, it's like a nail bomb detonating in my skull.

My mind flits and won't stay still. *A little goes a long way?* Is he referring to my affair?

It wasn't so much an affair, more a validation that I was worthy of attention. He was a playful flirt, a charismatic presence. Elbows pressed together at work and conferring in hushed asides: neither wanting to be caught looking, both sneaking glances.

'I'm not interested,' I said.

'In me?' His brow furrowed like a bloodhound and I'd laughed.

After that, my stomach flip-flopped every time I saw him, mussed hair and high cheekbones. A cheeky smile. Flashes of the Christmas party burst into my head. A disco ball shedding every shade of rainbow onto the dance floor, bodies flickering to the sounds of a deafening beat. I remember Miles weaving through the crowds, two glasses in his hand. I couldn't hear what he was saying, so I pulled him outside and pinned him to the car. I don't know what got into me, but it took a long kiss and another drink to get it all out.

We drove down the drive, our glasses thrown from the car roof where we'd left them. The warmth of his hand in mine made me feel as if I could say anything, be anyone. It was wrong and wonderful, and I'd never known it could be both at once. We parked at the beach, ran into the shadows behind the beach huts, our bodies slippery with sweat. I didn't want it to stop, and then I did, and I wince with the memory.

He asked me if I wanted to see him again. It was unrealistic, the same as creeping into the back corner of a crowded restaurant and holding hands under the table. He didn't need to bother himself with any of this. His life wasn't routine and predictably dull. He didn't live with someone who tuned him out or requested he saw a therapist for someone to talk to.

I agreed to see him the following evening. We found a restaurant overlooking the sea. There we were, sitting in full view of fifty people, laughing and flirting as if we were invisible. It wasn't like I found a strange man in my bed the following day. He wasn't strange at all. He simply wasn't my husband. I created a fake name in my contacts, so if he called, Jack wouldn't know.

Jack. Detached, inaccessible Jack. How far had I expected this to go?

If Theo had seen me talking to a man in Sainsbury's, how easy would it have been for Jack to have seen me in a car park, a hotel, a restaurant, hand-in-hand with someone other than him? What if he had lied to me and never left, that memorable weekend? Certainly, the affair has thrown a spanner into our marriage. Or has it? Since Jack hasn't confronted me about it, I still have some mileage.

Jack and I used to be inseparable. He was dashing and exotic, a taste of foreign places, and it was his confidence that won me over. He pursued me, asked if he could call me, which I took as a compliment. But as the months went by and the calls increased, he would question me about where I'd been, who I'd been out with. Dad called it *possessive*. Not in a suffocating way, more in a healthy she's-mine way when other men were about. It lessened after we married and Kate was born. But after she died, it started again.

How would Jack have reacted if he'd seen me with someone else? A confrontation? No, not Jack's style. He'd be abrupt and distant, simmering below the surface. I hate that a two-night stand, which could have remained a tawdry little secret, has morphed like a deadly virus, and now everyone is being infected.

I turn off the shower and grab a towel. Water drips off my hair and creeps down my back. As I go over the conversation with DC Owen a second time, searching each word for a new meaning, my stomach heaves. It wasn't what he'd said – a line of questioning I clearly expected – but the tone buried in the context.

How are you going to prove that, Mrs Thorne?

If DC Owen doesn't believe a word I've said, what makes me think I've got a chance with Patti Franchek?

10

FREYA

I'M WALKING AROUND LIKE a robotic mannequin, back straight, head up, as I wrap myself in a towel. Silence presses back at me and I see the shadow of Kate on the landing. Jeans rolled at the ankle and ripped at the knee.

'Can we go to Waterstones, Mum?'

The *yes* comes only in my head and my heart feels like there's a tear in it. I talk to her at night before I go to sleep and first thing when I get up. I talk to her when I do housework and when I go running. Especially when I go running. My throat thickens. Everything looks different now, as if the entire world senses my heartache and is reacting to it.

It doesn't stop me from standing on the landing, measuring every sound. Our bedroom to the left, Kate's room to the right. Dad's old bedroom, across the landing. I flip the light on and poke my head around the door. A desk, a chair and a bookcase with a small trundle bed on the corner. Kate's room is empty and ours is tidy. Bed made. Drawers closed. Blinds open.

A flash of colour catches my eye. The trailing edge of a ribbon peeks out from under the pillow. My heart pounds into overdrive. I spin around and shout. 'Kate!'

The echo of my voice recedes into the walls. Thick, ringing silence. Then I remember. The ribbon is hers. I sleep with it every night.

Out of the corner of my eye, I see Jack's laptop on the ottoman at the end of our bed and I look because I'm Bathsheba Everdene unscrewing the lid to Fanny Robin's coffin. What if there's some kind of conspiracy between Liv and Theo? The strange offer to come and clean the house. What were Liv and Jack whispering about in the kitchen?

The screensaver is a photo of Kate with dimples and dark hair, and I open the file marked *Family*. Selfies with Kate's best friend Emma, lips puckered and heavily pencilled eyebrows. Kate and Jack at the flying field. Kate in the driving seat when I taught her to drive. The three of us at Sprinkles, eating Belgian chocolate crepes and Ferrero Frenzy Sundaes. I scroll through aeroplane drawings and flight simulators, treading deeper into Jack's territory. I see a file marked "Us." Inside is a single document with words that knife me to the bone.

> *I don't want you to see the sad stuff – the gut-ripping grief I feel. I don't mean to shut you out. I love you, Freya.*

Did he leave this note for me to find, predicting one day I'd go through his computer? I recognise it as the perfect illustration of what is failing in our marriage. His absences, his need to be alone, are harder to forgive. I asked him to go to therapy with me so we could engage emotionally, but after three sessions the chasm between us became wider. It seemed as if we'd hit a dead end and I turned my focus inward – and I've been there ever since.

Visions of Jack press down on me until my brain throbs. In the weeks after Kate died, we hardly spoke, each incarcerated in our own heartache, hollowed out and purposeless. For months, we watched each other's faces for any signs of frailty, the type where you fall apart and do something you'd never dream of doing. Like Jack being offered therapy, but preferring to leave me alone for an entire weekend to climb that mountain of grief himself. When he came back, he went up to Kate's room as if his leaving had reversed time and she'd come home again. He sat on her bed, reading her Dr Seuss book, *Oh, The Places You'll Go*. She was his flying buddy, eager to help him in the shed and accompany him to the field. Now there's no one but me. And he never asks me.

Opening my drawer, I rummage for my underwear. While I'm tugging all the contents to the front, I realise the little green leather box with Mum's earrings is missing. The splinter of a Christmas scene tracks its way into my mind, Mum peering into a gift bag, tissue floating to the floor, and earrings pinched between her fingers. She tossed back her hair and asked me how they looked. I still have the photo. That last time Jack truly looked into my eyes, I was wearing those earrings and he'd said how beautiful I looked. Now I have the ridiculous urge to find them.

I wrench the drawer from the runners, turning the contents out onto the bed, picking through lace and silk, until I'm sure they're not here.

The Uber alarm goes off. *Focus. One thing at a time.*

I only have fifteen minutes until the Uber arrives. I scoop everything back into the drawer and pull on jeans and a shirt, wondering if Edward has touched these too. I tell myself to stop thinking about it. I need to get to Jack.

Outside, my neighbour Trisha's son is standing under the tree, coaxing Chester into the flats.

'Good morning, Arthur,' I say, and he says, 'Good morning, Freya.'

He tells there's a man called Dezza upstairs, which I assume is short for Derek. He's looking at a loose valve behind the toilet. So we sit on the wall and wait for my Uber.

'What happened to your face?' He recognises bruises – all categories of them.

'We got banged up in a car crash,' I say. 'No more car.'

'Bummer. Can you see out of your eye?'

'Looks worse than it is.'

He glances over his shoulder at a second-floor window. 'How long does it take to mend a leaky toilet?'

'Depends. You didn't flush one of your Spitfires down there, did you?'

'No. I'm thirteen now, remember?'

'So tell me about Dezza. What's he like?'

'Helps me with my homework and drives me to school. Mum goes all pink and sweaty when she talks about him.'

'What does he do?'

'Security, mostly.'

'Sounds like he's good to have around.'

If a man helps a kid with his homework and drives him to school, it's time to dispense with the worry and stop being so suspicious. Arthur looks up at my house and his eyes seem to glaze over Kate's window for a while.

'I heard you calling her the other day. I call my dad when no one's around. I don't want him to think I've forgotten him.'

Which I find strange because his dad was generous with his fist. Funny how kids think their parents are heroes, no matter how brutal they are.

'Kate used to do my chemistry homework on the bus,' he says.

'That's cheating.'

'She told me you'd say that. I asked her to marry me once. She told me to piss off the first time. The second time she said she'd think about it and the third time she said it would be a long wait if I were up for it. Her being seventeen and all.' He lowers his head and looks at the shoelaces I want to tie. 'When she died, did you have to see her?'

I tell him she looked like she was sleeping, but it's a lie.

I remember the photograph the coroner showed us and the verdict at the inquest. Death by misadventure – an accident because of a risk Kate must have taken by climbing over the boat railings. He told us there were 'travel abrasions' on her forehead and knees since the tide had carried her body to who knows where. She was waterlogged and scarred. I could barely look.

Death's a punch in the gut, a twenty-four-hour flogging. It's the first thought in the morning where the crushing weight of loss is at its heaviest. I begged God to rewind the clock, so I could piece together those last moments and replay each scenario with a different ending – one where she swam to safety, or she never fell at all. Even if she had to die, I'd be there to hold her.

'You've got a Peregrine falcon up there,' Arthur says. 'I know it's a Peregrine. I looked it up.'

'Beautiful, isn't he?' I squint at the bird all puffed out on Kate's windowsill. 'Talking of unusual things, have you seen anyone lurking outside our house recently?'

'Only the post lady. I fancy her. So does Roger Daniels in number 26.'

'Well, I got this letter. It's a bit creepy.'

'Is it a bomb threat?' he asks.

'No, nothing like that. If you see anyone hanging about, you'll let me know?'

'I'll take a few pictures if you like.' He smiles and taps his phone.

Despite everything that's happened, I no longer feel like a helpless victim. A surge of hope emerges and Arthur and I part ways with a high five.

11

FREYA

As Ambrose pulls away from the kerb, I notice a parked car where a cap shades the driver's face. Maybe he's scrolling through his texts and whiling away the minutes of his daily commute. I tell myself he's a delivery guy, or he's pulled over to make a call. It doesn't stop me from looking through the window as we glide past.

I scroll through the news. The librarian Elisabeth Sanders worked with has given a brief interview. She confirmed Elisabeth loved art galleries, swimming in the early mornings and dining at 1812. I try to map a lone swimmer on one of my runs. Now I wished I'd paid more attention.

Jack waits for me with a nurse at the front entrance of the hospital. My stomach spasms at the sight of him and a sob erupts. It's his raised hand and the shoulders trying so hard to be straight. He puts out both arms to comfort me when I should be comforting him. My mind pushes out that thought: *Was it my fault?*

We weave through the traffic, brakes jabbing at every corner. Ambrose looks up occasionally to peer at us through the mirror. He is too polite to ask about our cuts and bruises, but I can see he's tempted.

While I lay my head on Jack's shoulder, I can't stop thinking about bodies floating in the sea, even as far as the Brownsea Island Ferries or sinking beneath a seabed of oyster shells left over from the Saxon period.

I don't know which is worse, Elisabeth Sanders' parents knowing their daughter is dead or agonising over the weeks she was missing – held like a prisoner in a basement, an attic, a boarded-up house. Somewhere I had passed and never thought to examine, a neat Victorian that contradicts the horror of what goes on inside. Already I'm thinking about Kate as we veer closer to the flower shop. I turn to Jack, grimacing in the seat beside me.

'Go on,' he says. 'Take her some flowers.'

I expect he's studying my face for a single taut muscle, the tiniest shift of expression, but there's nothing.

No one sees the sad stuff, Jack; because I'm too damn good at pretending.

Ambrose parks at the flower shop and I choose a bunch of peonies. Soon we're on our way, sweeping past houses and impeccable gardens until we arrive at the churchyard. I leave Jack in the car nursing a headache and I realise I mustn't be long.

I walk up the path towards Kate's grave. Sunlight dapples

the headstone and there's a single white rose in the stone vase. Emma might have left it. Somehow, the thought of Kate's best friend comforts me.

I try to keep my prayers light-hearted, but my gut crumples and writhes. I never got to see Kate one last time. You don't, with deaths like hers. I hate to think of her pressed down by waves, scenes of family and friends tumbling through her battered brain as she fades in and out of consciousness.

Jack said I collapsed at the funeral and wailed so loudly it frightened him. I couldn't put away her clothes or wash her sheets for months, anything to catch her smell. As I look down at that mound of earth, I see her clearly, and it takes my breath away, a dark-haired child making daisy chains in the garden and dancing all by herself. It's like an eerie song that keeps playing in my head.

I arrange my flowers around the white rose, preparing myself for hitching breaths. Yet my body responds differently. Something makes me uneasy, a shift in the atmosphere, a presence.

The silhouette of a man catches my eye. He leans against a tree, foot flat against the trunk. Sunglasses hide his focus and the angle of his head suggests he's studying a headstone.

Through memory rather than conscious thought, I keep thinking I've seen him somewhere. Shoulder length hair curls outwards beneath the rim of his cap and his sweatshirt barely hides a paunch. I want to march up to him and demand why he's here. He could be Edward. He really could.

Jack's tired face in the car window beckons me and my head is swimming. As I leave the churchyard, something emerges in the man's expression. Unbidden, the words land in my thoughts.

Curiosity. And something else.

Disgust.

12

EDWARD

THE WIND BLOWS IN off the sea and the trees are whispering again. Edward is the spectator, the bystander. He is everyone and no one.

His colouring is unremarkable. It amazes him what people miss when they scan a crowd. Even the police. If anyone thinks putting on an accent and a disguise is unbelievable, think again.

He follows Freya to the hospital and then to the flower shop. It's an educated guess where she's going after that. He arrives a few minutes before her. The scent of wet grass is thick in the air and an October wind rushes across the graveyard. Under the shadow of a tree is his father's headstone. They say a man can hold his breath underwater for up to two minutes, but the way Edward remembers it was less than thirty seconds.

He tries to recall a string of words his mother taught him. All he can come up with is a disjointed recitation. What good does a prayer do now?

Then an exquisite nuance of perfumes, more intense than the smell of grass. A fresh wreath of roses, lovingly placed against a nearby grave. He stoops and takes one. Brushes it under his nose. Fruit. Honey. Green tea. Clove.

As he surveys a row of headstones, he spots one about fifty feet away. The vase is empty, and he remedies it. Of course, it's not his business, but he's curious about why there are no fresh flowers on this grave.

Katherine Mae Thorne.

He retreats to his shadowy corner, huddling with his back against the tree. Takes out his phone and conducts another search for Nisha Kalani. Two in Manchester, one in Somerset, three in London and shit knows how many in India.

A high-pitched whining fades in and out of range and he knows it's the synapses in his brain realigning. A sensory release, a rush of blood, as if an acupuncturist has pierced a vein and cleared a blockage. He does not know when it occurred, only that it is has.

He hears footsteps. Freya is dressed conservatively, and the rich colour of her skin and hair draws frequent glances from men. She veers between the headstones, stopping at her daughter's. Her chest rises and falls, but he is not close enough to read her thoughts.

Today, her face throws him. He didn't know ramming a car could be so disfiguring. But a silent strength seems to brew in her head.

Is he worried? Maybe.

She's pulled a two-week sickie and her days are a little less structured. That doesn't mean he can't sit outside her house and make her squirm. Or inside, for that matter.

Fear is another beast. It scares and surprises. It picks locks.

He doesn't do heavy breathing when he calls her, but the wind whispers against the mouthpiece and he expects it freaks her out. Even though his head is angled towards his phone, he watches her, spooling no doubt through a montage of Kates, re-running the first newsflash in her tired little mind – *missing, kidnapped, a runaway – accidental death.*

He wants to tell her that grief has no mercy. It cuts deep inside, leaving enough scar tissue for a coroner to find. Running won't separate her from pain. It hasn't separated her from him.

A letter from BALPA and the Civil Aviation Authority states that Jack fell asleep at the yoke. His co-pilot will attest to it. Edward has left it in Jack's hangar for Freya to find and yet here she is in her private greyness, wasting time. She's had every chance, or at least the illusion of a chance to make things right, and now he's curious to see what she'll do.

She stiffens, her gaze travelling towards him. He is confident she sees him and her sharp senses have sent up an alarm. He knows this for reasons he can't describe. He is rarely afraid, but with this woman, he has been uneasy more than once.

The breeze has changed direction and he can smell earth and wet grass again. The sky is thunderhead grey, clouds moving rapidly northeast.

He watches Freya race along the path to the car, gazing back as if enticing him to give playful chase.

He won't, of course. That would be a dead giveaway.

13

FREYA

I SLEPT FITFULLY LAST night, dreaming of Jack lying in a hospital bed, plugged into a spider's web of IVs. A car horn must have woken me, brake lights blinking through the blinds as if someone was refusing to let me sleep.

'Morning,' I say, hearing the clunk of the shower door. 'How are you feeling?'

'Sick to the stomach. Like my head's in two places.'

'Want me to get you a painkiller?'

'I've had one, thanks.'

My eyes stray to clouds of steam that have whisked Jack away, leaving patches of skin visible through the glass. The jagged edge of his shoulder blade one minute and the curve of his buttocks the next. I'm trying to fathom how he can lift his chin and if his pain threshold is higher than mine. I want to tell him what I found on his laptop, those precious few sentences that mean so much to me. Despite my hesitation, I go rigid when he speaks.

'Liv texted a number for the towing company. I'll call them about your keys.' Silence and then... 'Have you started smoking again?'

'No. Why?'

'I found a packet downstairs in the kitchen drawer.'

I wait with disproportionate dread that he'll interrogate me, but he doesn't. He towels himself dry and I help him dress. He unplugs his phone from the charger, and we go downstairs. He's already dialling the number for the towing company.

I stare at the cigarettes in the kitchen drawer and decide not to allow myself to be thrown off guard. I can't have missed them all those years ago when I swore to kick the habit for good. Taking a small notebook from the kitchen drawer, I jot down everything that's happened, from dates and times to descriptions.

Then I check the news. There are pictures of forensic officers on the beach and cordons to stop runners and walkers from walking along the promenade. I'm about to call our crime reporter to see if there are any more leads, when my phone rings. It's probably our insurance company. But no one speaks and all I can hear is the ragged cawing of a crow in the background. I try to form an outline of a face. A name. A place. Then the thought is gone like a trace of perfume you desperately want to follow. I hang up and my gut nudges me as if it knows something I don't.

Jack's voice blasts through my thoughts. 'They said the keys weren't in the ignition.'

'If they don't have them, who does?'

'Let's catch our breath and think about changing the locks.'

I move to the kitchen window and peer out. 'Trisha's new boyfriend is a locksmith. You might ask him.'

'What do we know about him? Tax evasion? Embezzlement?'

'Jack. I'm sure he's fine.'

The rusty yelp of the letterbox brings me to the hall. On the mat is an envelope and I'm thinking here we go again. I open the front door and shield the sun from my eyes. The only living thing twitching in the street is a man with the sprig of a ponytail, hunched over the rockery next door. He is usually at his upstairs window at night, sweeping a torch along the ground like a guard at Colditz.

I approach him, waving the letter. 'Did you see who posted this?'

Rabbi Aviel looks up, shrugs and points at his bellflower and candytuft. 'You think I have eyes on the back of my head?'

'I'm sorry to bother you. I can see you're busy. But someone's been posting things in my letterbox. I wondered, that's all, because it would help if you had.'

He scratches his beard with the tip of his secateurs. 'The postwoman?'

'What? No. There's no stamp. It was hand-delivered. If you see anyone loitering, would you let me know?'

'I'll keep an eye out.'

Which means it's unlikely he saw the bearer of the jam. I

stomp back into the house and rip open the letter. Inside is my charm bracelet, the one I lost in the accident.

Dear Freya.

When you answered the phone, I didn't have the words. There's so much I want to tell you. You drink red wine and flat whites. You like watching people. I like watching you.

You wore a lovely cream dress at the Christmas party. Your lover ran his hand down your thigh – an intimate gesture, don't you agree? You don't know half of this, which is why I want to fill you in with the other half. Lover-boy gave you a ride – quite a lively ride the way I saw it – once on the sand and twice behind the beach huts. Looked like he was in it for the long haul. Let's not fool ourselves into thinking it was a one-night-stand. He still looks. You still yearn. You know where I'm going with this. Guilt. Without someone to talk to, you can't unload, and you'll drown under the weight of it all. You may catch your breath between letters, but I'm not going anywhere. I wouldn't dream of it.

There are opportunities for discovery in the most unlikely of places.

Edward.

Since last year, there has been a glut of promotions and award celebrations, including Liv's private parties that never run out of fizz. I can't deny I haven't been hammered and shamefaced at a few. Kate's death had everything to do with that. I want to believe the sender has got the wrong address, but it's me he's writing to, me he's watching and my marriage he's threatening. I tell myself to set a match to it, or stuff it in the wheelie bin, but I take a photo. I need to keep records of every letter before they go to the police.

I add the name Edward to my contacts, so at least my texts have a name. Pull up the last string of texts he sent and type in a response.

> **Freya:** Thanks for the letter. I've called the police.

No reply. The text goes through, which means the number is active, and just to be sure, I send another.

> **Freya:** They can trace calls within thirty metres.

That should rattle him, until three blinking dots cavort on the screen. It's hard to think what I dread more. The dots disappearing or the reply itself.

> **Edward**: Nice try. But do you think I'm stupid enough to call from near my home? They're welcome to come here, but all you'll be doing is wasting police time.

That was his sign off. Not a hint of sarcasm. Whichever way I look at this, it's positive and perhaps I can reason with him. Perhaps I can make him go away.

'More post?' Jack's voice makes me jump. He tugs the letter from my hand, face knotting with confusion. 'What party's he on about?'

'The Christmas party last year.'

'Didn't Stan drive you home?'

I nod, but I'm lying. Liv's driver is more legless than his passengers. He keeps a bottle of brandy in the glove compartment and you have to hammer on the window to rouse him. Once, he offered me a cigarette – which I'm not sure was a cigarette – while singing, 'I'm a joker, I'm a smoker, I'm a midnight toker.' But I can't tell Jack.

'Beach huts? One-night-stand?' Jack snaps. 'This has gone far enough.'

14

FREYA

It's forty-five minutes before Patti arrives. She's narrow-hipped and light-footed, the type to sneak up behind you without making a noise. Behind her compassionate gaze, something deeper emerges, as if she's already picked up a significant detail.

'How are you?' Her eyes scurry up and down my face.

'Someone rear-ended us. I don't remember much except an explosion.'

'Airbags. You lose it for a few seconds.'

I'd lost it for a few hours, and when I came to, I thought it was snowing. Toxic dust. I can't remember travelling in the ambulance to the hospital, nor can I recall much of anything since coming home. Sometimes I have flashes of memory, a brief crack in the clouds where the sun shines through, and the sensation of my head bumping against the side window as the car careened downhill, spinning and skidding until it stopped altogether.

'Do you remember seeing the car behind?' she asks.

'Bright lights. That's about it.'

There's a jagged silence and Patti's eyes remain focused on mine. 'So you've received another letter?'

'Yes. And my charm bracelet.'

On go the gloves and her frown deepens as she studies the letter. 'The Adult Safeguarding Team will make a risk assessment. I'd suggest an SPO – a stalking protection order – only you say you don't know anyone called Edward.'

'No, we don't,' Jack says. 'What type of man are we looking at? Is he dangerous?'

'Potentially, stalkers can be, and sending letters is a way of having control.'

I go cold as if I've done the ice bucket challenge for motor neurone disease. 'But he says he watches me. Knows where I go.'

'Not necessarily. The intent could be to deceive, to insert himself into your life. Are you keeping a log?'

'Yes, I am.'

Patti drops the letter into an evidence bag and snaps off her gloves. 'We'll have it tested. It doesn't mean there'll be any fingerprints. Stalkers can sometimes involve a third party to watch the victim and drop off letters and gifts. Have you told your neighbours?'

'Yes, a few.'

'Where do you work, Freya?'

'I'm a PA at the *Daily Echo*.'

'Ah, a keen follower of crime news.'

It's clear from her expression she already knows where I work. But why crime news? Why not any news? Patti is staring right through me and she sees what, exactly?

'Do you remember the Christmas party he's talking about?' Patti asks. 'Or was it a bit of a blur? They usually are. All that free booze.'

'I remember it clearly,' I say. 'It was at the Highcliff Marriott. Jack was away that weekend so I went alone.'

'Was it fun?'

'As work parties go. It's just reporters and news editors. Nothing special. Except I had a falling out with my best friend.'

I mention Aynur Kaplan, only because I saw her at the supermarket last week with her daughter Emma. They left without saying hello. Walls have gone up, and I don't remember when she stopped texting or coming around. The world I once knew diminished after Kate died. The flood of sympathetic calls from relatives and friends quickly thinned to a trickle, and there are no more coffee mornings or parents' nights. One by one, they have faded away.

'Neither of you has seen anything unusual?' Patti asks, eyes sliding to the window again.

'What are we talking about exactly?' Jack asks.

'Unfamiliar cars parked in the street. Money passing hands. It's usually pretty quick. So, maybe not.'

We both shake our heads. She's referring to drug deals,

which would be more Trisha's department than ours.

'We lost our car keys, the ones from the crash,' I say. 'There have been other things. Cigarette ash in the kitchen sink, half empty wine bottles, footprints. DC Owen mentioned something about a witness. Perhaps this person saw something.'

'DC Owen, you say.' She slips her notebook into her pocket.

'Yes. Welsh, I think.' I daren't tell her about the hang up calls or the texts I've received and sent. She'll only think I'm encouraging it.

'Any direct threats are a criminal offence. If that happens, we'll set you up with a temporary phone so we can monitor yours.'

For a while we hold each other's gaze. Before she asks me if that's what I'd prefer to do, I jump in with another question.

'I wanted to ask... I keep thinking about Kate. Aynur organised a booze cruise from Poole Quay. There were cocktails and shooters, quite a lot of drinking. They all watched the sunset over the Purbeck Hills. After that, Kate vanished. She didn't text us when the boat docked. Jack called every friend he could think of. No one had seen her. We found our car in a pilot's parking space near the RNLI Lifeboat Station. So Liv and I explored the quay, and Theo and Jack searched the nightclubs. But a couple of weeks before, she went to that student union place.'

'The Fire Station?'

'Yes,' I say. 'She was too young, but with makeup, well, you know how it goes. I wonder if she'd met someone. Someone we didn't know about. Not all drownings are accidental, are they?'

'In Kate's case, the police looked for anything that might have indicated a crime. They checked the CCTV from the quay that night and saw her getting on the boat, but she never made it off.' Patti frowns, eyes floating upwards to catch the image. 'Her toxicology report stated she was twice the drink-drive limit. Did she have seizures?'

'No.'

'She wasn't taking any medication?'

'Not that I know of,' I say.

'There was no change of clothes in her car, so she hadn't intended on swimming. I can't see her climbing over the boat railings, can you?'

'Yet, she fell.' I re-enter the nightmare from which I wake repeatedly. 'What if Kate had argued with someone? Things got out of hand?'

'It's only natural to believe something terrible happened.'

I tell her about the people I'd talked to, boat captains, lifeboat crew, even residents in a block of flats opposite. I used my own Facebook page to appeal to people to offer information, but it seemed to hit a brick wall. Mostly, the comments were kind, sending condolence GIFs and emoji hugs. National news vans idled in the street that week, "snappers" taking photos of our house. I realised we were the story that every reporter wanted. On the fifth day, they found her. That's how long it took for her body to rise to the surface. I remember the clip from Sky News, cameras panning to a picture of Kate's smiling face as if she were unaffected by the tragic event. To me, it is as raw today as it was then.

Patti presses a card in my hand and taps it with a fingernail. She wants to refer me to You First – an independent advocacy for support.

'If you think someone's following you, Freya, drive or walk to somewhere with CCTV. Keep in touch.'

I'm only half listening, mind hopping over the letter, the words... *Lover-boy gave you a ride. He still looks. You still yearn...* and I'm looking at Jack and asking myself, how much does he know?

Grief comes like a slow rising mist. Not for Kate this time, but for what I've done to Jack. This is the woman I've become. Broken and secretive, and the bristling pain in my muscles is my punishment.

I don't want to lie. But I can't tell the truth.

15

FREYA

I WAKE LATE TO a thwack of bin lids and the recycling van lumbering down the street. Pain branches out from my spine and along my shoulders. Pinpricks of light blink on and off behind my eyes. Great. Another day in stalkerville.

I roll sideways off the bed and glance out of the window. Dew glistens on the leaves outside and the sun bleeds through the blinds like a cracked egg. I hear burbling water. Out of the bathroom pours a cloud of steam. Jack must have left the hot tap running before heading out to his hangar.

I get the familiar paradox of loving my independence and hating it at the same time. Isn't a woman alone in the house a stalker's fantasy? I try hard to put it out of my mind – to keep myself busy – but it's no good thinking I'm safer outside than in. Edward might be slender enough to drop through the smallest gap and quiet enough to be at my side in seconds. Exercise and fresh air are what I need.

I inspect my forehead in the mirror. It's ugly, the bruise, a surface wound where the real one is deep inside. I try to piece together every second of the crash, only this time, I imagine my leg snapped in two, bone tearing through skin and gleaming white in the moonlight. My muscles pulse with pain and my neck is on fire. I feel a wash of compassion for Jack. He's more worried about my mental health and my floundering attempts to cope.

I take a pair of scissors and trim a few wispy strands of hair around my hairline, then tie it in a loose ponytail. My phone rings twice and then goes silent. If Edward had found a phone carrier that didn't ask for identifying information, it explains why his number is untraceable. He may be my biggest enemy, but I refuse to be a victim. If he broke into the house right now, I wouldn't run. I'd fight. I find myself anticipating the moment with great pleasure.

I focus on the one thing I need more than anything. Getting my strength back. I squeeze fresh oranges, pineapple and lemonade, and chill it in a jug. This time Andi Wynter's name flashes across the phone screen, accompanied by a designated ring.

'Hope you don't mind me calling, but I wanted to say how sorry I was about the accident,' she says. 'How are you?'

'It's like trying to web all the filaments in your brain back together. Nothing's sparking.'

'Is there anything I can do?'

Since she's got an exclusive on the Sanders story, I ask her for news.

'I spoke with County coroner, Rebecca Griffith,' she says. 'As we know, the cause of death was strangulation. Confidentially speaking, Elisabeth was likely drugged, which might explain the lack of defensive wounds. The toxicology report will reveal more.'

'So, no DNA?'

'If there were fingerprint impressions on her neck and anything under her nails, then yes. But Rebecca wouldn't elaborate. When the police told Mrs Sanders Elisabeth was dead, she went quiet. They asked her if she understood what they were saying and she said she did. But when they described the nature of Elisabeth's injuries, she wanted to know who'd found her, because it must have been awful for the person who had. I just wanted you to know.'

I tamp down the tears as she hangs up. The case is pressing on me, stretching out in every direction. As much as I need air, the small voice inside my head tries to talk me out of it. *You can't run far enough.*

I ignore shafts of pain in my neck. What I need is a run. Weed pollen is still high on the allergy tracker and I ram a few tissues into my pocket. I shout to Jack through the open back door, and he walks towards me, his face a tapestry of swellings today, some yellow, some red and some blue.

'Do you think that's wise?' he says. 'Being out on your own?'

'I'll be fine. Promise.'

He kisses my forehead and closes the door behind me. I try running, but my neck is so stiff, I resort to a fast walk instead.

Trisha's binoculars are already burning into my back from the flats opposite. I send her a text.

Freya: You spying on me?

Trisha: Maybe.

Freya: So, who's the new boyfriend?

Trisha: Now look who's spying.

Freya: Don't know where I can get a couple of security cameras and two new locks?

The grinning emoji tells me she'll go the extra mile, always has, and we'll have fully functioning CCTV before you can blink.

The sky bruises over and I can feel the first spots of rain. Searching the hedgerows for cameras, I study the eaves and the upper corners of every residence, including the Cliffside Dene apartments. Just because I can't see any doesn't mean they aren't there. I stop for a moment and google traffic cams in the area. The first link that pops up is BCP Council CCTV Camera Locations. I check the section for Westbourne. Although they mention Durleyhurst Road, there's no sign as to the exact site, which confirms DC Owen's statement.

I gawp at the crash site. The obliterated stone wall stands there like a memorial, grass flattened and dents in the chain-link fence. Tyre marks show the culprit. I could make a witness appeal notice, asking for any information on a serious collision, with a phone number to call, the type you get with hit-and-runs where deaths occur. It might flush out the witness DC Owen alluded to, and I make a note to do it.

There are no more coastguard helicopters scanning the shoreline, turbines whistling, rotors rattling, and no sign of the outer and inner police cordons which had secured the scene. I take the road that cuts between the dunes, listening to the wind in the hedgerows, the sound Dad always called "nature talking."

When I think of Bournemouth, I think of pubs and cocktail bars and fireworks on the pier. The view from the Isle of Wight to Old Harry Rocks, and the little clinker-built sailing boat we had in the summer. In Thomas Hardy's time, it would have been pinewood, stretching from the Solent west through the New Forest to Dorchester. I wonder how similar Mum would have been to Bathsheba Everdene, his feminist and impulsive hero.

Sharp pains dig into the small of my back and I decide not to walk as far as the pier. I barely glance towards the beach huts where Elisabeth once lay. Instead, I focus on a yacht dithering in the water, halyards clanking before turning about. It gathers speed, bow cutting the waves, spray pelting the crew.

I trudge through wet sand towards the shoreline and stare at the distant pier, arches and pillars like four dinosaurs, heads and tails welded together. The sea rolls in under them, waves crashing into a milky turquoise blue.

My phone pings with a text.

Edward: Tough slogging it out after an accident, isn't it? Makes you feel defeated.

I turn a half-circle, sneaking a glance behind me. Edward could be a runner, someone I see every morning. A little girl walks along the shoreline, sand hammocked in her anorak. Her mother stands halfway up the beach, eyes narrowed at a sandpiper, stick-legs submerged in the foaming tide. Swimmers brave the water. Dogs chase sticks.

I glance up at the cliffs, where a row of houses shrink back on the flattened land. I see a man with binoculars, cap drawn low over his face. At first, he appears to be watching a couple sitting on deck chairs, their baby dribbling on its dirty bib as it waddles towards the surf. Then the binoculars pan towards me, and for a moment, his gaze appears to be soldered on mine. But the sound of a ferry's horn draws his binoculars towards the horizon. He's simply another walker.

The car accident has realigned the gears in my brain, and my instincts are sharper. Although my stalker teeters at the outer edges of my imagination, I can't go around thinking he's every man.

Dredging the rest of my water bottle, I find a bench and google police scanners and high definition optical zooms. Dad's equipment isn't outdated. It's cumbersome. As I sit there for the next fifteen minutes, hunched over my phone, I realise Edward knows everything about me. As much as I want to return the favour, the playing field is one-sided.

The sound of a man's voice makes me jump. I look up and see the silhouette of a familiar face. Wiry. Charismatic. He opens his mouth to say hello but shoots a glimpse at my forehead and exhales in a low whistle.

'What happened?'

'Oh, that,' I say. 'Some idiot went into the back of us the night before last.'

'Are you OK? Is Jack OK?'

'We're both fine, thanks, Miles.'

Miles is not alone. Standing behind is a woman dragging a reluctant schnauzer. Lashes weighted with mascara and a hoodie zipped so low, it hints to the path of an ample cleavage. I study the reporter I've admired from afar, the queen of our sister paper, the *Dorset Echo* in Weymouth. Jessica is sleekly exquisite, the type to toy with a dried apricot for lunch and a lettuce leaf for dinner. I'm already comparing her long legs to my bowling pins.

She studies me with a scowl and him with a frown. Miles isn't classically striking, although his lips and jaw capture a rare instance of it. He must get used to the pause in a person's expression when they look his way. The weak smile. The blush. Strange for me to be burdened with such minutiae, insignificant things that a week ago meant nothing.

'This is Jessica,' he says.

'You're everyone's girl Friday,' she squeals. 'I've heard so much about you.'

She stretches the last syllable of the word *Friday* to an impressive length. It's such a patronising term, as if I'm sloshing bleach in a toilet one minute and answering phones the next. I'm cringing at her little girl voice, which is sweet when it's coming from a child, but nauseating when it's not. I see why he's drawn to her. Dark hair and a model's cheekbones.

'I'm sorry,' she says, examining my forehead. 'Must have been awful.'

'He rammed us pretty hard. Twice, actually. You should see the fence near the car park.'

'That was you?' She pulls a face. 'Drunk drivers, always preying on older people. They're not as confident as we are, more trusting, you know?'

Older people. Did she just say that?

'Are you sleeping?' she asks.

I give a weary sigh. I haven't slept in nearly a year. If you call drifting off at night to the sound of Kate five years old, sleeping, then no. I feel Kate's heart beating against mine until it stops like a clock someone has forgotten to wind. Then I wake up and remember. That's why I can't sleep.

'Don't be so hard on yourself.' Long hair whips across her face and she bats it away. 'It's OK to be down after what you've been through. A lot of people, more than you'd imagine, pass the day drinking. Then drinking turns to drugs – and I'm not talking about the hard stuff, more painkillers – well, the days are long when you're all by yourself.'

'I don't live by myself. I'm married.'

'Of course you are. Your husband must be very supportive.'

Her words sound like a futile reassurance a doctor would offer to a dying patient. I feel myself doing it, giving her the look that says, 'Really?'

'I'm going to bring you something special,' she says.

'Oh, no, that won't be necessary.'

'Nope. I insist.'

'Let her,' Miles says. 'She's got great taste.'

He strokes her hair and kisses the side of her face. It's the worst thing, the pain that burns behind my ribcage. It's not as if he left me for her. But I can't stop thinking about that night on the beach, the taste of his mouth, his hands exploring.

The schnauzer pulls on its lead, jerking Jessica sideways and Miles with her. They are tangled together, all laughter and intimacy. I feel sick and disoriented and I'm only able to form one coherent thought. Miles and Jessica are in love.

'Look after yourself,' he shouts as they are dragged further away.

I wave and everything goes slowly, and the back of my neck turns to ice. So I walk off in the direction of the sea, kick off my shoes and roll up my jeans. I let the water wash over me and I stand in the sun for a bit, untangling my ponytail with my fingers.

Last week, when I was doing some late night shopping, I saw Miles and Jessica in a tapas bar on Seamoor Road. They were drinking strawberry cocktails by the window, noses almost touching. I felt the strange and lonely isolation of exclusion, then a rare moment of horror at what he and I had done. If no one had a grain of evidence, even after all my carelessness and Miles' hints at work, I'd truly believed our secret was safe. Until now.

The nostalgic chill of autumn is in the air, filling me with anxiety mixed with misery. I'm doing the very thing I need to avoid. Doubting and questioning myself.

16

FREYA

JESSICA'S VERBAL BARBS WEREN'T meant to hurt. There's a naïveté about her, a desperation to be taken seriously. She has a brain, a good one, and a defiant message to those who think looks gets you everywhere.

I take the path uphill towards the road and stop at the broken fence, picturing the ambulance crew plucking us from the twisted wreckage. Scrapes along the kerb show me where the car pinballed from side to side and slewed off the road. I don't see any pole cameras in the car park or further up the street.

At Spyglass Point, houses stretch out on the shaggy bluff, lawns reaching as far as the vertical edge. A clouded yellow butterfly hovers over a privet hedge and I can hear the throaty chirp of a sand martin. As I approach my street, my phone pings.

Edward: It's rude to stand people up.

My muscles shrink as I focus on the blinds behind every window and the possibility of a face. He's enjoying this, seizing me on my home turf, where I thought I was safe. He seems to know every detail of my whereabouts, and he's watching me, gloating – the sadistic bastard. I want to tell him I have no interest in meeting and not to ask me again, when another text dashes across the screen.

Edward: Let me guess – you're trying to work out where I am. There's no maybe about it. You either are or you aren't.

Freya: Why are you doing this?

Edward: Someone needs to watch over you. Think of me as a kind of bodyguard.

Feya: I don't think of you at all.

Edward: We both know that's not true. You think of me all the time.

Freya: I don't know who you are.

Edward: That must drive you mad.

His words are flippant, almost arrogant. He seems unimpressed by my questions, responding with obvious mockery.

Edward: I'm not going away, Freya. The sooner you face up to that, the better.

Freya: I've called the police.

Edward: Bet you haven't told them we're texting.

The screen seems to freeze, as if my tormentor has finished playing his game. Buried in his last text is the threat that he may have made screenshots, something with which to blackmail me. This is the man who'd hinted at being Elisabeth Sanders' killer. I shouldn't be talking to him.

As I turn onto our street, I see a van parked on the kerb outside the flats with a large padlock for a logo. *Parker's Locks & Burglar Alarms*. I wave at the man sauntering towards the front door, chest straining against a tight shirt. He has a parcel tucked under one arm, which, by the smell of it, I'd bet on fish and chips.

'I'm Freya,' I say. 'Trisha might have mentioned me?'

He reaches out a greasy hand. 'Derek Parker. She said you needed cameras. I can install a couple tomorrow, if you like.'

'Tomorrow? You're a life saver!'

I could have dropped to the ground and kissed his feet when he said how little it cost, but the crack in my neck is louder than a gunshot. For the first time, I have a plan, one that isn't motivated by fear. An offensive plan.

I open the front door and Jack's sitting at the kitchen table. He points to the phone in his hand – Captain Duffy, his flying buddy – on loudspeaker, caught at some contest with a gyro receiver in his plane. I mime a teapot and Jack nods.

'Sorry about that,' Jack says, ending the call. 'You know Duffy. You ask him the time and he'll tell you how the clock works. Who's that guy outside?'

'Trisha's boyfriend. I've asked him to install a couple of cameras. £200. All in.'

'What? Like CCTV?'

'Exactly.'

I reach up and kiss him, hoping it might soften him up enough to pull out the wad of cash he's been hiding in his wallet. He'd made £600 on eBay, sold a Sopwith Camel he'd kept since the seventies.

'The doctor says I'm not to have too much caffeine, but don't take my word for it.' His voice trails off as he heads for the couch. 'Your phone was ringing in the night. Might want to turn the sound off.'

What bothers me is that I hadn't heard the phone ring and Jack, ever the sound sleeper, had answered it instead. I check my phone and see a call received at 2.45 am, which must have been the one Jack answered. Then another at 3.00 am. Since there was no notification on the lock screen this morning, Jack must have answered it too. Only this time, the caller left a message.

I hear Jack shaking out the paper, so I tuck myself out of sight and press the phone to my ear. The accent is local but not familiar: *Meet me beneath the Big Wheel at 7.00 am. Don't be late.* It explains Edward's resentment at being stood up.

I know if I tell Jack about my affair, the marriage will be over. But if I tell him a half-truth, that I had been drunk, flirted a little with Miles and that he'd tried to kiss me, surely it's my word against his? Except that Jack would pay him a visit at work and Miles would be accused of sexual harassment. Hardly fair, if I'd initiated it.

But Miles is the only one who can help me. He has access

to records, better than anything I could find in the public domain, and he has contacts who could help me find Edward. I dial his number, the ringing drags on and on, and I leave a message. Then I change my phone settings to silent.

———◦———

Snoo – Kate's raggedy old teddy bear – is soft in the crook of my arm when the doorbell interrupts me from a nap. I lever myself off the couch and open the front door to a ring of loud 'Hellos!'

I'm irritated at the intrusion. It's not like Liv and I were best friends at school, but somehow she's inserted herself into our lives more since Kate died. Tonight, she carries two bottles of wine and Theo delivers a dish covered in silver foil. She sweeps into the kitchen, hunts in a drawer for a corkscrew and pops the cork.

'I hope you've been resting,' she says, as Theo retreats to the sitting room to talk to Jack. 'It's time to take a break from the commuter swarm. All those tired masses looking forward to a glass of wine and dinner when they get home. I must say, I'm a little envious.'

'You're not. You couldn't rest if your life depended on it.' I see my tone brings the hint of a smile. 'What's for dinner?'

'Lobster.'

I wince inwardly because Jack hates lobster. 'I saw Miles and Jessica Tremel on the beach. Was she a model?'

'All I know is she used to work for the *Daily Mail* until her split from Dogg-Martin.' She can see I'm lost. 'Won a Grammy last year for *So Rap (I Think I'll Scream)*?'

'Not exactly a career move, is it?'

'Dogg-Martin?'

'Bournemouth.'

'Don't be ridiculous. Bournemouth is a hotbed of scandal and intrigue.' Liv squeezes my arm. 'I'm proud of you. Couldn't wish for a better assistant. You could dress up a bit. House of Fraser is only around the corner. I've seen this lovely Barbour dress. Pale grey marl. So you.'

I ground myself by looking at impeccable nails and flawless skin. Liv's Twitter handle *@HerOlivianess* gives her an edge. If she's not campaigning to save our rivers and chalk streams, she's talking about the absurdity of closing down Beales Department store. While she's completing the morning print edition or off sourcing ideas and going to events, I proofread, fact-check, and update her contacts. Hardly a call for haute couture.

Liv lowers her voice. 'How's Jack coping?'

'He's distant. If he's not worried about Theo, he's talking to him on the phone. If he's not on the phone, he's escaping to the flying field.' My right foot jiggles, the only sign of my nerves. Liv's gaze focuses on it, brow creased, and I press my toes into the floor, willing it stop.

'And you?' She steeples her fingers, her eyes deepening with concern.

'I don't sleep and I'm anxious. I'm still seeing Dr Meyer.'

I take a deep, meditative breath, terrified she somehow knows every shameful thing I've done. Her face advances and recedes as she tells me how fabulous Sean Meyer is, I'm unable to speak or even blink, my thoughts racing to find a foothold.

She straightens as Jack and Theo walk into the kitchen, and hurriedly changes the subject. 'I've got to write an article on the pay gap and gender equality. What's the betting it will threaten some horrid little man?'

'You always get horrid little men,' Jack says, pulling out a chair. 'Especially when you print something nobody likes. Remember the article about the monumental crappiness of British politics? Don't expect an RAF Coningsby Spitfire and a Hurricane flypast when you die.'

Liv's face puckers with laughter. I catch Jack's eye as he jabs a pea on his fork and dams the sauce with a wall of mashed potato.

Theo leans into me and lowers his voice. 'You know Dr Meyer's big potatoes? Great therapist. He helped me get over the dregs of a bad flirtation. I made someone utterly miserable.'

'I hope she's not utterly pregnant.'

'It was someone I met at the bank. Told her if she wanted to hump an old man, I'm in the book.' He laughs. I flinch.

Theo unscrews the lid off a miniature bottle. 'Want some thinner?'

'I'll pass, thanks.'

'Liv insists I keep off the hard stuff. But what's the point?

Look at you. You did drugs and booze magnificently.'

'Prescription drugs, Theo, and it was only once.'

I feel the phone buzzing in my lap and, for an instant, Theo's eyes drop. I cover the screen with my hand and excuse myself. Creeping upstairs to our bedroom, I shut out the noise behind the door, hoping – or perhaps nervous – that Miles won't want to help. Something loosens in my chest and I take a deep breath.

'Hey, you.' His voice is breathless, as if he's walking somewhere.

'I'm sorry to bother you, Miles.' My mouth is suddenly dry and sticky. 'I need your help. I know this sounds crazy, but I think the man that rammed us is the same man who killed Elisabeth Sanders.'

'Wait, slow down. What makes you think a drunk driver killed Elisabeth Sanders?'

'Because I think he killed my daughter too.'

There's a moment of silence. The temptation to hang up is almost irresistible, to retreat from the shame, rather than confront the reality that he doesn't want to be involved.

'I don't know, Freya. It's a bit of a stretch.'

Be normal, I instruct myself. *You don't want him thinking you're a nutcase.* 'Miles, I'm not making this up. I wouldn't have called you if I didn't need your expertise.'

'If what you're saying is true, then that was quite some stunt he pulled. Not completely out of the realms of possibility. A little unlikely, that's all.'

I sit down on the bed, my thoughts grabbing on to something that will somehow explain how likely it is when Jack's voice floats upstairs, wanting to know if I'd like a slice of lemon meringue pie. I press the phone to my chest, open the door a crack, and tell him I'll be down soon.

I move into the bathroom and perch on the edge of the bath. 'Miles, all I need is a name. The police must know who he is.'

'It's an ongoing investigation, Freya. Which means they don't.'

'You have contacts. Friends.'

'That's not how it works, Freya.'

'How does it work, then? I thought all reporters probed the police for information. Just look at Liv.'

'Maybe it's Liv you should be talking to.'

I try to keep my voice calm and less injured, desperately trying – and failing. 'Please, Miles. I don't trust anyone else.'

Silence again, as if his mind is sorting through how to find a killer and a stalker with no electronic trail. Someone so completely off the grid, there's no way Miles can pull Edward's entire life apart and study it. His options are shrinking with every day that passes.

'I realise killers don't want to be found,' I say. 'But mix that with a stalker and you have a psychotically entitled mind that believes his target belongs to him. He's bound to make a mistake.'

'So you're saying, if we can find your stalker, we'll find Elisabeth Sanders' killer?'

A shiver of dread inserts itself beneath my ribs. I see a nameless figure, bending over a stained and lumpy mattress on a concrete floor. 'Something like that.'

He blows out hard. 'My week's looking hectic. But I'll reshuffle some things around. I can't promise anything though.'

I tell him I understand. When I end the call, doubt tumbles inside me, and I think about the face in the car behind, slipping in and out of the darkness, a spinning and recurring nightmare.

17

FREYA

WHENEVER I HAVE AN appointment with Dr Meyer, I reflect over the past year, realising I've not been using a tried-and-tested method to manage my grief. The alternative would be to lose my mind or jump off the nearest cliff, whichever was quicker. I'm picturing my battered body, surrounded by rubberneckers who'd rather tweet about my death than call for help.

I glance at my phone. A new day, with warmer temperatures and the promise of rain. I take a deep, shuddering breath when it starts to ring. I stab at the screen to connect the call.

'Hi, this is Ben Newey at NFU Mutual. How are you?'

'Fine,' I say, scowling, which pulls the bruise tight above one eye.

'I'm calling about your claim. In order to complete it, we're going to need the other driver information such as name, address, car registration, model—'

'Sorry, Ben. Can't help, I'm afraid. It was a hit-and-run.'

Before he says, 'Sorry to hear that,' I hang up. Ben will have to face that challenge head on.

I walk upstairs to Dad's old room, where we keep the filing cabinet. While it's not an organised system, I know where the no claims certificate is. Except that the hanging file marked CAR DOCUMENTS is empty. The thought of a third party having taken it makes me nauseated and I'm slinging files left and right, and there it is, slotted between two old phone books. I allow myself a few seconds to catch my breath.

I meet Jack on the landing and he leads me to our bedroom window. 'Take a look.'

I'm expecting a headless cat, dangling from a tree branch, but I'm staring at Theo's Vauxhall Corsa parked in our drive. My mouth opens and closes and no sound comes out.

'They dropped it off early this morning. He won't take anything for it. So don't offer.'

Theo wants to help. Does it mean that whatever hints he was making to me about my affair at dinner have been forgotten? Or does he see me as a kindred spirit, consigned to cramping shame?

'It's really ours?' I ask.

'Yep. Now you can drive to Dr Meyer's.'

I turn and twine my fingers in Jack's and his heart thuds against my cheek. Hugging him comes with the thought of why adultery, although not the worst crime in the world when you consider murder and abuse, is unforgiveable. I wonder if Jack has sensed some unknown element that tells him I'm keeping one terrible, mortifying secret.

'I called Patti,' he says, kissing my nose. 'She spoke to a DS in the Adult Safeguarding Team and warned me about a rash of fraudsters. Apparently, they're claiming to be police. We're to call the main number before giving out any information.'

As Jack goes downstairs and out of the back door, I have the perverse urge to laugh. The fact is, how are police to be taken seriously these days? It's all so surreal, so ridiculous. I suddenly wish I could talk to Aynur. Her logical mind sees things differently and she can usually map a path to the solution. But no amount of apologies will ever heal the rupture and I'm simply wasting my time.

I tame my wild hair into a bun and dispense with makeup. The sound of whispering brings me half-way downstairs, and I strain to hear Jack on the phone outside.

'... and psychological evaluations. Letting anyone inside her head is a risk. No... she came off all the pills ages ago... didn't do a damn thing. And these letters... he knows too much about her. I think she's making it... I don't think Edward exists.'

Does Jack honestly believe I'd engineer an elaborate hoax to feed my desire to be loved? If I can read his face as well as he reads mine, I'll find guilt there. Not a flicker.

I hear the familiar clatter of his phone on the hall table as he walks back in. 'Oh, there you are. Derek's installing the cameras today and rekeying the doors tomorrow. I'll get the keys and start the car for you.'

He brushes past me and takes the keys from the peg in the

kitchen. When I hear the soft rumble of the engine, I check his phone. The last number recorded isn't Derek's, it's mine, dated yesterday. Which means he's deleted the call he just made. And there's a text from a caller without a name.

Meet me in Moose Kitchen. 10.30.

I'm seeing black spots as I settle into the driving seat. Who is he meeting and why? I'm aware of a strange stir of emotions and I'm not comfortable telling Jack everything, not if he's in the habit of meeting secret friends. I drive tentatively to get the feel of Theo's car, the blind spots and the sloping dash. I stamp on the accelerator and squeal away as if I have a clear destination in mind. The road is familiar for so many reasons and I see visions of Kate in the passenger seat, eyes a smoky green. I cherish the things we did, sitting on the beach and talking as if a mother's advice could ever be enough. But now, I feel the gnawing, slicing anger that Jack doesn't believe me and it keeps playing on a loop.

A car looms ahead. I brake and hear the screech of tyres, almost ramming a Fiat. A young woman framed in her rearview mirror gives me a wide-eyed stare and on the rear bumper is a sticker, *Baby on Board*. Blood pulses in my head, a deep bass which isn't the antisocial noise from a passing car for once. She turns left at the junction and keeps looking back at me as if I'm about to do it again.

I do a mental about-turn and rehash the incident, only this time I cruise up behind her slowly and responsibly, and she gives me a thumbs-up because I'm a hero.

I park in front of a secluded block of flats on Richmond Park Road. I'm a little early, so I pull up my old Facebook page. I miss Kate's head teacher and I miss the parents' group, but I've posted nothing since Kate died. The impulse to use it to explore Trisha and Derek's accounts has been gathering since Edward's letters arrived.

Trisha's profile picture reveals half a face and a flash of red hair. She's a French translator and works from home. I have limited access since we aren't friends on social media. Her "about" information includes East Devon College and Bournemouth University, and a month ago was the last time she posted about cat protection and early morning swimming groups. Derek Parker's name comes up under "In A Relationship With" and I'm wondering if the change in Trisha's status is a little rapid. He supports Liverpool FC and posts about Race at Your Pace Bike Challenges and Ryder Cup Team Europe. Favourite TV shows; *Unforgotten. The Voice UK.* My thinking being that once I eliminate them from my list, I can focus elsewhere.

I ring Dr Meyer's bell and glance at a car pulling in, but all I see is half an inch of bumper as it parks behind another vehicle. Something deep in my brain – the part that listens to the changing sounds – reads the driver's hesitation. I turn back to the door to survey the scene behind me through shiny red paint.

Call-me-Sean ushers me inside. He has a degree in psychology and, according to his website, offers psychotherapy and hypnotherapy. I peg him around forty-five – sallow skin and dark hair and very rocker chic. He gestures to the couch while he takes the armchair. The sound of his clearing throat breaks the spell and I'm off like a racehorse about my stalker and the car accident – because he'll cut the session short in fifty-five minutes.

'He's following me. Seems to think I'm having an affair.' For a second, I recoil at the word *affair*. It should be safe to tell Sean everything, but I hold back because I'm not ready to share. 'I've answered a few of his texts.'

'Is that wise? Baiting him could make things worse. Remember that guy who stalked a journalist four years ago?'

'I'm not a journalist.'

'That doesn't exclude you. Frightening you makes him feel powerful. Stalkers see themselves as victims. They believe they've been toyed with or led on. Have you ever thought it could be someone you know?'

All the time. I tell Sean I know many people, which is a lie, and I watch them too, which is the truth. You always know when someone is watching you, that prickly sixth sense you can't ignore. But what Sean is keenly observing and tactfully articulating is that my stalker derives pleasure in scaring me. He knows me inside and out. If that's not creepy, I don't know what is.

'Jack's been talking to someone on his phone. There's no contact name.'

'How does it make you feel?'

'Suspicious. I've been reading up about multiple personality disorder. Take a man with two distinct personalities, each with a unique characteristic. If one commits a crime, the other wouldn't remember a thing about it. What if Jack sent those letters?'

'How do you explain the car accident?'

'I can't.'

'Don't you think you'd have seen evidence of this type of behaviour before now? Because you would. You'd know. Whatever you're believing results from what your stalker is telling you. Not necessarily what's happening.'

I want to tell Sean that Jack questions my memory and says I'm overreacting. If Jack knows I've betrayed him, then Edward may be his invention, a way of getting me to admit my guilt. But it sounds so absurd. So un-Jack.

I gaze at the French doors, where a butterfly rests on a buddleia, trapped in a haze of sunshine. I feel the heat of unexpected tears behind my eyes. Edward is becoming a regular presence, like a lodger who won't move out. I'm aware Sean must have followed my gaze, because my cheeks are tingling again.

'Have you offended anyone recently, Freya? Difference of opinion?'

'Why would my opinion matter?'

'It matters to him.'

Who hasn't committed some variation of wrongdoing against a friend? Seriously, has Sean never flirted with someone else's wife, taken umbrage over someone's opinion, got leery over a girlfriend's text messages? Well, hasn't he?

'Did you get along with your father?' he asks.

'Dad was amazing. My second term at Danes House was memorable. Two girls started shouting, "Lion lip. Bum lip. Harelip-Scare lip." Dad shouted back. "Knob off, ya feckin' sluts! Your arses take up half the shaggin' school!" It was long overdue. They knobbed off for a time, but they were always back for more. Dad's parting words to me were poignant in my third year. "Don't be worryin' about the bullies. They're dirty little heathens with tits for brains."'

While Sean's head is bobbing with laughter, I'm thinking about Dad. How he introduced me to Jack. She's *practical,* he'd said, as if cooking and cleaning were a spectator sport and I was its gold medal athlete. Any thoughts on studying English Literature at university disintegrated the day I met Jack. He steadied me at a time when my dating world pitched dangerously towards sexual predators. It's taken months of being swept along by the rapid current of life to get me to a place I can finally call normal. Except there's nothing normal about the unsettling presence of a man skulking around our house at night and a husband who thinks it's me.

Sean's mouth is moving again, and I can't hear a word he's saying over the constant chatter in my head.

'I'm sorry. What was that?' I ask.

'Are you still recording your thoughts?'

'Making lists is an obsession of mine. Story ideas. Leads.'

'I was thinking more about rating your emotions.' He rubs his hands on his jeans and looks at the clock. 'You can look back in a year and see how far you've come. You could join a survivors' group?'

'Not sure it would help.'

'Why?' he asks.

'I don't know.'

'If you could give a reason.'

'Something to do with listening to rejection issues, abandonment, anger.'

I try to ignore the dust on the windowsill and the coffee table. Does Sean dust? Probably not. Probably pretends he can't see the fine layer of grey on every surface.

'Were you angry when your mother died?' he asks.

I glance at the window to avoid eye contact. The tears come quickly. 'She never said goodbye.'

'But you know she couldn't.'

'It's something to do with her not taking me that last time. I suppose I should be thankful.'

'Is it fair to say you weren't able to tell her how you felt?' he asks.

'I was alone in the world, and I didn't get to tell her that I'd lost the most important thing that mattered. Do you know how that feels?'

He nods. 'I lost my mother when I was fourteen.'

I'd say Sean's overcome the hardest part. Establishing trust. Now there's no distance between us.

On the way home, my phone pings with a text from Edward. I turn down a side street and pull over. Attached is a link marked *Sanders diary reveals final week*, an article in a national tabloid. It conveys how the pressure of unwanted gifts and telephone calls weighed heavily on Elisabeth. She said colours were vivid, noises too loud and people spoke at half speed.

Edward: Fascinating, don't you think?

Freya: Not particularly. What's it got to do with me?

Edward: Is this how you feel?

Freya: What would you know about feelings?

Edward: I'm really sensing a tone.

His arrogance points at my shortcomings. Digging, needling. Prying. Even though his thirst to instil fear has intensified, I hadn't expected Elisabeth's words would be so devastatingly familiar. My fingers race over the keys.

Freya: Stop texting me and don't come near
my house!

Edward: Careful, Freya. If you block me, the videos I have of you go viral. Yes, video(s). You and your lover. On the beach. In the car. Quite a sordid little collection.

The first video he took of me on the beach confirms he has more. Even as I'm threatening to toss my phone out of the window, it'll make no difference. Either I own up to the police with all the texts and calls I've failed to mention, or I find this bastard before he incriminates me.

18

EDWARD

HE'S HAPPY, ALTHOUGH IT takes him a minute or two to recognize the sensation. It's a variation on the constant: Determination. Grief. Hate.

Since Dr Meyer's second floor office is at the end of an apartment block, his windows face the car park and gardens. Edward pulls his cap low and tucks a tracker inside the rear bumper of a blue Corsa. He is now able to locate Freya's car, access her trip history and receive notifications.

Returning to his car, he goes through Freya's running routine in his mind. He is every bit as fit as she is and doesn't find the exercise in the least gruelling. Her route used to start at the pier before the accident, going through Lower and Upper Gardens to Prince of Wales Road. Left on Milburn, over into Seamoor and into Alum Chine Road. Then Chine path to the promenade and back to the pier. 3.5 miles.

Her routes vary, sometimes unfolding in surprising ways. Today, she didn't go running at all. She's ignored his threats about talking to the police and it's driving him crazy. Breaking into her house and taking things to frighten her is no fun if he can't watch her fear.

Fumanti's soaring vocals fill the car, and his lips curl around the word *Espirito*. He glances at his face in the wing mirror. His mouth is too rigid and his eyes have a ring of blue around the iris. He almost doesn't recognise himself. His therapist often asks about his father, as if the old man's a fossil that needs dusting off and cataloguing. He insists Edward's feelings of inadequacy stem from his father's rejection. Or that Edward has been over-spanked and under-loved. He goes through the many layers of Father, trying to uncover one incident, a speck of an idea that causes these triggers, and he finds one. The time Father told him about Nisha.

'It sounds crazy, but I love her,' Father said. 'Not more than you. It's a different love. You'll understand when you're all grown up.'

When Mother sacked Nisha, Father threatened to leave too, but it wasn't the type of leaving where he took a suitcase and walked out of the front door. It was the sedative kind where lights flare into space and there's an entire universe of nothing.

It wasn't Father's affair. It was Mother begging him not to leave, her voice like the staccato of machine-gun fire, carving its mark in Edward's mind. Something shifted that day, and now it can take him several seconds to search the files in his brain for the right one. He wants to curl into a ball and sleep for hours. But like a concussion, he might never wake up.

Nearly an hour later and Freya is walking back to her car. She wears a white blouse showing the faint outline of a bra and her hair is coiled in a glossy French knot. She gets into her car – a gift from Theo Hunter – and proceeds down the drive. It strikes him in all his meandering that he needs to decide whether to take her, sedate her and call it a suicide. Or continue in this voyeurism, which he hates to admit he rather enjoys.

She turns right, curling around the roundabout and exiting at the second turning. There's only one place she could be going. Sainsbury's. When they reach the car park, she slots between a Volvo and a Golf. He feels more focused, more optimistic, because inside his car is a syringe filled with a relaxant, needle capped, and ready to go.

He returns to his car and while he waits he thinks of Elisabeth, the girl he'd met a few months ago – long dark hair to her waist, eyes like Freya's. She mentioned getting over a boyfriend. She wasn't getting over him at all. There's only so much ex-talk Edward could take. He hadn't hit her, hadn't shouted at her. He just wanted to remodel her.

He wasn't the problem, it was the noxious influences of the outside world, other voices interfering with her head. But she wouldn't let him help her. That's why he had to tie her up. To be fair, he couldn't expect a woman to love him, not if she was shackled to a radiator.

Freya's life centres on the simplest of tasks. Shopping. Reading. Cooking. Chatting to the neighbour. When the house is empty, Edward spools through her hard drive, rewinds and halts at every photo. Now, he wishes he could reboot her existence and return it to factory settings.

He could take her here, use the needle and dump her in the boot. But, *here* is too crowded, and the longer he waits, the less confident he becomes.

He needs air. He can't breathe. Opening the door, he steps out and weaves through the cars towards the entrance. He can't keep his mind straight and he fears making a mistake, given the pressures of the past few days.

It's just a theory, but what if Freya already knows everything about him? What if she knows the colour of his car, right down to the sticker in the back window?

Look at it this way, he tells himself. If she knew, he wouldn't be here. The twist in his stomach fades and he can breathe again.

He has a side view of the shop door, and when it opens, he flinches slightly. Freya glances towards her car, eyes clipping the heads of every shopper. She walks only a hundred yards before looking down at her bag.

Forgotten something? Or dropped her keys?

In those few seconds, Edward feels a crunch of adrenaline. He smells hot tarmac, he smells car exhaust, and he smells sweat. Then she swivels, almost facing him but not quite. The rush he feels is both instantaneous and exhilarating, and he crouches down on one knee as if he's dropped his wallet. The movement is so natural she won't suspect, out of the three men closest to her right now, he is the one to fear.

He hears her footsteps retreating. Then the slam of her car door. Edward gets to his feet and watches her reverse, slotting into a queue of vehicles departing the car park.

Dr Meyer doesn't think Edward has a problem. His mind simply processes information at an alarming rate. Dr Meyer also says Edward doesn't socialise enough. After giving it some thought, Edward assured the good doc he did, if it counted sitting in restaurants and coffee shops and soaking up the vibe. Maybe only he can see the people he stalks and everyone in this world lives in his imagination.

But that would make him mad, wouldn't it?

19

FREYA

There's a vacant table inside the door and I take a seat. Moose Kitchen is busy at this time of day, tables pulled together to accommodate a large party. Half a dozen patrons, eager to try the Canadian-inspired cuisine, are waiting in line. Not only do they block my view of the arched windows that dominate the restaurant's façade, but the tables along the back wall.

Inside my peopled fortress, I see a flash of grey between two waiters. Jack sits at the far side of the restaurant with his back to me. I can't work out if the man opposite is someone he knows well. The person sitting beside him is obscured by the table in front, but a hand lightly pats his arm. A woman, I think. He leans closer to her, only it isn't loud enough to warrant such familiarity.

I scan the menu for a coffee in case the waiter comes by again, and question how long I can sit here. I can't move two tables over to get a better view of Jack's companion. There's a big chance I'll be spotted.

'Hi, what can I get you?' the waiter asks, snapping me from my prying.

'Coffee, for now.'

'Are you ready to order?'

'I'm waiting for a friend.'

The patrons are all seated now and I have a better view of Jack's table. But if he were to turn suddenly it means he has a full view of mine. The woman beside him is wearing a light blue shirt. Her hair is straight and falls below her shoulders and if I could guess I'd say the style was a lob.

I can't believe Jack would be attracted to the woman, and her motives for an intimate encounter wouldn't necessitate a third party. No, this is a business meeting, because the man opposite Jack is in his early fifties, jowly, and with a hint of a beard. He stares at Jack intently, while spooning soup into his mouth.

The waiter brings my coffee and eyes my menu. 'Do you still want to wait for your friend?'

'Yes. Thank you.'

My mind scrambles for reasons why Jack would be meeting two strangers for lunch, changing his routine without telling me. It could have something to do with the airlines, a hearing about his sudden departure which might have been more serious than I'd earlier thought.

I lean back in my seat so I can catch a glimpse of the woman's nose and chin, but her head is angled so far down I assume she's sipping her soup.

The man opposite pulls out a white card from his jacket and slides it across the table. He taps it a few times, his chin lowered, which tells me it's an invitation to call. Jack spreads his arms out, palms up, shakes his head a few times and then slips the card in his jeans pocket. The man signals for the bill and slides a wallet from his pocket.

Jack looks over his shoulder to glance at the window, his eyes skirting the room briefly. His gaze would have no reason to linger in my direction, he's not expecting me.

I have the urge to leave before I'm noticed. Taking a large gulp of my coffee, I place a tenner on the table. Five for the coffee, five for taking up a table. The bus stop is the perfect hiding place, where I can watch the front door from behind dark tinted glass.

Ten minutes later, Jack comes out alone. Usually, this would award me a sense of peace; my husband trotting down the street alone. But something feels off.

Maybe his aloneness is what's haunting me. Or the meeting he's just had. I shake off the thought and follow him at a safe distance. He turns to study a tall blonde striding the other way, thumbing through her texts without lifting her eyes. His eyes dip to a small boy flying an aeroplane in one hand and dragging his mother with the other.

My mind is too jittery to process that the man I'm following is no stranger to me. He is my husband. I should be able to run up to him and feel his hands on the small of my back. But somehow I'm rooted to the distance. Fascinated by it.

Tempted to let it run for another ten minutes just to see what happens.

My phone shrills and I let it ring.

A spatter of rain, then a full on downpour. Jack ducks into the doorway of a photographers, and I slide under the awning of Tapas Plus. The rain falls even harder, pounding relentlessly against the pavement and pinging off the gutters.

I look down at my phone and my skin prickles.

Edward: Now you know how it feels.

I look up and down the street, and at the people behind me waiting to vacate the restaurant, all staring at their phones as I am. There must be some logical explanation as to why Edward can see me. I gaze across Bourne Avenue at the cars, hoping to see a face pressed against glass. A man walking a dog in the park, or huddling in the bus stop opposite.

Freya: Too chicken to show yourself?

Edward: Far from chicken, Freya. You had your chance remember? Stood me up. Not polite.

Freya: I didn't get your message until it was
too late.

Edward: Excuses. Excuses.

He's clearly capable of setting up an ambush and I need to be extra cautious. I don't want to be attacked while getting into my car. Or expect he has somehow managed to enter it, like they do in the movies, and hide between the seats. I text Jack and ask him if he's on his way.

I angle my shoulder into the slowly abating downpour. I should be able to see him, edging out towards the pavement and strutting through a shaft of sunlight. Any minute now, I tell myself, I can pretend to bump into him. His arms will envelop me and he'll say what a lovely surprise. We can go home together.

I look down at my screen hoping to see three dots to indicate Jack is typing. I force myself to think of the simplest explanation. He hasn't seen it yet. When I look closely at my text to him, there's a read receipt which shows me he has.

I don't care how cold it is, how much water seeps into my shoes, I march towards Jack's doorway and find only two women standing in front of a sign that says *Shop Closed For Renovations*. I ask the one with the green umbrella if she'd seen a man, about this tall, wearing a navy blue sweatshirt. She shakes her head and shrugs, and her friend looks on with equal bafflement.

How far could he have gone? He must have taken a bus, which isn't Jack's favourite mode of transport, especially not after twenty-odd stops to the library.

That's when I get my first inkling. I continue along the pavement as a car whooshes through a puddle and sends a spray against my shoes. I'm running to the nearest bus stop for the West Cliff route, following a row of brightly coloured umbrellas that snake into the shelter. I search for a man who might be looking for me.

Edward: Is it me you're looking for?

Freya: Why are we wasting time texting? Why don't you call?

Edward: So you can hear noises in the background and hope to follow me? You haven't thought it through, Freya. You don't know what I look like.

Freya: Don't count on it!

Something between a groan and a huff of frustration leaves my mouth.

I want to ball my fists and scream and scream until my throat is raw. I dash between the crowds towards the car park, so I can get home without being followed.

20

FREYA

Jack is sitting at the kitchen table, sipping a cup of tea. It takes a moment to register that he arrived home before I did, which is strange if he caught the bus. I try to smile, but it comes out as a grimace.

'Bad day?' he asks.

'A little headache. I'll be fine.'

'I made you a sandwich. Cheese and pickle.'

'Thanks.' I take the plastic wrap off the plate and sit opposite him. If he had time to make a sandwich, he must have got a lift. 'Anything exciting happen?'

'Cameras done. Take a look.'

I go outside and search the eaves. Small and black with tiny pinhole lenses. They would be inconspicuous if our gutters weren't white.

'And I sold a plane,' Jack says, as I walk back in.

Sold. I dwell on the word because it means he either hand-delivered the plane or went to the post office. 'Which plane?'

'The one you say looks like Gromit's.'

Small. Red. Easy to carry. My appetite is returning. 'Were you in town earlier?'

'Briefly. Running a few errands with Theo.'

I pick at my sandwich and tell him I'm going for a run. He doesn't look up, continues staring at his phone which is angled so only he can see it.

I change into my running gear and this time, I take Durleyhurst to Alumdale and then cut back through a path in the woods. I keep running, dodging dog-walkers with retractable leads, years of stress etched into their faces. I run faster, my heart rate spiking, my eyes darting right and left. Behind me, I hear footsteps over my shallow breaths and I don't look back. A man, I think, judging by the heavy tread. I slow down and wait for him to pass, a grey hoodie and a face that stares ahead in semi-hypnotic fog. He's built and he's fast. Could he be Edward tracking me from the front, listening for my footsteps behind his?

To my right is a chain link fence where one side has been cut and bent inwards for access. Undeterred by the NO ENTRY sign, I crawl through the mesh. I like running here because there are no obstacles, no dog's leads to leap over, no crowding on the path. Just me and the forest.

I came here with Dad when I was a kid. It was two years after Mum died and there was no meat in the fridge. Typical dad pulled out his rifle, chambered a few rounds, and off we went to hunt rabbits. When the neighbours reported gunfire in the early hours, Dad resorted to setting snares, which he should have done in the first place. But he said the rifle made him look "manly" and he might attract a chick or two on the way. Like there'd be any women gawping at him at that time of day.

I hear something, a rustling, plenty of forest noises feeding my panic. Could Edward have followed me here? I wait for the inevitable; a hand around my throat, the searing pain of a knife between my ribs. The space between knowing and not knowing is jarring and the stillness is deadly, like a trap. But a squirrel bursts across the path in front of me and skitters into the undergrowth. I nearly stagger and drop to one knee. The sound of my gasp drives a bird from a nearby bush, shooting upwards into the sky.

Slowing to a jog, I labour through the trees until the road is visible. Commuters stand at bus stops, mothers and children out for a stroll, everyone enjoying a blaze of sunshine before the clouds roll in again.

When I get home, I turn on the news. Someone found the largest hoard of Anglo-Saxon coins, an England cricketer made racial slurs, and hundreds march in Manchester. And then, the ticker running across the bottom of the screen tells me they questioned a man in connection with Elisabeth Sanders' death. Police had detained him last night, but ended up releasing him due to insufficient evidence.

The phone rings, jolting my nerves. I let it go through to voicemail. It rings again. And once more after that. Something out of the window catches my eye in the second floor window of the flats opposite. Trisha waving. She's confided things in the past – illegal things – that make her approachable. Not to mention the proximity of her home to mine, which means she might have seen something. Since Arthur is walking towards the bus stop with a slow, dawdling gait, Trisha's alone upstairs.

As I ring Trisha's bell, a car rockets down our street, sending a cresting spray of rainwater onto the pavement. It stops outside our house and the blur of a driver tosses a flyer towards our front door. Bloody salespeople.

Trisha's voice through the intercom has the scratchy timbre of a smoker's cough. She buzzes me in and the sound of clunking crockery tells me she's in the kitchen. Without makeup, she rocks it like a redhead. She wears her hair in two low plaits and her oversized T-shirt barely covers the top of her thighs. There's something sensual about her androgynous appearance that appeals to both men and women. I notice she's had her ears pierced again. Two cartilage hoops and three studs.

'Don't you ever pick up your phone?' she asks from the doorway, slotting a biscuit in her mouth.

'That was you?'

'Who'd you think it was?' She says, between chews. 'Ted Bundy?'

'Close.'

She gives me a funny look and motions for me to add the number in my contacts. 'Milk and sugar?'

'Please.'

The front of our house is the dominant view from her sitting-room window and on the coffee table is a pair of binoculars. I pick them up, trying to curb a recurring feeling of suspicion. A close-up of rain glossing the pavements and a shaft of sun pouring along the road is all I see.

I clear the crushed velvet sofa of its jumble of cushions and refrain from touching a thicket of green buds in a sandwich bag. The police have arrested Trisha several times. I know, because the *Daily Echo* was looking at issues involving drug problems in the King's Park area in support of Operation Planet. Andi Wynter accompanied a sergeant from East Bournemouth's Safer Neighbourhood Team and saw a young woman handing out a little "Jolly Green" to a few grateful takers. Three guesses who it was. Since they couldn't prove she'd been peddling anything more than a gram of catnip, they gave her a conditional caution. It's no wonder she keeps changing her number.

'You look a little stressé,' she says, handing me a mug.

'Oh, it's nothing. You OK?'

'It's a quiet day until you sit down to record your podcast and the cat has a two-minute-long coughing fit. Then your son liquidises a banana without the lid on.' She squints at me. 'So what's really going on?'

I bring her up to speed about my stalker. Judging by an open mouth, she's already unearthed the word "intruder" buried in my account. As for the name Edward, she's as clueless as I am.

Of course, she presses me about the man with whom he claims I had an affair.

'If you must know, it was a mild flirtation with someone at work,' I say. 'Few lunches, nothing more. Well, you can't, can you? Not when you're married.'

I want to tell her it was crazy amazing. How I was burning meals, leaving taps running, forgetting appointments. Not to mention what a liar I've been to Jack. It's hardly a onetime mistake like I was in the wrong place at the wrong time. Not when I did it twice.

'Is that why you go running every day? Because it looks like a lot of punishment for nothing,' she says. 'And don't tell me a girl's gotta get rid of all that winter padding. You look ripped to me.'

'Wait, have you been watching *me* through these binoculars?'

'Never mind that. So this guy saw you two together and now he's trying to blackmail you?'

'Yes. Now he's following me and calling me. It's sick.'

Don't get paranoid, Frey.'

'I'm already paranoid. How can I not be paranoid when I've got a peeping tom?'

'Have you called the police?'

I take a sip of tea and nod. 'DC Franchek. Heard of her?'

Trisha casts a glance at the ceiling and shakes her head. 'I bet she insisted on handling it her way. They always do. And I bet she said your safety is at risk. That's so you don't mess up any other investigation she's got going on.'

Trisha has a natural talent for peeling back life's layers. All the time she's talking, I'm having a disturbing conversation with myself. What if there's a better way, a quicker way to find my stalker?

'Patti seems to think she'll catch him.'

'Right,' Trisha says. 'But gonna totally disagree with your cop friend. Don't tell. And she's off her rocker if she thinks this stalker's easy to find. I'd bet Chester's dinner he's got more names than a drug user. Are you taking anything to help you sleep?'

'Do I need to?'

'You look wired. Might try smoking a little...' She points to the sandwich bag.

'I'll pass, thanks.'

True to say, I've seen a little orange tip glowing in Trisha's window at night and wondered how many hours of sleep she actually gets.

'It's been a few months,' she says. 'I thought it was fireworks at first, but who sets off fireworks at 2.00 am? This guy was standing in the street with his back to me, hurling stones at your bedroom window.'

My lungs feel swollen, likely to burst. 'What did he look like? Was he tall? Short?'

'It was dark.'

'Trisha, think. This is important.'

'Tall, fit maybe.' She looks like a horse whinnying. 'I was into my third gin, but I think about it every so often.'

I know a lot of fit people. You do when you run. I think of the man in the grey hoodie in the woods. How fast he ran, how sturdy he was. While I take a moment to grapple with why Trisha had heard stones rattling against glass at 2.00 am, I'm reminded she has chronic insomnia. It has something to do with her ex-husband and the abuse to which he subjected her.

'Do you know anyone in law enforcement?' I ask.

'You tell me. I've been arrested three times.'

'I didn't mean active. I meant retired. Someone who could find this person.'

'You've always wanted to be a reporter, Frey? Report your way around town and find him yourself.'

'That comes with a level of weirdness. Me, a phoney reporter, canvassing the street hoping to find a man with a fake name. What happens when I get arrested for impersonating my boss? ("Liv, I'm calling from a prison payphone...")'

'Don't work yourself into a heart attack.'

'Easy for you to say. You're not tortured with guilt.'

'I'm here for you, Frey. Remember that.'

If Trisha's scouring my face for signs of a psychotic crack, I bet she's found a few. Fear washes over me like an immense wave as we try to figure out the best way to expose Edward. She slides away from my questions about her life with joking answers. I can't help feeling a tremendous tie with her, like a sister.

When I get home, I pick up the wedge of cardboard on my

doorstep sealed with gaffer tape. I rip it open and the ground yaws beneath my feet.

You didn't waste any time, did you, Freya? A police officer and now a pair of eyes in the eaves. Remember what I said? Digging has consequences.

Edward.

21

FREYA

JACK IS ON THE phone in the bedroom, voice booming across the house. 'Let me spell it for you. Foxtrot-Romeo-Echo-Yankee-Alpha.'

He hangs up and almost jumps when he sees me standing at the door. 'That was Patti. No fingerprints on the letters, I'm afraid. But there was a witness who saw our crash.'

'Does this witness have a name?' I check my phone and see a missed call. 'Jack?'

'What?'

'A name? The witness?'

'It was some woman who lives on the same street.'

Some of the flats along Durleyhurst Road have sea views. The night of our accident was warm, as I recall, and many have wide balconies and sliding doors. This witness shouldn't be hard to find.

I hand him Edward's note and he reads it without breathing. His eyes flicker back and forth, rereading the words in case there's a hidden meaning behind them.

'Trisha saw a man a couple of months ago,' I say. 'He was standing outside our house in the early hours, throwing stones at the windows.'

'What would she know after polishing off a bottle of grog?'

'Jack, I'm serious. Trisha saw someone. It's important.'

I'm losing the instinct I'd once had for Jack. Those permanent points of reference are no longer fused inside me and when I look at him I see blank space. Now his focus is taken up with the blue cardboard, which served as some kind of wrapper.

'I know exactly what this is,' he says.

I follow him into the kitchen to where we keep our beer and I see it before he opens his mouth. A box of classic ales from Sainsbury's, cut down one side, an exact match to the piece he's holding in his hand. He unfolds it to correspond with the brewer's names, *Hobgoblin, Cumberland, Pedigree.*

'I wondered why it had been cut.' He looks at me and his jaw tenses. 'If he's been in our house...'

Together, we scroll through surveillance video on Jack's iPad. So far, we've captured a few pedestrians, a runaway dog and a paper bag that swirls in a semi-circle before wafting down the street. Out of nowhere, a car slows outside our house. My mind rewinds to the one I'd seen earlier, white, and speckled with mud. But Trisha's voice at the intercom prevented me from investigating further. The face isn't visible through the windscreen, but an arm extends across the passenger seat as he lobs the letter at our front door.

'We've got him,' Jack says. 'We've got the bastard.'

'You can't see his face.'

'The plates. Right there.'

Jack assures me the police will enhance it. But what if the number plates are fake? Stolen from another car? Apart from anything else, it's yet another incident that can slither through a loophole unchallenged. For the first time, I feel unequal to this, overwhelmed by the events that have built up over the past few days. There are wounds that go beyond the ones in the mirror and this letter is another deliberate act of torture.

'Patti Franchek? Jack Thorne.' I think he's talking to me except for the phone pressed against his ear. 'We've had another incident and I have video this time. I'm on my way.'

When he hangs up, I tap him on the arm. 'I'm the primary victim, Jack. I should go.'

'You're not in a fit state, love. I can tell by the way you're rubbing your temples. You've been getting them often?'

'What?'

'Migraines.' He takes a bottle from his pocket and rattles it. 'Here. Take a couple.'

The comment causes a spasm of rage. Jack has every right to talk to Patti, to receive her counsel, as I have done. But his allusion to my health is jarring. On and on, he goes about my absent-mindedness. I can't imagine what it's like for Jack to study each of my mental fractures and not know how to repair them, to hear me talking to myself – entire conversations

– while I'm cleaning. Something about him feels off, like an underlying whisper from a source I can't identify. He grabs the car keys and the door slams, leaving me in a vacuum of aloneness.

When my mind clears, everything becomes cold and hard. *Get it done, Freya,* I think.

I text Miles. Meet me tomorrow at Waterstones. 2.30.

The response is almost instantaneous. *I'll be there.*

I keep feeling as if I've been cast off my regimented path and led and down a dark, windy track to who knows where. Had I not been so starved for any kind of human interaction, I wouldn't have thought of calling him in the first place.

I study the flats, my hand pressed against the window. Trisha's typing. The man two windows over is pacing around the room while on the phone, and one floor below, a child is dribbling a ball, mother standing over him with an extended finger. My focus shifts to my hands, where ragged fingernails could do with a lick of varnish. At the tip of my little finger, where sunlight refracts through the glass, I notice a chip.

I heard stones rattling against your window.

As I stand in breathless silence, I realise it could be the impact point where a car kicked up a stone, or simply a fault in the glass itself. But Trisha said stones, plural, which means another conscious act that took place over two months ago that failed to get my attention. It explains why Edward's persistent contact is escalating. His preoccupation with me stems from not only his involvement in the Sanders case, but mine too. Where I have no proof of his association with Elisabeth, he has a video of me with Miles.

I pull up the Dorset Police Facebook page. Below the *We're Here for You* post is an appeal.

> #LatestNews - Enquiries into the circumstances of the death of Elisabeth Sanders are being carried out by detectives from the Major Crimes Investigation Team (MCIT). DC Franchek said: "A detailed investigation has been launched and I would appeal to anyone with information that may assist our enquiries to contact us."

There's an anonymous free phone number and links to Crimestoppers online. I'm hoping a witness saw something a little more specific than a man in a hoodie. Who doesn't wear a hoodie?

My focus veers outside, to where the wisteria twines against the glass, leaves pearled with raindrops. Before I can throw open a window to smell the perfume, my phone screeches to life, startling me. It rings twice and then stops.

I ram my face between the blinds. A skinny child and a blousy mother walk along the pavement to the flats. Theirs is the only movement in the street. If Edward wants one last session in the boxing ring, my fists are up, and I'm dancing.

Then a text.

Edward: Do you know what my favourite game was when I was a child?

I don't want to engage, but I've already started typing:

Freya: No.

Edward: Hide and Seek.

Freya: Very funny.

Edward: I wasn't trying to be funny. I'm simply choking on the silence over here.

Over where? He's already got me pacing around the house, looking behind doors, glancing up the narrow staircase to the landing.

Freya: What's your name? Your real name?

Edward: Edward Besant. It's French. Like it?

I don't respond, allowing the silence to choke him as much as it's choking me. It's not his real name. He wouldn't have given it so freely if it were. My screen goes black and then lights up again with his next text.

Edward: You married people, I don't know how you do it. Pretending to love each other, all smiles, one lie after another. Has Jack ever been to a hooker? I bet he has. It's not like you'd ever know.

Something in his tone trips a feeling of unease. I want to block him, but I can't tear my eyes away. A tremor starts around my mouth, and the noise in my throat isn't quite human. He sends another text.

Edward: Don't go alone to the woods. It's where fools stray and their bones are never found.

22

FREYA

IF I HAD PUSHED a little harder, I might have drawn him out, but he's smarter than that. I am beginning to understand the rhythm that is Edward, his texts, his threats, his all-consuming presence.

I google the name Besant. It goes back to the early 1900s and describes a François Besant married to Cordélia Dufault. A quick skim of Twitter, Facebook and LinkedIn confirms Edward doesn't exist, although a YouTube documentary for human rights activist Annie Besant shows up twelve times on the images tab.

If Edward had ever displayed any type of psychotic disorder, he may have seen a doctor through the NHS, or been referred to a private therapist. I scroll through local website links which list three predominant names, Dr Sean Meyer being the first on the list.

I make a note to book another session with Dr Meyer. To his credit, he hasn't written me a prescription for antidepressants.

Medication is only part of the treatment and talking to him is the best therapy for me. I haven't slept in days. At night, I fall into a jagged sleep, waking at every noise and then dozing for the rest of it. During the day, I want to run as far as I can from this gut-gnawing guilt and tell Patti Franchek everything. But it's safer to keep my troubles to myself.

There's a letter from our insurance on the kitchen table about our old car. Distorted scenes slot in my head and a scream soars into the night. I remember the car ploughing into us and a chorus of grinding and popping. I'm lying somewhere with the shadow of someone above me.

I count off the people I know. Theo had access to our house. He had keys. Even though he's still fit, he'd never have dragged a woman across the beach, let alone killed her. Where would he have kept her all this time?

My mind jerks back to the dinner party. I remember whole chunks of it, the brief interlude between the main course and the dessert where Liv and Jack disappeared into the kitchen. When I looked over, they sprang apart like guilty adolescents. I try to ignore the images and voices that clamour for attention, needling and coaxing because they know I'll engage.

The more Edward permeates our lives, the more convinced I am that he's poisoning us. I empty the water jug down the sink and a carton of milk, and as much as it pains me, Jack's stash of beer. I clean out the fridge and start all over again. I'm saving lives.

On the news, the police talk about evidence discovered in

Elisabeth Sanders' computer, but they don't say what. They keep showing pictures of the beach and close-ups of how she used to look. The picture they don't use is the one I saw; a woman so still and sad and utterly defeated.

It's almost midday when Jack hauls a toolbox from the back door to the front. I hear Derek talking about pins being cheaper and rekeying being the way to go. Even though we're paying Derek for the job, Jack insists on keeping an eye on things. I realise, with a surge of relief, that the commotion provides a landscape of routine. Even Rabbi Aviel is outside, watching their progress like a foreman.

I take a packet of jammy dodgers and join Arthur outside. He reminds me of a barn owl, amber eyes and hair sticking out at the sides of his head. He's kicking up a few divots in the lawn, and there's a downward slant to his shoulders.

'Shouldn't you be at school?' I ask, patting the wall beside me.

'I threw up this morning.'

'I'm sorry to hear that. Something you ate?'

'Nah. There's a bug going around.' He smiles and tucks the biscuits I give him under one arm. 'Why are you having your locks changed?'

'We lost our keys in the crash. It's just a precaution.'

Together we watch Jack and Derek discussing cylinder plugs. Two kids chase each other down the pavement, football pinging off the gutters and rolling into the street.

'I've received another letter, a few weird calls,' I say.

'You could just change your number. But if he hacked your phone, he can hack anything. For all you know he works for British Telecom.'

'Awful thought.'

He's sees my eyes drop to the scar on the underside of his wrist and pulls down his sleeve and says he'll be seeing me. I hope he's not taking a razor to his skin, needing to feel pain to drown out the tears inside. Any feelings of abandonment from his father dying aren't new to me. There's always the internal conflict between who we are and who we think everyone expects us to be.

I squeeze past Derek and Jack, and no sooner have I put my phone on the coffee table than it rings. My muscles twitch as if fighting to stay calm. It's either Edward leaving a creepy text or Miles cancelling our meeting.

A voice says, 'How are you holding up?'

I almost collapse on the couch with relief. 'I'm fine, Patti. You?'

'Good. Although, I wish I had better news. There were no fibres or prints on the evidence you gave us. Your video footage – I traced the car to a lifeguard. He said a child around ten or eleven gave him the envelope with a tenner attached. The tenner was in exchange for delivering the envelope. No questions. Easy money. I'm still looking for the kid.'

It's a minor victory. Our cameras have forced Edward to retreat. 'You mentioned something to Jack. A witness to our car crash.'

'We don't give out names, Freya. Please know she was accommodating.'

Accommodating could mean the witness gave an outline of what she saw without providing much detail. I'm sure Patti hears the disappointment in my voice, but the thing is, I can work out which house by knocking at every door on the street.

'We need to establish a pattern,' she says. 'Sometimes we see things flatten off before they escalate. You are changing your routine?'

'I don't go to work every day, if that's what you mean.'

'I mean running, going out on your own.' I hear her flicking a pen and shuffling papers. 'The DC you spoke to about your accident, you did say Owen?'

'Yes. Why?'

'We don't have a DC Owen.'

The world tips and greys at the edges, pin-striped shadows quivering on the opposite wall. I silence the noise by ending the call.

It won't matter where I go or how often I change my routine. Edward will never go away.

My fingers flip between the hangers and I select a sheer long-sleeve top and hook it on the doorknob. I scoop my hair into a bun and then apply a little shimmer and eyeliner.

Before I leave, I wash up a few dirty plates and mugs Jack has left idling in the sink. Mum's voice floats through the years: *A clean house is the mark of excellence.* It's not like she's going to come back and ensure I'm following the housewife's protocol, but I ensure no trace of crumbs – or smears of jam Jack has left on the draining board – are left for prying eyes.

I'd rather lose myself in the drone of city traffic than watch my street. The nearest Waterstones is in the Quadrant Arcade, where readers loll on couches and a cup of coffee fills an entire afternoon. I park at St Peter's, which is not a car park. I'd like to say I have an agreement with the vicar, but I haven't been to church since I was sixteen. I could, however, be looking at Mary Shelley's tomb or admiring the west transepts and baptistry. There are plenty of other tourists milling about.

When I get to the high street, bus engines rev, horns blare as they pull away from the kerb. I skirt a pile of rubbish spilt from a toppled bin and bump shoulders with a woman as she hurries by. The Arcade decants a crowd of shuffling school children, gazing at their phones and giving running commentaries on their Insta-feeds, and a parade of businesswomen clatter by with Costa flat whites and sticky toffee coolers.

The homey smell of coffee and muffins hits me as I enter the book shop. My fingers brush over a few thrillers, and I hear the ping of a text. It's Jack, saying we've got more locks than Dartmoor Prison. I text a thumbs-up emoji.

A heavy hand on my shoulder and I wheel around. He's grinning, which is not a bad thing and separates me from my nerves. Something about him locks my body in place, and I absorb him as he absorbs me. He does that jolty thing with his feet, going in for a kiss on the cheek that doesn't quite work. Him, moving to his right, me, moving to my left, our lips almost touching. Despite the crisp weather, I'm sweating, embarrassment tugging for my attention.

He pays for two cappuccinos and drops his change in the tip jar.

'Thank you for meeting me,' I say.

'Not at all. You look great, by the way.'

He selects a table by the window and pulls out a chair for me. I see a press card peeking over the lip of his shirt pocket, the *Daily Echo* logo in large print. I don't ask him where he's been. It's too needy. But I marvel at how easy it must be to gain access to places the rest of us can't. If his face wasn't plastered on that card, I'd ask to borrow it.

He slides into his chair and dumps his bag on the floor. A bee bumbles over an array of potted plants and I look down at the glazed arcade, stragglers strolling in and out of shops. I'm thinking he's about to pepper me with questions, but he doesn't. He launches in with the fun stuff, taking the edge off my biting nerves.

'You weren't sleeping with me for the sake of your career? You know, angling for a promotion?'

'Really, Miles? It never entered my head.'

His eyes dart around the room, though the café is practically empty. I can't look at him without sensual images forging themselves into my limbic brain. Two people running riot on the beach and standing in the frothy lip of the sea. I'm trying to tamp down the Before and After, wishing I could blot it from my memory.

'I hear you've thrown your name in the hat for Andi Wynter's assistant. I think you'd be brilliant,' he says. 'I understand the need for a change. Can't be easy working for a friend. Especially someone like Liv.'

'It's not that. It's just... she can be a little critical.'

'That's putting it mildly. So, what's happening?'

I tell him everything, from finding Elisabeth Sanders to the car crash. His mouth slackens when I describe the letters from Edward that threaten to tell Jack about us. I expect him to argue, but he simply nods. I want to reach out to hold his hand, but instigating any kind of contact expresses approval, and I can't go there. Everything is rotating around me as if I'm driving on a roundabout with no exit.

'Blackmail isn't something you predict unless you're a celebrity.' He takes a sip of coffee. 'Does this bastard have a last name?'

'Besant. He says he caused our car accident. I know this is going to sound weird, but I think he's been in our house. I'm scared.' My face reddens as my mind slips back to us. I promise myself explicitly there'll be no more *us*. 'I need to ask you something. The Christmas party. I don't remember much, that's all.'

'Oh. Right. If it makes you feel any better, no one does. Liv was the perfect hostess, and Andi spent the evening doing a partnered hustle with her wife. I was doing a little freestyle in the corner with Drew. I had to help him up a few times.'

'Did anyone see us leave?'

His eyes float to the ceiling and back at me. 'You were talking to Liv's driver. He was flirting. He does when he's had a few. You were pretty verbal about how your daughter died: everyone was uncomfortable. You know how they are.'

'How are they?'

'People can't cope with grief. They don't know what to say. Anyway, you were out of your tree.' He ducks his head a little as if *being out of my tree* exonerates me. 'I gave you a lift. I think about it sometimes.'

I open my mouth, but my throat's sealed shut, and I brace myself for the agony of hearing him say what an idiot I am or that I have some kind of neurosis, but he does no such thing. I sip my coffee and remember how he once pressed a finger along my upper lip to catch the foam. His eyes drop to my mouth, and his fingers twitch.

'What we had was wonderful, Freya. It was one night, well, two, but no one knows.'

'Edward may have proof.'

'What kind of proof?'

'Photos. Video. Us on the beach. In the car.'

He leans back and takes a breath. 'Shit.'

I open the video Edward took of me on the beach when I found Elisabeth, and push my phone across the table. 'If I keep going to the police, all the videos he took of us will go viral.'

A small crease appears between his eyes, and I know what he's thinking. It's my privacy this stalker has invaded. My marriage, my career, my reputation. I could lose everything. So could he.

'Freya, look at me. I trawl hundreds of online networks. There's bound to be someone who knows him. Andi and I have been having brainstorming lunches at work and the more reporting we do about the Sanders case, the more sources come to us. We see trends we didn't think to look for before. Readers are getting involved and we've already had a significant response. It's slow going, yes, but we will find him.'

Miles holds out his phone to me.

Elisabeth Sanders' killer still not found
By Andi Wynter
Senior Crime Reporter

Forty-year-old Elisabeth Sanders' body was found on Alum Chine beach at around 6.45 am on Tuesday by a jogger. She was reported missing two weeks ago when she failed to show up at work.

Chief Investigating Officer, Joshua Petersen, of Bournemouth Police, said: "We are continuing to make enquiries to identify the person responsible. I would urge anyone with any information, or who may have witnessed the incident, to please contact us."

To speak to police, visit Dorset.police.uk or call 101, quoting occurrence number 44100000617.

There's an old graduation photo of Elisabeth and one with her mother and a sentence on how a "runner" found Elisabeth. I'm glad for the anonymity. Andi was the first reporter at the scene, which means the officer I'd spoken to had alerted her. His radio obscured his name badge and it wasn't until he unclipped it to make a call that I remember seeing the name Petersen.

Miles reads the summary. 'It says here that Elisabeth lived with her boyfriend, Max Lalonde. He was unaware Sanders was depressed and lonely, or that she used the internet to meet other men. Apart from statements from the police about pursuing several lines of enquiry, there's not much else.'

'It makes you wonder, doesn't it?' I say. 'He could have lashed out.'

'Something tells me the story's about to change. Different angle.'

'What do you mean?'

He gives me a look, more lingering than the first. 'There could be others the police aren't telling us about. There's one woman dead. *One*. Now they're calling this The Alum Chine Killer. Sounds like they're jumping to conclusions.'

'Maybe they're including other missing cases.'

'I know I'm reaching here,' he says. 'But remember the woman who was attacked outside a nightclub in Poole? She was dragged into the back of a car and almost strangled. If it hadn't been for a crowd of men who witnessed the incident, she'd be toast. Then there was the attack on a woman outside the pier gift shop.'

'Nian Zhen.'

'Right. Except she kneed him in the groin and ran.' He raised both eyebrows before he spoke again. 'Pity she was too drunk to identify him.'

'You agree there are similarities. Of course, it all makes for a good story.'

I try to visualise the cord used on Elisabeth Sanders. But all I can see is her neck, bloody and puckered, and I can almost hear her final ragged breath and sense the regret she must have felt.

'There's something else,' I say. 'Elisabeth Sanders was wearing a ribbon similar to the one Kate wore. What are the odds of two girls wearing the same thing?'

'You mean two separate incidents, one common thread? Possibly. But whatever you saw, you weren't in your right mind. Think of what you're going through now.' He puts an elbow on the table, his hand resting against his forehead. 'I'm just throwing out a few thoughts. But are you having therapy? I'm not saying you *should* have therapy. That would sound condescending, insulting. Or shorthand for "*you're crazy*" which you're not. Painful experiences don't become tolerable because you talk to someone. It's like getting a health check. Life's great. You want to improve it.'

'Tell me about it.'

'I was going to meet Jess for lunch,' he said, 'but I bailed after you texted.'

A flush prickles up my neck to my cheeks. 'A beautiful reporter versus an average girl Friday. I am flattered.'

'It's the same for me.'

'What is?'

'The average part. I'm not into glossy, if that's what you think. I'm not into self-deprecation either.' For a second, his dark eyes hold mine. 'You've never struck me as being uncomfortable in your skin. Are you?'

'Only when people point it out.'

His knee is warm against mine. The anticipation of touching without inhibition, the promise of another night. Has he told Jessica about us? I like him, the feeling of being with him. The hitch in his breath. The smell of his cologne.

A couple sits down next to us and I realise they keep glancing over. We make an odd pair. Me, the quintessential battered housewife – black eye visibly blacker – and him, The Everyday

Man, and he doesn't even know it.

'You could go away for a few days, get your mind off it,' he says. 'There's a conference in investigative journalism in London.'

He's captured me again, and by the shimmer in his eye, I'm hoping he's going to ask me to go with him.

'What about a trip to Paris?' he asks. 'You'd love Paris. You could spend the day at the Palace of Versailles...'

You. Not us. I try to keep the plug of emotions from my voice, but everything comes out in scratchy whispers. There have been a few times in the past year that I've wanted to search for him, to catch his hand in mine, to see if he'd pull it away like Jack does. I don't know what I want anymore. I'm still seething after Jack remarked on my recent failures.

'I shouldn't have asked you to come,' I say. 'I shouldn't even be here. I'm sorry.'

I'm not sure sorry is the right word, or even the point. It seems weak in the scheme of things. Sorry. The verbal Band-Aid. The cure all. I'm trying to make sense of the person I was and the person I am now, because *sorry* doesn't do it.

23

FREYA

As I walk back from St Peter's Church, I'm unsettled by a man stooping to open his car door. A red Mini, four cars from mine and parked in the same row. He is in his mid-thirties, dressed in khaki trousers and a navy polo shirt. Director of music – or stalker? He seems to watch me through the passenger window as I unlock my car. I wait for him to slide past.

I reverse slowly, slotting in behind him, resisting the urge to return the stare he gives me through his wing mirror. He turns into the street, and I could have sworn he looked over his shoulder more than once before accelerating as far as the lights.

The phone shudders in the cup holder, and I ram it against my ear. I strain for any sound, a cough, a barking dog, something I might recognise. What my mind mentally maps is the crash of distant waves. That part, at least, is familiar. It strikes me that the caller might enjoy this too much – and before he says something in a gravelly bass, I jump in.

'You may be interested to know that your number is not as private as you think.'

I hang up. If Patti Franchek deems these calls severe enough to get a warrant, she will likely find the numbers borrowed or stolen. I've fantasised about setting a trap for Edward and taking a swing at him with a tennis racquet if he came through the door. But what if he died? When I think it through, would it satisfy the Crown Prosecution Service that I'd acted in self-defence?

I glance up at Trisha's window as I pull into my drive, her blinds are angled to shut out the light. Does a computer hacker and lock changer make Derek suspicious? Is Trisha really a French translator?

Jack's voice bellows as I open the front door. Something about his phone battery. Of course, it's dead if he doesn't plug it in at night.

It's hard to tell what he's thinking. One side of his brain is in the moment, the other side existing in the past, seamed down the middle like a walnut. He tells me I've burnt a hole in his favourite shirt. As strange as it is, I don't remember doing any ironing since we arrived back from the hospital.

His next gripe involves the beers I threw away and a fresh carton of milk.

'Freya, you think this stalker is trying to poison us. He's not. You think he's on some kind of revenge kick. For what? You believe the police put Kate's case on hold when they ruled her death an accident. There's no fresh evidence to suggest otherwise. I'm not saying everything you see and feel isn't real. You see where I'm going with this?'

'You can't deny the letters aren't proof.'

'The letters, yes. But...' He trails off and then takes a breath. 'I'm only going to ask you because I must. Were you... are you having an affair?'

'Very funny.'

'I want to believe you. I want to support you, but your behaviour doesn't make it easy. I don't want any more nasty surprises.'

I shake my head. 'What are you talking about? You think leaving a letter on your workbench isn't a surprise?'

'So you have been going through my things?'

'Oh, come on, Jack. I didn't know the airlines were about to "retire" you.'

'That's not true. They gave me the option to rest, take time off, but I wanted to retire.' He looks into my eyes and I feel a flicker of hope. 'Airlines rarely fire pilots, Freya, not unless there's alcohol abuse or unwanted fraternisation. I didn't do either.'

'So why the letter?'

'It was a warning.'

I'm ashamed of my character assassination when all along, I'm trying to find a reason to bring him down to my sordid level. My complaint is petty by most people's standards, but my standards no longer bear any relation to most people's.

I'm being squeezed into a corner, and I'm afraid Edward may, because of his twisted mind, send Jack the proof he needs.

I might think differently tomorrow. But somehow I doubt it.

24

EDWARD

THE MOON SHINES THROUGH the ribs of the old tree, painting stripes on the car bonnet. Wind howls and thunder clatters in the distance. Edward pops a wedge of chewing gum in his mouth.

What a crappy day, and it will be another crappy night. He doesn't want to go into it, except for a name. Arthur Miller. The last time Edward was here, he noticed a flashy car in the street, the same car that appeared on the Miller boy's Instagram feed. If the little shit keeps taking pictures of everything, from nesting birds to girls, he may be monitoring unfamiliar cars and registration plates.

The second thing was Freya in Waterstones with lover-boy. Edward stakes money the meeting was to rekindle the affair. Her hair was coiled in a knot and her eyeliner flicked at the corners of her eyes. He hates this new side of her, hates it with a depth he's never hated before in his life.

For a split second, he thought she was Elisabeth and wished

he'd never met her. He also wished he hadn't killed Elisabeth. Not in the sense of regret – at least not *genuine* regret – but because there was evidence to be dealt with. Just before she died, he'd realised he'd spent two entire months fantasising she was someone else.

Elisabeth knew. She'd known for several months what she'd signed up for: a man who could only give half of himself. On one level, Edward knew her suffering was so extreme he didn't want to think about it. Except that thing she'd said before she died.

What was it? His mind does a cartwheel and there it is, like a flashing neon sign.

'They know who you are and you'll never hurt anyone again.'

They don't know who he is. They don't *know*. Here he is outside Freya's little cottage, about to do it all again. It's true he wants to be immortalised. But he doesn't leave his signature behind, or allow a pattern to emerge. No fingerprints to analyse. No scenes to preserve. Not a single clue to his identity. He doesn't leave evidence. He takes it.

His mind does a mental run-through. He pulls on his gloves and shrugs on his backpack of tools. The Thornes are too dim to realise the cameras pose no threat to him. He can easily turn off the power supply, or jam the signal if they are wireless. Or he can use the back alley. No cameras there.

He sprints silently down the side street, invisible, like a trail of dry ice hovering along the pavement. A cat stalks along the fence, tactile hairs shimmering along his snout. Instead of yowling and scampering off into the shadows, the animal crouches, penny-sized pupils closing to a slit.

Edward gives it a wide berth, slips between the slats in the fence, knowing he will assemble them neatly together when he leaves. Using a small glass cutter, he scores the pane above the lock, lifts it carefully from the frame and props it against the doorstep. He unscrews the bulb on the back porch enough to turn it off. They'll assume the breaker has blown or the bulb has burnt out. Then he reaches in for the lock, and he's inside.

Now comes the fun part. He walks through the house to the front door, slides back an upper bolt and unlocks the dead lock. By opening it a crack, Freya will believe it's how he got in, yet the cameras will show no evidence. He then leaves Freya's gift on kitchen counter. He wonders how Freya will explain that to the police.

He partially unscrews the bulb for the kitchen lamp. Below it is a bottle of Malbec, a peppery blend he quite likes. He pops the cork and selects an antique Fleur de Lys goblet from the cupboard. It pays to take his time.

He notices an empty whisky bottle in the bin, the same one he'd used to inject the sedatives. It should have knocked them out cold. The thought gives him the chills, raises the hairs on the back of his neck. It's like he's high on hatred, his mind laughing and shouting and calling Freya every name he can think of.

He can pick up their voices in the house. The fact is, he's

thought of everything – down to a bug under the sofa. He doubts they pay attention to furniture imprints, or drywall shavings in the bathroom, where a pinhole camera hides inside a light switch.

Upstairs, he sees the first hump – Jack lying on his front, wrapped in the duvet and head partly tucked under the pillow. Freya is lying on her back, one knee bent, the hollowed out scar of her navel exposed. He can't think of another woman who looks this good while sleeping.

On the bedside table is a small notebook. Flicking through the pages, he sees dates and times, and a list of all his gifts. He is flattered she is keeping a record. If it weren't for a tiny light on the charger pad under the bed skirt, he wouldn't have found her phone. He takes it into the bathroom and downloads an app from the dark web, paid for with untraceable cryptocurrency. Expensive, but it allows him to monitor her calls and emails remotely.

Returning the phone to the pillow, he argues with himself over how much sedative they've ingested. She stirs a few times. He waits ten precious seconds for her breathing to return to its regular rhythm. He traces her shoulder and down to the knuckles of her hand; the membrane covering his fingers allows him to feel every tiny bump. Being next to her feels perversely like progress.

He knows chloroform isn't everything it's cracked up to be. It can take minutes to knock someone out and intense strength to hold them down. The recovery time can be up to half an hour accompanied by shivering, headache and vomiting, and that's if they haven't suffered a heart attack.

Her limbs are so pale in the moonlight, he almost believes she's dead. Lowering his face to hers, he feels warm breath against his lips. In his pocket is the syringe. He slips off the cap and a bead of liquid hesitates on the needle before dripping onto her skin. He aims for her thigh, thumb resting on the plunger. It's just enough to put her to sleep. Hopefully not for good.

But as he drives the needle in, her hand bats the syringe to the floor. He has pierced the skin, not enough to put her under, enough to feel the prick of an insect bite. Her moaning tells him she is waking. He crouches, hand patting the carpet until he finds the syringe again, never mind the noise.

Rage fizzes in his blood. Inching out of the bedroom, he bolts downstairs, pressing his back against the kitchen wall. Spittle builds in the corners of his mouth and a frozen bolt of terror goes through him. He, who is so guarded, so careful, has failed.

The thud of a foot on the stairs and the swish of a hand against the wall. She's already in the kitchen, a vision in underwear, and rubbing her thigh. She leans over the sink and looks up at Trisha's window. If she focused on the surface of the glass, she would see his reflection behind her.

Every muscle in his body contracts. He is still. The slightest movement will produce a sound and give him away. He could swing his hand hard, power his elbow into her throat and she'd be his. He has a split second to think things through and instinct cautions him. She is carrying her phone.

Her face turns towards the kitchen lamp and she flicks the switch and nothing happens. Directing her torch at the front door, the beam hits the night latch which is no longer engaged. He wastes no more time and twists around the kitchen door to the living room.

There's a moment of regression to childhood, that bubbling sensation in his stomach when a parent is about to corner him for some deceit. As he curls his hand around the back door frame, he calculates the angle and closes the door slowly so as not to amplify the squeaky hinge. But he has no time to lock it or replace the glass.

He's back in the car in thirty-seven minutes and forty-five seconds – a better time than he'd expected.

What a game this is.

25

FREYA

THE LIGHT FROM THE open fridge tells me it's some kind of mosquito bite. My thigh throbs and stings and I cool it down with an ice cube. Moonlight blisters through the window and a car shoots past, tyres sticky on wet tarmac. Thoughts of Edward slice through me, the stench of him wafting in like smoke, silent and toxic.

Everything else is as it should be: keys on pegs, tea towels on hooks, Prue Leith's *Cookery Bible* and *Madhur Jaffrey's Indian Cooking* book on the kitchen table where I left them. On the upper shelf by the window is the miniature clay house Kate made for Mothering Sunday. The only variance is a burnt out bulb and wind twining through the house, batting the blinds and stirring the curtains. When I see the front door is ajar, an icy finger of unease tingles down my spine.

My eyes glide to the dead cherry tree three doors down. It stands like a brittle ballerina in second position, and fastened to a bony joint is a wind chime. The sound is oddly soothing.

Chester slinks along the flat's wall, crouching and using his paw to scoop something from a hole in the brick. Other than that, the street is a cindery streak, and a cold scud sends leaves skittering down the pavement.

Locking the door, I refrain from turning on the main kitchen light. Otherwise my stalker will be drawn to the house like a moth. Something registers in the corner of my eye. Flicking on my torch, the light forms a silver eye over a package on the kitchen counter. There's no barcode or destination address and my skin tightens at my name scrawled in black ink. Freya Thorne. Nothing else. Inside are yoga pants and a sports bra, and I detect the faint leathery trace of a man's cologne. Before I start thinking that Jack failed to mention it yesterday, I find a tag with the words, *Made for each other. Your friend, Edward*.

My ribs feel too tight and I can't breathe. My first thought is to check our CCTV. But a creaky floorboard warns me of movement. It could be Jack turning in our bed or the bones of the house settling. But it's not that type of noise.

I turn off the torch and listen for the pop of a knee or the intake of breath. Moving towards the fireplace, my fingers creep along the wall and collide with the poker. It teeters against my thigh and I lunge for it, hand snapping at thin air. A loud clang confirms it has cuffed the coal-scuttle before coming to rest on the hearth. My hand is shaking too much to pick it up.

I can't breathe. Oh God, please don't let Edward be in the

house. Please make Jack wake up. I open my mouth to yell, but my voice sounds like I'm choking. I wish I didn't have to do this alone. I need Jack. I need him downstairs.

Calm down, Freya. Calm down. I scan the familiar outlines in the sitting room. Nothing moves. There's no one here.

The phone beeps in my hand and I almost jump. 'You home, Frey?'

I sag against the wall. 'Yes, I'm here.'

'What a relief. I thought there was a burglar inside your house. Why are you creeping around with your torch on?'

'I heard something,' I say.

'You mean you, creeping around your house with your torch on.'

'What time is it?'

'2.05 am and guess what? Best date of my life. Seriously, Derek's amaaazing. Did you know he shaves? I mean, everything. His body is like one of those hairless cats.'

'Good. Great. Listen. I don't want to spoil anything, but someone left a package in my kitchen. You didn't see anyone out there?'

'No. But check your camera app. And Frey? You might sign up for self-defence or learn how to shoot. Google Parkstone. I can teach you a few basic moves tomorrow. Want me to come over?'

'No, no. It's OK. Listen, do me a favour. Google the name Edward Besant. See what you can find.'

I say goodnight and hang up. As I place my phone on the

draining board, I see Jack's favourite glass goblet stained with a slop of dusky pink. My fear grows, mutates, and then a sudden jolt of lucidity. I had lipstick on yesterday and I must have used the glass myself.

I open the camera app and select the channel – frames and frames of normal activity. No matter how many times I drag the slider forward and back there's nothing to see. What would Patti make of me calling her so early? Especially after telling me about support workers at You First and to make use of the stalking clinic – which I haven't.

I find a bottle of whiskey in the cupboard and pour myself a few fingers. Now that I'm warm and mellow, I speed-dial Patti, and the robotic sound of her voicemail greets me.

'Patti, it's Freya, Freya Thorne. Listen, sorry to call so early. Someone left a package in my house and my video's not working. We're OK. We're fine. Can you call us tomorrow?'

I clamber upstairs and shake Jack, and he's rubbing one eye with the heel of his hand.

'What? What time is it?'

'I don't know. Someone's downstairs. The front door was open and there's... there's a package in the kitchen.' He's so groggy, I have to pull him upright. 'Jack, did you hear what I said?'

'OK. Relax. Stay here. I'll take care of it.'

Whether it's the sudden shot of whisky or a sense of relief that Jack has picked up the lamp from his side of the bed and is going downstairs, I don't know. But scenes of him chasing a hooded figure flirts at the edge of my consciousness, followed by images of him jabbing his fists at a ghost.

I'm standing on the landing, peering over the banister. Why is he taking so long? Why is he dragging his feet? It's ten whole minutes before Jack comes back upstairs, shaking his head.

'All clear. Did you lock the front door last night?'

'I thought I had.'

Of all the scenarios I'd imagined, of all the mistakes I knew were inevitable, leaving a door unlocked had to be the worst.

26

FREYA

THE SHOWER IS SO hot, it's boiling my skin raw, and steam snakes its way into the bedroom. My thigh no longer hurts and the tiny red mark has all but gone. I'm so tired, as if oversleeping wasn't enough. I must be coming down with something.

When I turn off the taps, the air is suddenly cold. I feel a twinge in my belly and then I'm almost bent double with pain. My period. The last time my cycle had a hiccup was after that fateful weekend. We were careful – *he* was careful. Six weeks and nothing happened. Six weeks and one day and I was sitting on the toilet with my jeans around my ankles and there it was. A small spot. A huge relief.

I google Parkstone Gun Club in Poole. On the website is the picture of a girl lying prone on a mat, cheek glued to some fancy rifle. It teaches gun safety and how to develop shooting skills. It doesn't promote a woman obsessed with revenge to maim or kill a stalker. I must be out of my mind.

I dress in a light sweater and leggings, and meet Jack in the kitchen. Eggs bubble and spit in a pan and he flips them over with a spatula. Judging by his rain-slicked hair, he's been outside.

'Morning.' I slam my backside into a chair.

'Patti said you called her last night. Before we indulge in a brief fantasy that we've caught Edward on camera, I checked the video and there is no video.' He taps his phone and shows me what I already know, slides and slides of low light street views. 'Were you aware the pane in the back door was loose? Someone propped it against the doorstep and unscrewed the porch light.'

He doesn't need to explain the improbability of glass remaining intact after a fall and we both scrabble around the only workable explanation. Edward had removed the pane and entered through the back door, left a parcel of clothes for me in the kitchen. The message is loud and clear. Our cameras, hunched under the gutters, had recorded nothing. I place my palm flat against my chest, fear mixed with a deep sense of shame. I've put my trust in a neighbour known to the police for selling drugs and, to my detriment, an ex. I've disregarded Patti's warnings not to respond to Edward. In the end, establishing anything about Edward is the most important thing and the only thing worth pursuing.

'I told Patti you were sleeping. She'll be here in a couple of hours.' He smooths the hair back from my forehead. 'I'll check the back fence. Why don't you go back to bed?'

'No. I need fresh air.'

'Do you think that's wise?'

'Jack, it's nearly daylight,' I say, shouldering my backpack. 'I've got my pepper spray.'

Jack shouts after me as I gun it down the street. 'Is there anything I can't stop you from doing?'

I run as far from the house as I can before slowing to walk. I check my news app.

> The police have questioned a man in relation to a string of sexual assaults in the area, especially near Alum Chine beach. He is not thought to be connected to Elisabeth Sanders' murder and has not been charged.

An article on the Robin Hood Car Thief, who steals cars from wealthy neighbourhoods and leaves them in destitute areas. This must be what Patti alluded to when she told us not to leave our car running in the drive. And a photo of Max Lalonde, Elisabeth Sanders' boyfriend, stocky and dark. Not someone you'd look at twice. He was away in Manchester on business when Elisabeth went missing.

A gust brings the smell of rain and I squint at the glare of headlights as cars pass me in the street. I used to listen to music on my phone and let it take me to far away places. Now I watch for strangers and listen for thudding feet.

House lights flicker behind lace curtains as the world wakes up. A car reverses from a neighbouring house, night frost clearing from the windscreen. For a brief second, I see the driver's face, chin down, his hand in a flat wave before accelerating up the street. Number 26. Roger Daniels' dad.

The sharp chill penetrates my lungs as I run slowly at first, down the hill towards the beach. Instead of taking my usual route, I veer uphill towards the tropical gardens, past a patch of grass where Dad had tried and failed to teach me to catch a Frisbee. Up ahead, a man runs on the spot; ear pressed to his phone. He glances in my direction and darts downhill and I can't decide whether his sudden departure is on my account or whether his phone call had naturally ended.

Images of an impending attack bounce around in my head, but that doesn't stop me. Following him takes me along a winding lane that narrows at the rear of Vesuvio restaurant. A small fence borders a *Treasure Island* themed playground, and a finger sign points to the entrance. I see rows of empty tables through the window. Movement through the glass seizes my focus; not someone inside, but the reflection of someone behind me.

I twist around, but all I see is a flash of grey. I find the indent of a path running between the trees and hike uphill, my legs grazed by jumbles of gorse, splashing through scattered puddles. Getting wetter. Colder. Every additional step promises me another sighting, as if he is a rare bird I have to photograph. Adrenaline sluices through my body, sweat and rain in my eyes. I need to sprint, to fly, to push myself. It's the only way to find clarity.

I run through dappled clearings, pain flickering in my neck – every muscle straining to get into shape. Pine dust swirls in the canted light and the woods seem to groan and whisper. I'm searching for the man with the phone when I stumble over a vein of roots and go flying.

As I lie on the ground, fighting for breath, I spot a tree on my right, sap oozing from an open wound. Someone has carved a heart surrounding the letter E. Then, as if changing their minds, hacked out the bottom rung and made it an F. The wood spins and time seems to freeze.

Get a grip, Freya. I haul myself up and dust off the dirt, my lungs on fire. I'm unsure whether to go along my intended route to the gardens or double back and go home. Two women stamp out a rhythm about twenty metres behind. They pass me with a good morning and a smile, and I decide to follow them to the beach. I run downhill, eyes trained on the path and the blur of gorse in the periphery of my vision. No sign of the man.

As I break through the dunes, sea air dilutes the scent of sap. It's weird to be here without Kate, the past shifting and darting in my face like a hummingbird. There are shadowy depressions beneath the cliffs, which she likened to the lost boys' burrow in *Peter Pan*. Anyone could hide there. Impossible to see under the stormy sky. I pretend she's running with me, leaping over seaweed and shying from the waves. We used to rent bikes and cycle to Corfe Castle, stopping for lunch at the Scott's Arms in Kingston, and we'd go to the New Forest Wildlife Park and see fallow and sika deer. My mind rebels against each thought because the tears will come, and when they do, I'm a mess.

On the shoreline, a woman crouches over a precious find, seawater running through her fingers. Then I notice a runner in a fluorescent shirt, hunched over to catch his breath, and behind him, a walker in a grey hoodie, taking a sip of water. The sea is ablaze in the early morning sun and waves charge up the beach, leaving a fringe of lace behind. I look up at the cliffs and, on its dwindling summit, the solid bulk of a tree trunk. Or a figure, perhaps, wind snatching at his clothes. I'm seeing things.

The walker has kept pace with me on the promenade, but there's no sign of the runner. I console myself that he has simply found somewhere to sit beneath the cliffs. I take a long swig from my water bottle and there's a tap on my shoulder. I lurch sideways.

'Shit, Miles!'

'I'm sorry. I didn't mean to scare you.'

'Are you following me?'

'Actually, no. But if that's an invitation, I'll take it.'

He coaxes a smile from me. There's no sweat on his forehead and his breathing is shallow and jeans and a striped shirt are hardly runner attire. He notices me studying the dog with a shaggy coat, gazing forlornly up at me.

'Jessica's. His name's Gizmo. So no pouring water on him,

OK?'

I grin, remembering the Mogwai in *Gremlins.* As we walk shoulder-to-shoulder, Gizmo obediently at Miles' heel, I want to ask is Jessica at home in his bed? Perhaps she's cooking up a continental breakfast and is waiting to serve him in lacy underwear.

'Are you OK?' he asks. 'You look tired.'

I give a weary sigh. 'Somebody tried to get into the house last night.'

'Seriously?'

'Cut a pane of glass from the back door and left me a gift.'

He stares at me, forehead rutted in thought. 'What kind of gift?'

'Clothes. Running clothes.'

'You called the police, I take it?'

'Jack spoke to them this morning. They're coming over later.'

He pulls me into a side hug. His eyes seem to search the beach for the same reasons mine do. I can't shake off an immediate feeling of panic that Edward, crouching in the dunes, might spy on this rare moment of intimacy. Memories of that night gather and murmur, and I shove the craving deep into my gut. The passing seconds eat at me and I change the subject.

'You smell nice.'

'Jimmy Choo.' He scowls. 'Jess thought I needed a shot of masculinity.'

'As long as she doesn't suggest a shot of plastic surgery.'

He looks down at me. The silence snaps tight. 'You're flawless, and by flawless, you don't need makeup. I think that bothers her.'

'She's perfect.'

'Depends.' He removes his arm. 'Is perfection what a woman looks like after surgery or before?'

'I doubt it's a question you've been asking yourself all week.'

'Just over a year, actually.' He kicks a pebble with his foot. 'There's something off about that hit and run you had. You don't think Jack might have contracted someone to do it? I mean, it would make him the casualty of a badly executed plan. Or a well-executed plan, whichever way you want to look at it. But he'd be blameless if he were in the car *and* got hurt.'

I shudder. Insane though the suggestion is, it *could* be true. 'Jack's not like that.'

'You never really know, do you? Whatever it is, it's a monumental cock-up. Do you trust him?'

Miles doesn't know it's my lies that are piling up not Jacks. I should be more concerned about the impact they will have on him. 'Of course, I trust him.'

'I have to ask. Am I in any danger?'

My head is aching. He rushed over to talk to me, not to unpack our two-night stand, but to protect himself from a psycho stalker. I tell him no, but I can't make that kind of promise. Now it's his turn to change the subject and he bangs on about Jessica and how she's playing hard to get.

'She's nothing like anyone I've ever dated. I suppose that's the mystery. It makes you want more when they tell you so little. It's hard to think of her with him.'

'Him?' My stomach flip-flops.

'Sorry, I shouldn't be talking about it.'

'No, you said you couldn't bear to think of her with *him*.'

'Hard to compete with a famous rapper. There's still a spark.' I hear the regret in his voice, and when I look up, he's not grinning anymore. 'It's a long story. Story of my life, really. You can't ask for exclusivity when there's someone else.'

He's looking at his feet and wincing, his expression showing several layers of pain. I want to hold him, but I can't because I'm looking at the face I once kissed. I take a few seconds to breathe normally, and another few to process what he'd said.

'So you're serious about her?'

'That's the idea. For better, for worse.' He pats Gizmo's head. 'It's a big ask, though, isn't it? Being together forever.'

I feel a surge of betrayal, but it lasts only a second. 'I'm happy for you, Miles.'

'Thanks. That means a lot.' He plucks a jelly baby from his pocket and chews it thoughtfully. Then takes out another. 'Catch.'

My hand grabs it as it arcs downwards, and I pop it in my mouth.

'You'll call me if you need anything?'

My immediate instinct is to say no, but something else creeps in. A spark glinting from the ashes. 'I will.'

He turns and leads the dog up the beach, and I'm alone again. I don't mind, and I watch him walk uphill to the car park, fear put aside for one more day.

27

FREYA

I SEE TWO SUITS across the street. It's Patti Franchek and a young man, strolling along like Laurel and Hardy. They've been interviewing the neighbours, naturally. I open the front door and Jack is pacing around the kitchen.

'What took you so long?' he says. 'Didn't you get my message?'

My words are cut off before leaving my mouth. Again, I failed to answer my phone. Patti Franchek and DC Lucian Hales are framed in our open front door, both smiling, both hopeful.

'I understand there's a pane of glass you'd like us to look at,' Patti says, motioning for Lucian to check the back door. 'And you received a package?' She studies the label on the yoga pants and looks me up and down. 'Right. Any idea what time he left them?'

'Before 2.00 am.'

'And the glass door?'

'You mean when did he break it? I don't know. We didn't hear anything.'

We all move into the sitting room. Lucian beckons Jack and me to the couch and it's Patti's turn to check the back door. Lucian pulls out a notebook and peers down at it.

'We had a call yesterday evening from a Mr Edward Besant.'

My body freezes mid-movement and my head shakes in a slow sweep of denial. Edward called the police? Why?

'Stalky Edward?' Jack asks.

'Claims you're badmouthing him, sending him threatening letters.'

'Sending letters, how?' Jack looks at me. 'We don't even have his address.'

'Thing is, Mr Besant says he's got heart problems. Been admitted to hospital at least three times. A fourth could kill him.'

'And that's our problem? If this is the same creep who is stalking my wife, then it's a scam.'

'I understand, Mr Thorne, but he's seeking legal action. He insists he has proof.'

'That means you have his number.' I say.

'Actually, no. He was calling from The Riverside Inn. We did check.'

Jack huffs out a series of breaths. 'We both know he's doing this to frame my wife. Isn't it what all stalkers do? She's the victim here. Not him. You only have to look at the back door and the gifts he keeps leaving. It's disgusting. A total violation.

And now he wants to take legal action? Can you do anything?'

'We've been going door-to-door, asking people if they've seen anyone in the street acting strangely. Your neighbours have been very helpful. Especially Ms Miller. She says she keeps a regular eye out. Her son described a few unusual cars which, of course, we'll look into.' He glances over at Patti, who is now standing at the doorway between the hall and the sitting room, and then back at me. 'You haven't been... you know, talking to him?'

'How can I? I don't have his number.'

'Right.'

While Lucian scribbles a few notes in his book, I ask, 'Surely, you've done a background check. You must know where he works, assuming he has a job like regular person. Is Edward his real name?'

'I can't tell you any more, Mrs Thorne. But I promise you we'll find him. We always do.'

I slump back against the couch and let out a loud sigh. Lucian doesn't know any more than I do and it's no good pretending just to make us feel better.

As Jack sees Lucian out, Patti hesitates. 'There's no glass on the ground which means he used a tool. Light as a pen and made from carbide tungsten alloy. Explains why you didn't hear anything.' She sits opposite me and leans forward a little. 'So, Freya, you usually go jogging every morning. Same route?'

'No. I've been changing it up.'

'Do you go to the woods much? Suspension bridge?

Squirrel's Leap?'

'I don't make a habit of it, if that's what you mean.'

'So where do you go?'

'The beach, mainly.'

She's looking at me with this weird expression on her face, as if she doesn't like my answers. It makes me prickle all over.

'You know what strikes me as odd?' Her scowl matches mine now. 'You don't seem remotely interested in the proof Mr Besant alluded to. When someone talks about proof, the question everyone asks is *what* proof. The only reason I can think of is that you already know.'

'I'm sure I don't.'

'Because it would be highly inappropriate, unethical even, to keep any information from the police, no matter how small.' She gives me a rueful smile and tucks the package Edward left me under one arm. 'Just let us do our job.'

I want to tell her she's looking at the wrong person. But I'm sweating and trembling and I know it's something she sees.

After she leaves, I run upstairs and google the name Besant again. I find a deactivated Facebook photo for an Edward Besant preserved by Google. It shows a man sitting in front of a window where backlight obscures his features.

I pinch to zoom in and see a framed award behind him on the wall, but the words are blurred. If I can find this much, then so too can the police.

I wonder what Patti knows.

The doorbell rings and I glance down at the street, feeling the swell of one of those oh-hell-it's-not-her moments.

'Surprise!' Her infantile voice wafts up from the sitting room. 'Hope you both like oatcakes and Dom Perignon.'

Jessica stands with one foot delicately placed in front of the other – a balletic fourth position like the royal duchesses on TV. She points at a large hamper, only I'm not looking at the hamper, I'm staring at the green sundress which dips to her knees, bodice straining across generous breasts. Except for her dark eyes, she's like Kate. The same toasted skin and full lips. My mind has a way of feasting on the tiniest details.

Jack pulls out a chair for her and gestures for me to sit. Jessica exchanges a look with him and her eyes flicker before she lowers them. I feel trapped and I want to scream into my fist.

'We're starting this book club and we'd love it if you could join.' She wrinkles her nose as if what she's about to say will be unpleasant. 'It's a small group, so don't feel overwhelmed. Probably at Liv's since she's got the nicest house. Not that yours isn't nice. It's quaint.'

Then she goes on and on about how her computer crashed today. I secretly revel in her trying to recreate unsaved notes on a *Day in a Life* piece. She mentions packing up her desk and looking forward to the move. Only I don't know what move she's talking about. Words gush from her mouth, fluttering in the air like a knot of sparrows.

'You seem tense, Freya. Are you sleeping?' She reaches out and squeezes my wrist. 'Miles and I are worried about you. Is there anything we can do?'

'The police have been fantastic,' I say, except I don't believe they've been *fantastic* at all. Suspicious, more likely.

Her voice is like a tape at slow speed, warping in and out, questioning if the perpetrator enjoyed acts of violence towards women. After all, he saw me, a woman driver. She's all wound up like a toddler's bath toy and I want to hit the "off" button.

'Therapy's what you need.' She looks from me to Jack. 'Don't you agree? You should try Dr Meyer. You'd love him. I mean, no pressure. I go to therapists *all* the time.'

'Well, I can count on your referral then,' I say.

'Absolutely. He's a saint. So qualified *and* handsome. Can't think why he's still single, but he's probably married to his job. Such dedication.'

Frustration pricks beneath my ribs and I want this to end, but Jessica keeps turning up the dial. She's won an award and is being featured in *The Guardian* this week, and Jack nods and nods like a bobblehead car accessory. I'll be stuck here for another ten agonizing minutes unless I butt in, but there's not a millimetre of a gap in the conversation.

Scraping back my chair, Jack anchors my wrist. 'Thank you for the hamper, Jessica. It was kind of you to bring it.'

'My pleasure, Jack. I thought it would cheer you both up.'

Jack? Not Mr Thorne? When did all this familiarity happen?

There's something I can't work out. She reminds me of someone who models bikinis but hates to swim.

Jack opens the kitchen door and escorts her out to her car. I watch them from the sitting-room window, blinds angled so they can't see me. His hand rests on the small of her back and she flicks a look behind her, wishing I'm watching or hoping I'm not.

Oh God, they're all in on this. Jack and Jessica and Liv. They're all part of a trap or a game or some sick fantasy they've cooked up. As I look at the hamper on the kitchen table, an idea occurs to me. Jessica's handwriting on the card is almost identical to the letters from Edward. I stare at the words – *Jack and Freya, with love from us all.*

'Freya.' Jack slams the door and lowers his head. 'That was rude. Just because you're having a shitty day doesn't mean you say "screw you" to everyone else.'

'What? No. That's not what I was saying. Come on, Jack. Does she really think she's more interesting than anyone else? It's exhausting... all this talk of me having therapy and with Dr Meyer.' I'm shivering from aftershock. 'Everything's changed. You've changed. Liv's changed. Why is everyone changing? That's why you've been reading my texts, checking up on me. Let's face it; I must be mad if I'm making all this up.'

He can stop me at any point. He can say he's had enough, but he listens. I'm not sorry for what I've said. If I could use a word, it would be *purged*, as if I've finally thrown up a rancid bowl of prawns.

'I saw Miles on the beach,' I say.

'Miles from work?'

'He suggested you might have known the person who rammed us. Did you?'

He takes a deep, pained breath. 'That's the most ridiculous thing I've ever heard.'

'If you plan to get rid of me, divorce isn't out of the question. Might be healthier for both of us in the long run.'

'I wouldn't dream of getting rid of you.'

'Bullshit. It's written all over your face.'

'Freya, you're becoming more and more unreachable, and I'm sick of sucking it up. Beer and wine, and God knows what else poured down the drain, empty bottles in the bin. Since when did we buy Johnnie Walker Black Label?'

Johnnie Walker? Let me think. I trawl through a flurry of supermarket images. Jack drinks Dewar's.

'You know what bothers me?' he says. 'You running off by yourself when you know there's a psychotic stalker out there.'

'I'm not going to let him dictate how I run my life.'

'Freya, it's your safety I'm worried about.'

'I can look after myself.'

He walks forward and squeezes my shoulders. 'Calm down. You're having a bad day.'

'We all have our good days and our bad days.'

'And...?'

'*And...?*'

Jack covers his face with his hands and turns a full circle.

'This week. Last week. Every week's bad. When's it going to end? No one's trying to threaten you, least of all me.'

The one thing I've learned about Jack is that he's a terrible liar. Can't hold it in. Goes sweaty and itchy and dances from foot to foot.

Me? My lips don't move, and the lie is safe behind a row of teeth, like a prisoner behind bars. My mind vaults back and forth as a new thought slinks in. Had Jack been drugging me to sleep at night? I'm obsessing. Minds can do that, fixating on false scenarios until you believe it's true.

He holds out his hands, fingers warm and firm in mine. I don't recoil, but I don't exactly grasp his hand as tightly.

'I'm not getting rid of you,' he says. 'You're my wife. We're both trying to get through the shittiest part of our lives.'

He pulls me to him, massaging the space between my shoulder blades with one hand. I should be grateful he is holding me. He could be at the Argyll Bowling Club with Theo, or at the flying site with Duffy. At least he's not checking our bank account for funds and asking – no, pleading – to buy the latest and greatest from Hobbycraft and Modellers Loft. He's here with me now, where he's always been.

He is the only one who can reach the deepest heart of me. When I can't express how much I hurt, Jack knows. He always knows.

28

FREYA

THE FOLLOWING DAY, I run towards Branksome Beach. The sun's rays break through the clouds, dropping sharp silver lines across the sea. I watch a group of early morning swimmers drifting in and out of the receding tide. Patti's words keep swilling around in my head. *Just let us do our job.* In my mind, this means no meddling, the type the police can trace.

On the way back, I see a man in his car with his head tilted forward, like he's sleeping. If he weren't at the crossroads of our street and Earle Road, I wouldn't have knocked on the window. With a little stab of embarrassment, I realise he's a she, and the phone in her lap tells me she's texting.

'I'm sorry,' I mouth. 'I thought you were someone else.'

This is the thing about Edward. He isn't with me every minute. I forget him, and then he comes scooting back with a terrifying jolt. I go through my notes in my head, trying to construct another way to spark my creativity. A snare. A plan. Anything.

When I get home, the sound of the lawnmower tells me where Jack is. I call Trisha. 'Any luck finding Edward Besant?'

'Want the good news? He doesn't exist.'

'How's that good news?'

'Let me rephrase it. The only Edward Besant I can find would be eighty-two now. Lives in London with his partner, Stan Nicholls, and used to work for a headhunter in London. That's not to say he's not ripped like Bruce Willis and can leap over walls.'

I sit down on the top stair, my shoulder against the wall. 'That's it?'

'There is another Besant. Andrew Besent Lyons. Spelt with an E. It could be a double-barrel surname, but I'd bet on a middle name. Bought a house in Compton Acres in 2009, that big one with the chimneys, around the corner. He enrolled his son, Charlie, in Preschool on De Mauley Road the same year. Has a registered income tax return. So does his wife, Miranda. Sound likely?'

'Not really. So Edward's created a false identity. We guessed that from the start.'

'He's probably involved in some kind of criminal activity, changed his name to escape arrest. Or to escape someone who wanted to hurt him. Truth is, I don't have a good answer, Frey.'

'Now what?'

'You keep watching your back. I keep my head down and be a good girl.'

I hear the emphasis in the last three words, but I know her

mind's spinning off the trails. Trisha is never a *good girl*. Can't be done.

I take a shower, catching my reflection in the glass door. Even though I run and attempt a few sit-ups in front of a good movie, not every part of me will be firm. Not the parts I want Jack to see.

Lately, I've sensed a change. Two nights ago, he emerged from the bathroom with a towel around his waist, got into bed and studied aeroplane parts on his iPad. Somehow I hadn't attributed his disinterest to the accident. That it may have been more life-altering than I realise. I've also noticed that my laptop is warm when I know I haven't been using it. He knows how to read my emails and restore them to unread. He knows I'm not a model wife, no matter how much I try. So he has reason to be suspicious. I wish I could turn the clocks back to before all this happened.

I dress in jeans and a long T-shirt and slip on a pair of old tennis shoes. The newspaper is splayed out on the kitchen table open at one of Liv's articles.

A business affair: Every office has one
By Liv Hunter
Lifestyle Reporter

Research shows that the more familiar you are with a co-worker, the more likely it is that you'll become attracted to each other. But what are the risks?

And before you throw yourself headlong into a relationship, remember there are potential problems ahead. What if it doesn't work out? Are you worried about your reputation or the best interests of the team? Are you really bothered about your co-workers' reactions when you reveal all?

Just how do you deliver the news that you are dating a co-worker? You've kept the lid on your relationship for months and now you've taken it to the next level. Only you know how your peers will take it. Have a game plan before you spill the beans. If you're still struggling with the big reveal, talk to HR. As for rumours, offices have policies against that kind of behaviour...

I persuade myself it's not about me. Aynur might have seen Miles and me leaving the party. Her deliberate silences may have nothing to do with Kate, but more to do with her disgust over my slutty behaviour. I wish I could scrub out that disastrous party. It isn't too much to ask, is it? A complete do-over?

Oh, Jack, why did I pull you into this mess? My best friend, my everything. I know he's forgiven me the small things but never this. One our wedding day, he said he'd never leave me in front of everyone who loves us. It went by so fast, from putting on my beautiful dress – a fitted Victorian bodice with a V neckline, long sleeves and silk tulle trimmed with lace, to driving to the church. The pews were decorated with hyacinth and lily of the valley, but I barely noticed as I walked up the aisle. Jack watched my every step, his eyes never veering from my face. Our vows were ambitious and eternal and moving. But now, I've broken them.

There's no way to put it right. Unless I find the one person who threatens us. I keep thinking about the broken glass in the back door – about what Patti had said. *He used a tool. Light as a pen and made from carbide tungsten alloy. Explains why you didn't hear anything.* I try to think about something else, anything else...

I grab my phone and find bullying is trending on Twitter. Liv's written a small piece about her trainee reporter who resigned earlier this year.

After Sara Farouq started her new job at the Daily Echo, an anonymous caller criticised her articles and began a bullying campaign. Farouq developed anxiety and

depression and had trouble sleeping.
Repeated threats forced her to resign.
#StopBullying #SpeakOut

Was that how Olivia saw Sara's decline? A young woman who couldn't handle the inevitable criticism? What I saw was far more insidious. Sara tried to remain upbeat, but the terror in her eyes told another story. A seasoned reader had subjected her to a campaign of abuse and no one did anything.

The door to the flats squeaks open and I can't help looking through the window at Trisha barrelling towards the skips with a bin bag, cigarette bobbing between her lips. Her body is sharp and willowy, face red from the sun. I hear the lid slamming and back she comes, scooping Chester off a neighbour's windowsill. It's hard to look at her, yes, *hard* when all she wears is a long T-shirt and you know she's got nothing on underneath. I can almost feel Dad's head on my shoulder, his voice chiming through. 'There's your woman now. Face like a smacked arse.'

Jessica's hamper is on the kitchen counter and I tear through ribbons and cellophane. Scones, jam and clotted cream catch my eye and soon our house smells of Earl Grey. Every sound seems loud; the clink of a teaspoon, the kettle's gentle hiss, and I pour boiling water into the mugs, tugging a tea bag back and forth.

Sweet grass wafts in through the back door, Jack doing

his final circuit with the lawnmower, a short one, given the garden's dimensions. A tube of caulk on the patio tells me he's about to fix the window pane. It gives me enough time to check his emails.

His laptop is on the couch and I punch in the usual PIN. Incorrect login. The screen tells me to try again and I can't be sure whether I'm typing it correctly. I hear the grunt of the lawnmower as it powers down and I close the lid.

The squeal of the back door and a soft click. Jack removes his shoes and walks across the room in his socks. He pats the cushion next to him and I sit.

'What?' I ask.

'Edward's letters. Funny, but the Y in *Freya* has a long tail like the ones you do.'

Instead of shrinking into the crook of his arm, I'm sitting upright. 'The Y has a tail drawn like a backward L, but with one notable difference, Jack. The bottom line doesn't curl into a loop the way mine do.' I'm already drawing my Ys on a napkin to prove a point. 'As insignificant as this might be to you, it's proof I didn't write these letters.'

'I wasn't saying you had. I'm saying Edward wanted me to think you had.'

A nugget of optimism grows inside. If Jack knows Edward can trap me in a lie (and let's face it, one more added to the pile won't make much difference) then he is open to the possibility that I've been telling the truth. Mostly.

I want to bury my face in the soft muss of his chest. It seems an emotional storm roars around us and that Jack is the only point of calmness at its centre, and the rhythm of his voice, his breathing, is the only sign of familiarity in this crazy world. When he quizzes me about Edward, which he will, he'll realise that it didn't begin with me finding the body of Elisabeth Sanders and the subsequent letters, but with my adultery all those months ago.

29

EDWARD

EDWARD STARES AT THE windscreen, eyes focusing between the tiny beads of rain one minute, and then the beads themselves. The pattering makes him drowsy and before long, he's dozing, dreaming of Freya's moistened skin in the shower. When he awakes, his skin is coated with sweat.

He knows drugs have changed his brain chemistry, but his body continues to demand them. His lodger's recent meddling balloons in his head. He keeps alluding to Edward's "stash" as if he's afraid the police will find it. Perhaps he's naturally protective, or nervous, Edward can't decide.

He rubs his hands down his jeans, until he feels the sting of denim threads and his palms are raw. He should have left by now, but his cravings have kept him here. He is parked outside Mountain Lodge and has a winning view of the flats and Freya's house. Her back door is a mess. He punched out a pane of glass, thinking the sound would have woken them. Nothing stirred. Understandable considering the sedatives he'd left in the whisky and a carton of milk. He deposited two half-smoked joints in the mouth of a downspout, lipstick on both filters.

Since then, he's been reading her stalking log and drawing doodles on the back page. It's a beautiful thing, leather bound with a silk bookmark in matching hunter green.

A van pulls up at the flats and Trisha gets out, cigarette smoke clouding her face. She stoops through the passenger window, grabs the driver by the scruff of the neck and plants a kiss on his lips. Like the chivalrous man he is, he wants to see her safely inside. She twerks her way to the front door, skirt hiked so high, Edward can see her underwear. When the door closes behind her and the van is gone, he is alone again, smelling wet gravel and exhaust.

Drizzle patters against leaves and plinks against gutters. Carriage lanterns outside the flats throw beams almost as far as the grass. He doesn't see cameras or motion detectors and he knows they don't have a dog. It would have barked when she went indoors. He also knows she empties her bins twice at night. Once between nine and ten, and again after midnight. He checks the clock on the dashboard. Two more minutes.

While Edward waits, he does another search for Nisha Kalani, making sure the beacon from his phone is covered by a jacket. This time he gets a hit in Mangalore. There's an old address for Nisha in Bournemouth and the dates and addresses match up. He stares at a Facebook video. She has a round face now and her legs are heavier at the thigh. Her hair is how he remembers it, long waves falling to her waist and those eyes, those striking brown eyes, are still the same. She pulls a child in a little red wagon.

He wants to call the number, but he has no idea if she'll remember him. Or if it will dredge up the worst of memories. The curious thing is he feels is love and shame and anger, all rolled into one. Sometimes the prickle of tears turn into heaving sobs, and he doesn't know why. Memories are intrusive. Erroneously romantic. Hideously disappointing.

For the past day or so, he has felt numb. His failure to take Freya dominates his thoughts. He's sick of watching the last of the sun, fat-bellied and lounging on the horizon, and he's tired of sleeping in his car. There has to be a better way.

He doesn't want to be a lifelong stoner, a chronic marijuana user. There's something squalid about a man scrabbling for a spliff from the detritus in his glove box, especially when he knows where to get a few buds.

When he met Trisha over a year ago, he knew she'd consume every part of him, leaving him empty like they all did. He didn't want to admit it at the time, but visiting her without an appointment seemed intrusive. Trisha wasn't the name she'd given him in The Vault, the name he'd murmured in the alley as he pulled her leg around his waist. The name he knew to be false. Which is why he'd followed her home.

The doors to the flats squeals open. He recognises russet hair and waxy skin. While she carries two bin bags towards the alleyway behind the building, he sprints for the tree, light-footed as a cat. He can hear the clink of wine bottles as she drops her rubbish into the skip. Then she saunters back, head down, looking at her phone. Pressing his body against the tree trunk, Edward melds himself to the bark. Before the front door swings shut, he slips inside.

Her bare feet pound upstairs, her shadow disappearing through an open door. He doesn't hear a click, doesn't expect to. She's cleaning the flat, because she never sleeps.

At the top of the stairs is a window through which the moon shines and Edward crouches in the darkest corner. He can hear rustling and coughing, then the slap of feet against linoleum, inching through the hall to the landing. She carries one more bag downstairs, this time, abandoning it inside the front door.

Edward creeps into the flat, flattening himself against the boy's bedroom wall. He hears the door close and the bolt engage. Then silence. He knows the drill. The toilet flushes in the adjoining bathroom and the mattress creaks. He will wait ten minutes, and if he's lucky, she'll crash for at least an hour.

He thinks about Freya, how wrapped up he is in her life. There's something about her, something invisible that he can't put his finger on, something he's on the brink of knowing. Rather than wallowing in indecision, he steps out of his hiding place.

He presses down carefully with every step; the sitting room floor giving the minutest whine of complaint. Then he listens. There's nothing but the *tick-tock* of a gold carriage clock on the shelf and rain spattering against glass. He can smell furniture polish and the slightest residue of wine. But he's not here for wine. He's here for weed.

Edward knows that unlocking his only means of egress is essential. Leaving Trisha's front door on the latch is the best way forward. He pats down the coffee table, the bookcase, searching behind ornaments and under the dining room table. Then he moves towards the couch, and slipping his hand between the cushions, he finds the bag. The buds smell herbal and woody and he is intrigued by base notes of kerosene and mineral oils. Slipping it in his pocket, he sees Trisha's bedroom door is ajar.

The bed is in the opposite corner, covered in a creamy quilt. Her breathing is imperceptible over the drizzle and he approaches the bed to be sure. This is a special moment, and such an interval between her waking and him watching her will never come again. He savours every last second.

A sharp rustle of bedclothes and her face is grey in the darkness.

'Who's there?'

He doesn't speak. Silence is sensual. The empty wine glass on the side table arouses him. He detects the perfume of black tea, crushed figs and currants, and his palate conjures flavours of incense and smoke. Certainly not Chateau Lafite, classic old school and elegant, but a full bodied red he'd be willing to share.

'Arthur? That you?'

The narrow beam of light from her phone warns him she

is accessing an emergency number and the groan of a hinge behind him reveals the boy is up.

'Mum, you OK? Mum! There's a man... an intruder.'

Intruder. The word is vulgar and offensive. It tells him he is an outcast. He doesn't belong. He pushes past the boy and runs for the door and voices break out all at once. He's on the landing, sliding down the stairs, the sensation similar to the drop at the end of a nightmare. He pulls open the front door and streaks across the lawn, glancing over his shoulder as he reaches the corner of the house next to Freya's.

A figure in pale pyjamas hugs the doorframe while another darts barefoot down the path to the road. He can't move, nor can he emerge from the shadows without her seeing. Trisha's rapid chatter informs him she's telling Arthur to get back inside.

'If you're out there, dickhead,' she shouts, 'the police are on their way.'

Somewhere between her chasing him downstairs and standing on the pavement, she's grabbed a lacrosse stick and she's cradling it like a pro. He trembles, knowing he must harness the fear and use it to run. But he can't move. His car is about thirty feet behind him and the sound of the engine will give him away.

She's smart. She'll run up the street, snapping photos of his plates. His best bet is to ease along the road, drawing her away from his car. But her phone torch brightens every shadow.

He looks down the street to where a public footpath runs

over Alum Chine Bridge. It's his only chance and he makes a run for it. The torch beam shudders along the road in front of him and her shouts get fainter and fainter.

A last-minute decision takes him towards a house. He jumps for the wall, but the bricks are slick with rain and suddenly he's lying face down, a brief shot of pain rooting him to the ground. Lifting his head, he's blinding by the beam of motion sensors.

He crawls under the leathery leaves of a rhododendron, one knee stinging from the fall. While he's gathering the energy to move, a musical moan echoes along the street. Sirens. What a bloody nightmare.

The back garden is his only escape. He races for the narrow opening between the shed and hedge, twigs snapping louder than an explosive. A surge of adrenaline and he bursts through. They're shouting and following him blindly. He wants to turn right – he can't turn right, there's another police car cruising up the road, siren pulsing in triumph – so left it is, towards the suspension bridge.

For about three seconds, he's running parallel to the police car, which is gaining on him, strobe lights blinking through the rain. It speeds up, passes twenty feet in front, turning sharply to mount the pavement. He changes direction to evade the block, slips between two cars and shoots across the road. He knows if he finds cover in someone's back garden, he will be swallowed by darkness. He races on, realising the risk is too great to circle back for his car. Best to keep moving and then he'll be home free.

He focuses on the squad car's headlights glimmering between the trees. There are only two cops. Edward crouches low, watching a torch beam flicking from side to side, arcing over walls and under cars, flickering between the tree trunks, until they disappear.

When he's sure they've passed him down the street, he streaks across the road and into the park. Maybe not home, but definitely free.

30

FREYA

SINCE THE POLICE HAVE been to our house, I've heard nothing from Edward. It's been a week and I've been dodging my early morning runs in favour of lifting weights and running up and downstairs for twenty minutes at a time. I miss the fresh air and a pale beach where choppy water sparkles near the horizon, but I can't risk being followed.

I strip the bed and wade through a tangle of sheets. The sound of a grinder tells me Jack's outside and I'm briefly distracted by his phone, which breaks into a neon jig, sliding along the surface of the bedside table. I jab the home button, and the PIN – the same number Jack uses for everything – no longer works. There's no banner notification on the lock screen, and I feel like I'm underwater, running out of oxygen. *Why is he changing his passwords?*

A knot sticks in my throat. I look over the banisters and find another surprise. The carpet is sequined with glass and a draught blows in through a jagged hole above the door handle.

A smashed pane, the same one Jack had just fixed. I feel as if I'm skimming along the surface of a wormhole and the door prickles in and out of view. Creeping around the smaller fragments, I walk out to the garden and I'm stamping the air with breaths.

Jack's hangar door is open. A small sealing iron sits amid a clutter of tools. Seconds dwindle. The air cools. I hear the roar of a car fading to a hum.

'Jack.'

He appears from behind the shed with a rake full of leaves. 'Hey, sleepy head.'

'What happened to the back door?'

He rubs his forehead and narrows his eyes. My stomach tightens and I can't work out if it's confusion or disappointment, and I don't want a silly argument to become an exit opportunity.

'Obviously I didn't do a good job. So I've called the glass man this time,' says. 'Where the lanterns are concerned, the bulbs weren't screwed in properly.'

'No Jack. We both know what happened. We *know*.'

He looks at me with big eyes. 'If a burglar could choose between a mansion filled with state-of-the-art electronics and a cottage with peeling paint and leaky gutters, why choose ours?'

'You know perfectly well this isn't some random burglar, Jack.'

Then he's on the phone to Patti, eyes hardening and words

punctuated by sighs. The complete outrage at what Edward has done with no video footage to prove it. We search the whole house this time, stopping only to retrace our steps. What we find missing is a clear message to me that all my painstaking work, my jotting down of dates and times has gone out of the window.

The fierce loyalty in Jack's expression is almost too much to bear, and he holds me in his arms, chin resting lightly on the top of my head. We see Patti's car pull up outside and I run out to meet her and Lucian.

'He broke the same window,' I say. 'This time, my stalking log's disappeared.'

'Shall I help you look?'

'We've already looked. Our cameras haven't recorded anything.'

Chins tilt. Eyes squint. Lucian lets out a low whistle. 'Where's your electrical panel?'

'Around the back.'

'Any cameras back there?'

'No,' I say.

Patti gives Lucian the merest tick of a glance, and he slinks off through the house. She gives me a slow smile that tells me she wants to talk. 'Apart from all this, how are you holding up?'

'I'm wondering, thinking, that maybe this guy thinks it's some kind of joke.'

'Jokers? Pretty rare. The fact that he got into your house without being recorded concerns me more. You might be interested to know your neighbour also had a break-in?'

'Trisha?'

'Yes. No one was hurt. Although in her case, we think it was connected to drugs.'

We go indoors. Patti scopes the kitchen, stopping at a picture of two women standing in front of a flicker of firecrackers and lanterns, skin decorated with Hindi patterns and eating roasted cashews.

'Diwali. My mother and grandmother,' I say, as if she needs to know. I also insert that my dad was Irish. 'Rory *a-double-Jameson's* Mathúna.'

'Oh, yes, the PI. I remember him. You have his smile.' Her eyes flick to a photo of Kate. 'Strong family likeness.'

'I suppose.'

She tilts her head and rubs her chin. 'Last time we spoke, you said you were seeing a therapist?'

'Actually, I have an appointment tomorrow morning.'

I hear voices and the brush of feet against the back door mat. The door squeals to a close and Jack stands at Lucian's shoulder.

'Found these in your downspout,' Lucian says, holding up a plastic bag with what appears to be two scrawny looking cigarettes. 'According to Mr Thorne, you don't smoke weed. Is that your understanding, Mrs Thorne?'

I stare into Lucian's eyes, startlingly yellow and locked on mine, and I'm quick to smother his claim. 'I don't smoke at all.'

His eyes drop to my mouth. 'You don't, by any chance, wear pink lipstick?'

'I do.'

'I would say that explains it but since you don't smoke, it doesn't.'

'Explains what?'

'Why there's pink lipstick around the filter.'

Jack looks from Lucian to me as if we're approaching game point in a tennis match, and the smile Patti reserves for me slips from her face. She thinks I'm crazy and she's probably right. Who else is taking a chunk out of our back door and leaving clothes that are my exact size? Or smoking joints while wearing my lipstick? The only person I know who smokes joints is Trish and she doesn't wear pink lipstick. Nor would she creep around unseen. To Patti, I'm both victim and perpetrator, a girl gone mad. It's the only explanation. And she wants to stop it before it gets out of hand.

'In that case,' she says, 'we'd better dust for prints.'

31

FREYA

A WHITE SCRIM COVERS the furniture, except for the back door where silvery-grey streaks cover the glass. Jack and I had to sign a form to allow eliminating prints to be taken. I question what the police may find. I told her we've had a fair bit of traffic over the past two weeks; Liv and Theo, Jessica and Derek. All of whom will need to be excluded. I overheard Patti say something about a shoe impression by the back door, possibly a size 10. She picked up one of Jack's and studied the sole. For comparison, she said.

I'm beginning to associate this house with violent attacks. Open doors frighten me, even when I know Jack is around. The idea that someone's watching me keeps tugging at my subconscious. Over time, I've developed a sixth sense, as if I can tap into that presence as easily if it's being telegraphed. But there's no neon arrow showing where that presence is coming from.

I'm losing my mind a little at a time until there is no more *me*. Instead, I'm someone with the same name who sleeps with my husband, eats at the same table, but isn't me anymore. Looking through news videos of Elisabeth Sanders is the only way to salvage my sanity from one day to the next.

A YouTube video, taken from a grainy CCTV camera, shows her leaving The Four Horsemen Pub at 10.45 pm the night she went missing. The live feed picked up the blur of a man to the far left of the frame, hunched in a doorway and dubbed *Mystery Man A*.

The beginnings of a plan flicker around the edges of my mind. If Trisha were willing to follow me at a distance, she could easily track my stalker. I couldn't expect her to do it for free. The only bank account I can secretly withdraw cash from is Kate's university fund and the donations we received from well-wishers. It makes me feel like a charlatan. Whenever I think of her, the smell of perfume springs up and there's a flash of laughter, long dark hair, and the stubborn set of her mouth. I try to hold it in.

Jack is in the sitting room staring at his laptop. On my way upstairs, I glance at his screen and see an article in the *Smithsonian Magazine* titled *The Myth of Fingerprints*. I can't tell –because his back's to me – whether he's doubtful the police will find anything significant.

I close the bedroom door and dial Trisha's number. 'You had a break-in?'

'Some creep, poking around the flat. Arthur's fine.'

'Anything I can do?'

'We're OK, thanks. Derek's a mess. Wanted to stay all day, but he had a big job at the Riviera Hotel.'

'I'm sorry, Trish. Just so you know, we had a break-in too. All our entryways have been dusted, door handles, drawers. Looks like Narnia in here.'

'Shit, Frey. How many break-ins happen on the same street *and* on the same night?'

She's right, but hers was drug related and I can't tell her that. It's another reason her eyes are glued to those binoculars and she can't sleep.

'I'm scared.' I say. 'Patti thinks I've been having an affair.'

'Bollocks.' She takes a raggedy breath and I realise she's smoking. 'She's only going off what the letters say, and half of it's a crock of shit.'

'I wanted to ask you about phones. What if the numbers Edward's calling from belong to other murder victims?'

'That'd be creepy. But unlikely. The phone has an ID number the police can use to track it, even if he changed the SIM card. I'd say he's using burners and changing them. That's what I would do.'

In my head, I picture Edward slumped over a magnifying glass, pulling apart every phone and using the parts to make something new. But of course, he isn't. Not if there are ID numbers specific to each phone. I wish I could close my eyes against the horror of him and the daily pleading that ignites my brain. *Please, please, please, help me find him.* I don't understand how he's able to stay hidden.

'I had coffee with that guy at work. Well, I was desperate, and he needs to know what's happening.'

'The *mild flirtation* guy?' she asks. 'Did anyone see you together?'

'Yes and no.'

'Well, did they or didn't they?'

'Yes. It's a popular haunt.'

'Sorry, it's hard to get my brain around all this. I mean, *you* in this kind of shit.' I hear her take another long drag. 'You're going to tell me the police have flagged your address and suggested a panic alarm? I'm beginning to think I need one.'

'I've logged everything, and I mean *everything*. He's like a postman on steroids. That's why I need your help,' I say.

'Look, Frey, I'm sorry this creep keeps blackmailing you. But you've gotta understand, I'm under intense police scrutiny. No, thank you, I'm sensing a trap.'

'I wouldn't dream of you doing it for free. I need two things. Well, three, actually. A camera inside your house and a camera inside mine. When I go out, you can drive behind me at a distance and we might catch this guy. Like you say, how many break-ins happen on the same street *and* on the same night? I'll pay you.'

'How much?'

'Five hundred.'

'That much?'

I can't believe the words made it out of my mouth. Five

hundred for Trisha's expertise and Derek's knock-offs. How am I going to explain the deficit to Jack?

'But there's an *or else*. You're offering me money, but if I don't do it, then what?'

If she wants me to tell her I've seen her behind the flats armed with wads of weed, I'll do it. But it's not my place to condemn her or to coax out the dirty details of her private life. So maybe it's time I dropped the snotty attitude – that's what Trisha is saying. I wait for the obligatory one minute of deep thought, but it's less than three seconds. Trisha already knows how eager a few bob makes you.

'What if Jack's winding you up?' she asks. 'You don't have a pile of money stashed away somewhere? Life insurances? Anything he would gain if anything happened to you?'

'Only the house.' I'm already counting our savings in silent torment.

'After Kate died, you got a little *verbal* with Aviel's wife. I opened my window. Well, you do, don't you.'

'You're alluding to another "Someone murdered Kate and nobody believes me" episode, where Jack bundled me into the car and took me to the doctor for psychiatric assessment. So, no. The Aviels are hardly the type.'

'My point is, you've made a few enemies on this street.'

For weeks after that, the world became misted over with tears and I couldn't eat. There were parties and work functions, and Christmas was the worst time of year to be without Kate. My dreams were warm and friendly until they weren't, and I kept seeing her in intermittent flashes, like beams cast by a passing car. When friends said how sorry they were, I responded that Kate wasn't dead. So yes, I've upset a few people.

'Bring the money tomorrow,' she says. 'After Arthur's gone to school.'

32

FREYA

Sunlight streams against the windscreen, soft and yellow against the glass. I turn the radio up and hear a live report coming from the BBC. Not the host's gravelly voice this time, but Detective Inspector Anna Seymour.

'A detailed investigation is under way to look into the circumstances of Elisabeth Sanders' death. A man was caught on a restaurant camera near the beach at 2.45 am on Tuesday 15 October, driving a stolen Vauxhall Astra. I would urge any witnesses or motorists who may have captured anything of relevance on dashcam to please get in touch.'

If Dad had been here, he would have already found him. That's why the police used him from time to time. He was like a bloodhound. Nothing escaped his scrutiny. A bubble of fear expands in my chest as a childhood memory emerges.

It was a week after my seventh birthday and I'd run outside to escape a swatting. I'd lied about touching Dad's camera. The spool of film spilling from the open back proved it. There was a narrow spot behind the shed and I'd dug myself in deep. The back door slammed and soon Dad was puttering about in what is now Jack's hangar. I asked God to make me invisible. But He must have taken the day off, or He was ignoring me for lying, because when I peered through an open knot in the wood, Dad's eye was staring back at me.

Like the man who's driving alongside me as if to overtake. The car is black and sleek, the type executives drive. When I accelerate, so does he. When I brake, he hangs back too. He slots in front of me to avoid a passing car, and I'm gripping the steering wheel and fumbling for my phone. If he thinks this is some kind of sick joke, it's not funny.

As I snap a photo of the plates, it occurs to me how much I wish this were some kind of twisted dream – the type where you're being chased down an avenue of writhing beech trees, or about to jump off a suspension bridge. I allow myself to believe it's one big nothing. Before it becomes one big something.

In his wing mirror, I catch sunlight on a cheekbone and the curve of a shoulder. Then the frame moves a fraction, and a hand snakes out of the driver's window. Not to adjust it, but to caress the reflection. My reflection.

I turn the steering wheel a little to the left so I'm now in his blind spot. But he mimics the manoeuvre and I'm framed inside his mirror again. The palm of his hand is flat against the door panel, which means he's driving one-handed.

My turn is only a few feet ahead, and as long as I don't indicate or tap the brakes, a sharp tug on the wheel will give him no chance to follow. Panic twists in my gut, and I take my foot off the accelerator to give myself space. As he hurries past the turnoff, I hit the brakes and downshift into the sharp curve. I'm cresting along a narrow street to the bank, my eyes pinpricked with spots. I roll down the window, filling my lungs with sea air. Even though it's not rush hour, ahead is a row of cars – tourists taking advantage of the sunshine.

While I believe the black car was Edward's, I have to consider the possibility that it wasn't. Maybe the driver simply thought I was someone else? An ex? A friend?

I pick a parking spot by the bank. For ten, twenty seconds, I'm looking at cars, studying every model before I get out. My breath is getting shorter and shorter, until I'm hardly breathing at all. I've always been subconsciously alert for predatory males, the unseen shadows that follow me down the street. Now I can't hear myself think over the blood roaring in my ears.

I realise my car is parked too close to the road, too visible, and I have to be quick. The sun is hidden behind the canopy of trees, tarmac cracked and sprouting with weeds. The air feels muggy here, as if all the humidity has been trapped beneath the bank's awning.

While I'm punching in the PIN to Kate's Uni account, I hear shoes crunching over gravel. There's no one coming towards the front door or advancing across a lawn split by a line of pine trees. I don't harbour any illusions that Edward isn't here in the car park, watching me. When the machine spits out my cash, I march towards my car and check the back seat. It's habit now, like stopping at a red light and staring at the driver next to me, imprinting their face in my brain.

A prickly sensation races across my skin and I check for sagging tyres and a hiss of air. Locking myself inside the car, I look around for those crunching shoes. But there's no sign of anyone. As I send Trisha the photo of the car and plates, I hear the rumble of an engine and a black car slides into a space opposite. A cold trickle of sweat slides down my ribs. It's not the same model, but it still makes me look.

On the way home, I check in with Andi at work. She tells me someone called in about Elisabeth Sanders.

'Another witness?' I ask.

'We've had a few crank callers pretending to be friends, but this was legit. Fergus Trainer had known Elisabeth since school. They used to go out. He told me she started seeing this guy, never mentioned a name. But here's the interesting part. When she tried to end it, he kept texting pictures of her and threatening to send them to all her friends. Frankly, they were a little creepy.'

'What kind of pictures?'

'Elisabeth sleeping,' Andi says. 'A sheet covers her nudity, mostly, but there're all different poses caught by a ceiling camera. It's not her house. Fergus didn't recognize the room.'

I wait for my thoughts to snap into place, but horror blasts through me like a live grenade. 'Did she call the police?'

'I already checked. There aren't any domestic reports.'

'It doesn't mean he wasn't abusing her emotionally or psychologically. Look at her comments on social media. Unless I'm way off base.'

'Oh, for sure. Everyone has shit they don't want to talk about.'

'Thanks for keeping me in the loop, Andi.'

People may think stalkers only have peripheral connection to their victims. But most have complete, unfettered access. Similar, you could say, to a husband. For a second there's a shape, the fragment of a picture, a half-remembered memory. It keeps echoing in my brain, taunting me. And then it's snatched away again.

We know some people in our street. But you can't know *everyone*. There are always drivers who get lost trying to cut through to the beach. Parked cars idling along the kerb, exhaust spilling into the air. The dog walker. The photographer. The estate agent. The house buyer. The delivery boy. Any one of these could be him.

I can't get into the house quick enough. Despite a cool breeze whistling down the street, my palms are damp and I can feel sweat evaporating off my forehead.

A curtain twitches in one of the upper windows of the flats, then a flash of grey as someone moves across the room. I can tell it's Trisha by the slow tilting roll of her hips. I hope she's searching for that licence plate.

The squeal of the front door and a spidery ripple of dread races across the back of my neck. It's only Jack. He gives me a stiff hug and I try to remember if he had a doctor's appointment I'd forgotten about. He slips off his shoes, leaving a trail sweaty sock prints on the floor. I follow him into the sitting room.

'Patti asked to see me, so I got an Uber. I knew what she wanted before she opened her mouth. Given, she said, that stalking requires repeated visual and physical proximity, did I have any idea who could have been writing these letters? I said no, because I don't. She reminded me that stalking can be hard to investigate and prosecute, and that I'm to be patient because you're bearing the brunt of it.'

'You're not offended by Patti hinting at your involvement?'

He shakes his head. 'She's only doing her job. I would have done the same.'

'I'm sorry I took the car.'

'When you need the car, you take it. Safer than being on the bus.'

Before he asks me where I've been, I tell him I'd reserved a book at the library for Trisha and went to pick it up. The room feels colder and if I believed in ghosts, I'd say Dad had joined us. *Ah, did you know a lie travels farther than the truth?* It's as if I'm standing in shallow water one minute and a rip current pulls me from the shore the next.

Jack flicks on the kettle. 'The glass man's been.'

'Already?'

'He was in and out in twenty minutes.' He thumbs the home button on his phone to check his messages. 'Earl Grey or Yorkshire?'

'Yorkshire,' I say, knowing he'll have to find a new box in the larder.

He leaves the phone on the table and I see several bannered notifications on his screen. Yet when I'd looked at his phone previously there was no such feature. While he rifles through packets on the shelf and rips into a new one, the wall between us provides enough cover for me to check them. I still can't access the phone with the old passcode. But the messages are from Duffy and Patti and plenty from Theo. It's the one to Liv that bothers me. The subject line reads "Concerned," but the snick of the larder door latch tells me there's no time to read more.

We drink our tea in silence and I'm looking at him, and he's looking at his phone, and a flicker of dread brushes the edge of my throat. I want to remove myself from the chaos of letters and stalkers, anything to distract me from a ticking clock that barrels its way into my head and reminds me I can't hold on for much longer.

I walk over to the sink and pour my tea down the drain. A salt-rich wind blows through the open window and I imagine the sea drawing a deep breath and exhaling as it crawls along the sand. I want to run, leaning into the bends, pushing myself harder and harder until I'm standing beneath the ironstone cliffs near Mudeford Spit. Anything to get away from this.

33

FREYA

I GO UPSTAIRS TO get Trisha's money, and a buzzing sound makes me freeze. A drone hovers about six feet from the bedroom window, and I don't know whether to duck or close the blinds. A warning pulse starts in my neck and then ripples along my spine.

Opening the window, I peer over the ledge. There's no sign of anyone with a transmitter and something that size wouldn't have the payload for anything larger than a phone. Had they taken a picture? I watch the thing drift down the street. Maybe it's Google updating maps.

I grab a book from the stack inside my bedside table, hook it under one arm and remind Jack where I'm going. He barely looks up.

Trisha's wearing skinny jeans and an off-the-shoulder T-shirt, and I detect a strong whiff of perfume. Derek must be coming over.

'It's all here,' I say, handing over the envelope.

Trisha licks a finger and flicks through the banknotes. She nods a few times as if her mind is making mental sums of the bills she has to pay. I settle on the couch and notice a model plane sitting idly on the table – a sand and spinach camouflage scheme by the look of it.

'You didn't see a drone out there, by any chance?' I ask.

'Probably MI5, Frey. Hope you ducked.' She eyes the book in my hand and reaches out a hand. '*Little Girl Dead*. That for me?'

'I told Jack I was at the library getting you a book. Better than telling him I took a chunk out of Kate's Uni account.'

'How's he doing?'

'How does any man do when he's just had his house fingerprinted for intruders?' I say. 'He's getting weird.'

'He's scared. Same as you. I'm glad Kate's not here to see all this. I'm sorry, I didn't mean it like that.'

'No, I know what you mean.'

Trisha hardly mentions Kate, and when she does, it's with an apologetic wince as if she's bitten something sour. I want to tell her to talk about Kate all she wants. I won't break.

I came here after it happened, slept on her couch and cried. Trisha made me kneel and thank God for the seventeen years I got to have with Kate. Liv and Theo arranged the coffin, the service and the flowers. When I think of Kate, she is never as vibrant as she is in photographs, but pale and undefined. A matrix of poses, faces and expressions, floating away, never to be retrieved. I look at my abdomen and know that no one can ever erase the tiny incision that marks the last remnant of her.

'I looked up that licence plate you sent me,' she says. 'The car was registered two years ago in Bournemouth. The DVLA don't give out names. Not without a small fee or a warrant. It's not listed on Car Check either. Makes me wonder if it's a stolen plate or registered to a movie star. Let's look on the bright side, shall we?'

I catch her wide smile and the glint in her eye. 'What?'

'Derek wants to move in. So I took a leaf out of your dad's book and followed him to a client and back. He'd pop his cork if he found out I'd been investigating him. But there're too many creeps out there; I shit you not.'

I can see the amusement on her face, as if she wouldn't allow her hopes to be pinned on a few perfect dates. Many of which took place in the back of Derek's van, the park, the cinema. I doubt they talked much. After all, someone as seamless and as hairless as Derek could be married.

I used to read Dad's paperwork when I was young. Mostly cases of missing people and cheating spouses, all with some reason or another to leave home. One night, Dad took me out to do a little surveillance. We sat in the car outside a large house on Lilliput Road, eating sandwiches and drinking hot tea. Dad let me use his binoculars while he used his camera to snap at something through the trees.

'There's your man now. David Ludlow, local MP, snogging with Nora Bingly. Will you take a look at that?'

Snap, snap, snap. I lifted my binoculars to an upper window, saw two mouths pressed together, tongues like moist slugs. I must have made a noise, because Dad chuckled and said I'd like it soon enough.

He told me that each street had a mood of its own. You could walk naked down one with your hair on fire and no one would notice. Others had eyes behind every window. He'd park in places that gave him cover, making sure the exit points were ones his targets were most likely to use. No U-turns. Too conspicuous.

I return to the vision that is Trisha, standing with one hand on her hip. Her eyes shoot up to the ceiling and nailed to the window casing is a camera, pointing at our house.

'You can't see it from outside,' she says. 'It's covert, like the ones in the Tower of London.'

'Those are smaller, Trish. About a tenth of the size.'

Tears prick the corner of my eyes and I thank her. She's my only friend, and that's what I tell her.

'Let me know where you want the other one,' she says. 'Derek suggests in the kitchen, pointing at the front door.'

'I prefer the bedroom, pointing at the bed.'

She grimaces as if my choice of room is odd. 'Are you drinking? Your eyes... you look drunk.'

'Oh, shut up.'

'*You* shut up.' She reaches for a pack of Silk Cut. 'Mind if I smoke?'

I push the ashtray across the table. The tip of her cigarette crackles as she takes a drag.

'I hope your cut doesn't leave a scar.' She points at my forehead. 'I can't tell you how many bruises I had before I finally came clean to my social worker. Of course, they weren't accidents.'

I hadn't considered what she'd gone through. Perhaps some secrets are too big to hide, and eventually, they're bound to come out. A black eye, a broken finger, a missing tooth. She's seen it all.

'I've got a few friends down the pub. Ones who use the dark web,' she says, fluttering her fingers like it's some kind of freak show. 'One, your stalker might have used that fake name before. Two, we have a description of his car. Three, he's tall-ish. Four, this is important. Your cop may already know him.'

'From a list of known suspects?'

'Maybe. Before you get too comfortable, we need to share GPS,' she says, cranking up the drama. 'Sometimes you can't get a location. Signal's blocked. But you'll feel safer.'

'I remember Patti saying something about GPS. I've been watching for signs of spyware and tracking, although I don't know how you'd tell.'

'It's unlikely someone accessed your passcode if you keep your phone on you at all times. Derek knows all about jail breaking and remote monitoring. If you like, he can take a look.'

I nod, but I'm not comfortable letting him loose on my phone, not until I delete all those texts from Edward. 'You mentioned self-defence?'

Trisha picks up the ashtray and slots her cigarette in the groove. She shows me how to hold my keys in a fist, blade pointing through my fingers. Then she picks the widest length of her sitting room and I cringe because no matter how much she tries to teach me to stabilise myself, shift my weight and throw an elbow, I'll forget it all in the terror of an actual attack.

'Groin kicks. You come in – hands under his chin – and drive in with the knee. When he grabs his nuts, you wrench him around and take him down. Got it?'

It all looks so easy when you're Trisha, lunging and flexing and jabbing a knee into an imaginary groin. She does shadowboxing. I know because I've seen the bag hanging in her spare room. It takes balance and proper footwork, none of which I have.

She gives me a mantra to memorise and says I'll be stronger for it. As I take a breath, her foot hooks mine and I topple to the floor. She's astride me; knees rammed under my armpits.

'This is what you don't want. So pay attention. If he breaks into your house, you'll have the advantage. He doesn't know every creak, every squeaky hinge.'

I don't want to spoil her day, but I think Edward has a pretty good idea.

'You're fit.' She stands and offers me a hand. 'I've seen you running for hours along the beach, kicking up sand like a marine.'

'That's a slightly inflated view of my faculties, Trish.'

While I'm wondering when she could have seen me running on the beach in the early hours, something flashes across the window and she lurches towards it.

'Oh, wouldn't you know it? Roger Daniels. Creepy little shit.'

There he is, carrying a transmitter. I'm almost relieved the drone belongs to him and not some perv in a mac. Now it's caught in the tree and we're both laughing.

I thank Trisha for everything and for agreeing to shadow me. With all the mistakes we've made, all our darkest secrets, maybe Trisha and I are alike. She must have sensed it when we first met, a vital piece I'd thought I'd tucked away where nobody would find it.

Jack's out in his shed when I get home, back door ajar, letting in a flurry of dead leaves. I hurry upstairs to the printer in Dad's old room and make a handful of flyers, asking for any information about our accident and include my number.

I walk to the end of the road, feeling uneasy. It's as though some joker has angled cars and wheelie bins slightly out of place, just enough to question if there's anyone hiding beyond my line of sight. The only noise that brings me peace is a plane droning overhead, contrails like streaks of breath against a blue sky.

I stop at the site of our accident and the first impact. A block of flats overlooks the cliffs and the telephone entry system is a bank of names. I'm about to press one when a car stops at the kerb, spilling a woman and three children and a handful of shopping. She tells me she's a resident, and doesn't remember hearing anything on the night I mention. When I hand her a flyer, she insists on pinning it to the noticeboard inside. I walk next door to the old Cliffside Dene Hotel, where two cameras are mounted near the eaves on the beach-facing wall.

Inside is a concierge. I tell the man at the desk I work for the *Daily Echo* and I'm doing a story on an accident that occurred a few nights ago. He doesn't match the bruise on my face with the crash, but his smile gets wider when I pull out a twenty.

'Funny you should ask,' he said, pocketing the money, 'a police officer was asking the same question yesterday. Wanted to review the CCTV.'

There's no way I'm going to ask to review it. He'll only ask for ID. 'Any chance I could talk to a resident?'

'I'll make a few calls,' he says. 'Might take a while.'

I take a seat while he calls a few numbers. The email icon on my phone displays seven unread emails. As usual, all are junk. Delete, delete, delete.

It's twenty-five minutes before the lift opens behind me. I whip around to see a woman with blonde hair and a Celtic tattoo creeping up one side of her neck.

'Hi, I'm Agnetha Pålsson, you are...'

'Freya Thorne.'

She juts her chin towards the doors, and we walk outside.

'I'm sure your story isn't for prying ears. So, you were the driver?'

She's a good deal smarter than the concierge. 'My husband and I were coming back from a dinner party and I should have turned left here. Someone went into the back of us. I wondered if you saw anything.'

'I'd just come back from work, opened the patio doors to catch the breeze.' She points to a second-floor balcony. 'There was a loud bang and two cars shimmied down the road, coupled together. They raced around the corner and I lost sight of them. I ran down the hill and saw a man leaning in through the driver's side of the car in front.'

I remember then that someone had opened the car window, but through the stabbing pains in the first few days and the periodic panic attacks, pieces are still missing.

'When he saw me,' she says, 'he ran to his car and zipped off. Before you ask what he looked like, he was a shadow in headlights. I'd say tall, taller than me, and as for dark or fair, I couldn't tell.'

'Did you see his car?'

'Could have been a G-Class Mercedes or a Jeep. It's a rough guess.' She rubs her chin and looks up the street. 'So the police haven't found him yet?'

'No. It was a hit and run.'

Agnetha would only have seen a car roof from her flat, and her focus would have been on Jack and me when she got downstairs. I'm indebted to her. So many witnesses are afraid to help, and she came out with no fear for herself. I give her my number in case she remembers anything else.

Turning into my street, I think I hear the echo of footsteps behind. I speed up a little, heart rate doubling. I can't resist a glance. A figure flickers behind a row of spruce, heels clacking closer and closer. When I turn, I see a woman rushing towards me, then sidestepping me for the bus. Why am I so afraid all the time? What purpose does it serve?

Kids swarm the pavements, some walking in groups, others in pairs. I look for one with a Spitfire on his backpack, tearing into a KitKat. I wave and he waves back.

I'm not inside the house two minutes before Jack calls from Dad's room. Something about mortgage papers and where the statement was we'd received two days ago. I can hear the runners on the filing cabinet, and a thought scuttles past, only I don't catch it in time. Two minutes later, he appears at the kitchen door.

Had we paid too much? You can never pay too much for anything these days. Had we received a letter about defaulting on payments due to overspending? My mind backtracks, searching for clues that might explain a significant disaster. In the hit and miss filing system of the Thornes, it comes to me.

B for banking.

Except this wasn't about the mortgage. Not directly. It was about all our accounts. But why does Jack want it now? Today? Right this minute?

I rail against him, bringing attention to his retirement and me having to work and how the money he once earned could have bought us a house with a sea view. His scowl tells me it's so much worse.

'There's been a large withdrawal from Kate's savings account, Freya. What the hell have you done with it?'

34

FREYA

I TELL HIM I took it to hire a capable private investigator. Of course, this brings back memories of Dad, and my eyes sprinkle with tears. When I mention Dad, Jack's expression goes flat, like a dog at the first sign of a threat. He's wondering what it has to do with a missing five hundred. Although, about now, his carefully ticking brain is linking the money to a few measly hours of surveillance. I mean, five hundred is a good deal for a couple of cameras, right? I'm not being screwed here.

I've pored over Dad's old books to find a way around all this, to do the investigations myself, but I'm treading on dangerous ground. It makes me regret not learning more about Dad's trade before he died.

'We could look for a PI online, but there'd be an enormous fee. So I asked Trisha.'

Jack lifts his chin like a man preparing for execution. I expect him to bombard me with questions, but he squints as if looking at me is agonising. We are standing in no-man's-land.

Not far enough away to be distant, or close enough to be touching.

'Do you honestly think Trisha can find this guy?' he asks.

'She's resourceful.'

'Because she smokes weed, hangs around addicts and screws half the neighbourhood? She'll be gone in the morning. Flat emptied and no forwarding address.'

'Give me a break, Jack. What does five hundred get you these days?'

'You don't think the police are doing enough?'

'In a word, no. It would be easier to let Patti deal with it all, but I can still picture the way she looked at me, which is the way you're looking at me now.'

'Well, how's this. We don't know who these people are or whether they're dangerous. All we know is Trisha's a single mum and Derek runs a security firm. Or a racket, whatever the hell it is. A few nights go, Trisha had a break-in, same as us. Only hers was some kind of drug addict looking for his next fix. But what if it was the same guy? Small world.'

He's right. A very small world with very large possibilities. I start patting cushions and tidying books away, anything to keep from feeling a failure.

'Let's stop all this skulking around,' he says. 'All you had to do was tell me the truth.'

I nod. Except lying isn't just in my head. It's in my bones.

'Shit,' he says, looking at the clock. 'I nearly forgot. Theo asked if I could get his prescription.'

'Of course. Go. That's fine.'

Keys jingle, the door slams and the car whines as it reverses out of the drive. I feel oddly discarded. I know he'll only be forty minutes, tops, but I'd like to have gone too. I'd like to have been asked.

I clamber upstairs and lie on the bed. My face is already wet, tears coming hard and fast. I'm not crying for the things I've done, but for what I've lost and can never get back. Jack knows every inch of me by heart, knows every mood and what chips away at my self-esteem and what builds me up. He can see it deep behind my eyes, a room only he can access.

The clouds in my head are growing more and more menacing, darker and heavier and ready to burst. I think back to my initial session with mental health services. I'd told the doctor I had panic attacks and kept thinking about death. He offered to refer me through the NHS, but recommended I talk to Dr Meyer. Then came the prescriptions for antidepressants which I never took, and endless talks about stress management. When really, I'd destroyed my marriage and kept fantasising about the man I'd slept with.

The seed of a memory tracks its way into my mind. The long weekend when Jack was away. We'd had another argument over a large box delivered by Fed Ex. A model fighter jet costing somewhere near two Gs. Jack was travelling to Wales with Captain Duffy and wouldn't be back until Monday night. We'd barely hugged before he left. I was in no mood for socialising with friends whose relationships were everything mine used to be. With grief baying at the door, all I wanted to do was party until I'd obliterated every image.

It was Saturday morning when Miles sent a text asking me out for a drink. I ripped tags off new clothes and stuffed them in a weekend bag. Ran off to meet a lover without thinking of the consequences. I question if anyone had seen me at the Harbour Heights Hotel. The man in the lift, dressed in a suit and carrying a briefcase, perhaps. We alighted on the same floor, and he walked behind me as I turned to go into the room. Had he seen a table laden with white chocolate and strawberry mousse and a bottle of Prosecco? Had he seen Miles smiling as if he knew every detail of what was to come?

There was a large window in the bedroom and I remember looking at a froth marbled sea, where a training schooner lounged on the horizon, its lights bright in the dusk. Miles stood beside me, smelling faintly of wine. He knew I was in a fragile place and I wanted to unload.

'I'm so glad you're here. This,' – he handed me a glass – 'you have to try. Let's say it's a concoction of all things Italy.'

I remember tasting notes of apple and pear and pink lemonade. He filled up my glass again with a mischievous grin, and we were laughing.

'Are you sure you want to do this?' he'd said.

Yes. I was sure. The words *let's wait*, or *maybe I need to think this through* kept sloshing around in my head. But I wasn't thinking about careers or how potentially damaging this could be. He was an adrenaline-filled rollercoaster, an exploration into a territory I'd never known.

His fingers slid up the side of my neck, hands cupping my head. My body loosened as he pulled me close. I hardly noticed the cry of a herring gull as it banked past the window. But I remember being afraid that he would excite me more than I could handle. Here my memory slides into black, and I wait, forcing the images to come.

Neither of us spoke as we lay under the sheets, moving together in a slow, gentle rhythm. Tiny berms rippled his belly, firm to the touch. Then I awoke in a hotel bedroom with him next to me, trapped in the realisation that I should never have been there at all.

In the morning, Miles watched me gather up my belongings and I made him promise not to tell anyone. It was the beginning and the end of something, and we both knew it.

'Freya—'

'You don't have to say anything.'

'No, let me finish. You're too wonderful to be left on your own for an entire weekend. If this is what you want... a secret only between us, then I understand. But there's still tomorrow.'

The silence seemed to swap hands, and I didn't know what to say. He wanted me to think about going to Paris the next day. I did. And we didn't.

On the way back to my car, I saw the same man with the briefcase. Had he been following me? How much following is too much?

For a time, I hugged the secrets to me, smiling and feeling their warmth. The affair numbed the pain in my heart until guilt broke the spell. He was a constant presence at work, a kind heart, a shoulder to lean on. A memory I've tried to throw off, yet he slips between my thoughts. Now, he's moved on, found someone else, and I'm pleased. At least, I should be.

I slide back to the present and close my eyes to capture the images. My mind does what it does best. Mashes up the truth with lies until I don't remember anymore. Whenever I get close to telling Jack, I always start with, 'I need to tell you something' and then I can't bring myself to tell him the *something*.

I slide off the bed and open the bedroom door. Something feels wrong, like a note jangling off key. A buzzing sound, not high frequency like Roger Daniels' drone, more consistent, as if the old radio in the bathroom emits static. But the dial is turned off. When I press my ear to the wall, it stops. Must be electrical cables or the water pipes.

I look down the stairwell and I'm frowning at a sea of paper, rustling in a breeze. I'm not understanding why Jack would have left rubbish on the floor. But it isn't rubbish. They're pictures of a woman and a man making love. Her face is clearly visible over his shoulder. My face.

No, no, not this. I can hardly breathe. This is not something I can tell the police and I can't show Jack. Because the man in the picture isn't him.

They're everywhere. Layers and layers of them in the sitting room and kitchen. Like the cargo hold of a sinking ship, the level seems to rise with each ragged breath.

'Jack!'

Where's Jack? Then I remember he's out and he'll be back any moment.

I wade towards the kitchen cupboard and pull out a box of bin bags. My heart feels as if it will burst and my throat is so dry I'm coughing.

I grab and scrunch as many as I can, some filtering up into the air as I lunge for them. My mind screams for me to hurry. I stuff them into the bags and carry them to the bins outside.

Please, Jack, don't come home. Not yet.

I find a few stragglers under the kitchen table as Jack's car pulls into the drive. Sweat clings to my back and legs. I reach for those last few pieces, tamping them down into the bin. No time to haul it outside.

I hear the car door slam, then footsteps. I'm looking for something to cover these obscene pictures, wet kitchen towel, tea bags, anything.

A key rattles. The lock engages.

I see the filter basket in the sink still full of coffee grounds. Just as the door opens, I dump a top layer of sludge into the bag and fasten it.

35

EDWARD

THE PROMENADE IS HEAVING, gulls screeching over scraps under the tables. The sweet, pungent smell of a joint wafts across the restaurant patio and Edward sees several eyes looking for the culprit, heads shaking as if they can't believe someone would do it in public.

He selects a table near the railing and shakes out a napkin. He takes a few more hits and mashes the joint under his heel. Quiet music plays and he's pleased to find no elaborate dishes and specialty cocktails with locally inspired names. The air is thick with baked crust and oregano. There's a reason he's here, and that's to finish what he started a few months ago.

Nian Zhen. The waitress. The one who got away.

He looks up at the sky and sees a contrail hanging above him like a giant worm. The sun is a dim sulphur glow behind a cloud and it seems warmer today than yesterday. He unbuttons his shirt and rolls up his sleeves. The waitress on duty is pretty. Trousers a little too tight and skin so dark, he wonders if she sunbathes naked.

His stomach seems to crumple in on itself and the rumbling is louder than a fridge compressor. Snapping his fingers, he orders tomato bruschetta to start, followed by chicken Milanese and a cappuccino to finish. He doesn't stare, he's too smart for that. But he can tell she's curious.

Had they met before? Met... that's a conscious action. Something she'd remember. But not if she were high and half-assed on the pier, begging for it.

His phone pings with a newsflash. A four car pileup on the A338 near the hospital and the Robin Hood Car Thief is causing police concern. It worries him too, all those ANPR signs, providing number plate recognition and driver's details. He's never as invisible as he thinks and, parked on Burnham Road at any time of day, could have raised a red flag. He didn't know the Audi came from a rental company when he stole it.

He studies his phone, a saved video of Freya sitting next to lover boy in this very restaurant almost a year ago. If she is the girl next door, he is the high-fashion model, slim and muscular with a lean face. She appears to be fighting the drag and pull of her sexual urges, and all hope hangs on his delivery. For one tiny second, she turns her head towards the beach, to the rolling waves and the murmur of backwash. Her charade of innocence makes Edward squirm. If he placed a consecrated wafer on her forehead, would it burn and leave a scar?

She is an interesting woman. Capable of beautiful dreams and such horrible nightmares. He might fit irritatingly into the elitist world of academia and stick out like a sore thumb, but he bets she regrets saying it now. He clamps his lips together, swallowing laughter. He enjoys the chase, the build-up, the hesitation. It serves as foreplay.

The thump of a plate tears him from the thought, and he nods at the pepper grinder that hovers over his meal. Five distinct flavours. Tomatoes, basil, balsamic, garlic, olive oil.

He savours his appetiser, wondering when Freya will come to live with him. He doesn't want her to worry about Elisabeth. She meant nothing to him, not the way he sees it. Things got snarly when Elisabeth wanted to see his house, and he couldn't blame her for that. There's so much catfishing these days.

They'd smoked a joint by the pool, kissed and laughed at something he had said. Her crop-top was blinding white, and the sky was on fire behind her. She jumped in and he followed, putting his arms around her waist. He wished he'd kept his mouth shut, but out it came – Freya's name instead of hers.

Her hands flew to his chest. She pushed and screamed, and the tone of her voice did something to him. He felt sick and shattered, as if he were going back and forth without purpose. He wanted it to stop so badly, he could almost taste the blood on his tongue. But there was a taste of something else, too. Rage. There were several minutes of a blackout, at least he thought they were minutes. It could have been an hour. Taking a sensory break from her screams was impossible and the way he saw it, he didn't have a choice. A length of double braided nylon, hanging from the pool railings, was a means to a timely end. He lay her in the dark room until he decided what to do.

He had a few options, the way he saw it. Either leave the body near the log cabin on Alumdale Road, or in the trees behind Squirrels Leap. Or drag her to the end of the garden and lug her over the wall. Apart from a narrow channel in the cliff, the sheer drop would make it impossible to navigate, and sandstone and clay sediment caught in hair or clothes would give police a location. His hatred for the one person who had caused all of this made him deaf to all of them. It was time Freya saw what she had done.

He walked to the chippy to get something to eat and noticed a car delivering food to a flat upstairs, its engine still running. He was quick. The driver was not. Driving the hatchback home gave him the means to transport the body to the beach. The gate at the top of the lane had been locked, but the pedestrian access allowed him to carry his burden to a narrow strip of grass behind the beach huts. CCTV kept an eye on the beach, but camouflage made him unidentifiable, as did shoes one size larger.

Many hours afterwards, he waited deep in the darkest shadow until a flick of pale light seeped across the horizon, moonlight burning a trail across the surface of the sea. Footsteps echoed along the promenade towards him, and in the moonlight, Freya's face was a mask of light and dark. When she reached the indent between the cliffs, his fingers curled around a stone, exploring the shape of it, the weight. It tempted him in. There was no run up and, as his hand reached its delivery arc, he released it over the dune. She flinched at the sound and it must have given her one of those uneasy, itchy sensations to be standing there alone. The sound caused the gulls to explode into the air like tossed paper in a gale.

The sun slid across the sea, spilling between the waves like runnels of mercury. It was then that she saw the fractured huddle in the sand. He wanted to watch. It was the best part.

News channels and CCTV have picked up the incident, but the description of the man is nothing like him. A persistent question arises from time to time. He was sure he'd worn gloves, but that doesn't mean he hadn't touched the cord prior to that night.

No point discussing it in his head. It's too late now.

Nian brings another plate. The chicken is plump, juices pooling into a gravy, and he smells parmesan, lemon and breadcrumbs. Does she see the man who picked up her up from the nightclub that cold night in February, drove her to the pier, and made love to her on the bench? Does she see *him*?

A few minutes later, a shadow falls across the table as he knew it would and he studies a shirt unbuttoned low enough to display the hollow between her breasts.

He gives her a twenty, but there's another fifty hanging out of his wallet. 'I was wondering what you were doing later?'

'I had thought of putting my feet up,' she says.

'And now?'

'Definitely putting my feet up.'

He can tell by her accent she's not from around here and those precious vowel sounds are as long as her legs. When she leaves to attend to another guest, he's alert in the subsequent silence. A tinge of regret passes over him. She isn't Freya, she's nothing like Freya, but he can pretend that she is.

He cowers under the scorching sun, faintness spreading through his limbs. He would have preferred a sullen sky veined with lightning to the haze and brightness of today. His lunch hour is over and, although satisfying, it has put him behind schedule. But being late for anything is imminently arousing.

He catches Nian's gaze two tables away and follows her into the restaurant. There has to be a rear exit. Fire codes require it. She leads him down a short corridor and through another door into blackness. As far as he can tell, there are no windows. A supply closet.

He steps across the threshold and closes the door. It's a cramped space, made even more restricted by two bodies pressed together. This is what she has reduced him to – this blind, animal craving – and the worst thing is it feels so good.

He can hear blood singing in his veins, the exhilarating sense of savage strength, and the lust that seizes both of them. She hooks the heels of her shoes into the shelves behind him and if this is what Nian calls putting her feet up, he's game.

36

FREYA

THE SKIES DROOP OPPRESSIVELY low, almost touching the rooftops. The falcon huddles on the sill outside Kate's window, feathers ruffled by the morning wind. A fierce eye stares back at me, unblinking. It pivots slightly, wings open in a spread of feathers, and I can see the ghost of its speckled bib. Then a blur of grey as it recedes down the street, voice fierce and plaintive.

It inspires me to do Trisha's workout: running up and downstairs, punching, kicking, swinging around the corner of the door and lunging at an opponent who isn't there. I'm laughing at myself as I dress. My eyes drift to the mirror and I study the network of lines at the corner of my eyes and the trailing edge of a bruise at my cheekbone.

I brush my hair and notice a curl with a blunt edge above my left ear. I lean forward to get a better look. For the briefest moment, I imagine I'm looking at the wrong reflection, that this vindictive, frightening thing is someone else. Halfway through that thought, I realise it's not that I don't cut my hair. I do. I simply don't remember cutting it here.

I open my dressing-table drawer and my scissors are the first thing I see. Blades half-open and wisps of hair curled around the screw. There is an element of the ridiculous, as if Edward is watching me through the mirror. I study the wall, the pictures, the light switches, for a discreet camera. I have stayed awake at night, long after Jack has gone to sleep, listening for sounds until I sink into the pillows. Now I'm too exhausted to know what's real and what isn't.

I check my phone. When I unplugged it early yesterday morning, it was fully charged and by lunch, it was down to forty-eight per cent. I rarely leave apps open, but something's draining the battery.

When it rings, I almost drop it. Trisha's voice is shallow, as if she's run out of breath.

'Turn on the telly. Turn on the news.'

I run downstairs to the sitting room and search for the remote. The face of a young woman fills the screen.

... Nian Zhen, a waitress at Vesuvio restaurant, has been reported missing since yesterday afternoon. Police have not released the identity of the man she was with or what his role was in the disappearance.

I'm thinking they shouldn't be showing this – someone should stop this – when Jack returns from his shed.

'Another girl's gone missing.' I point at the TV.

He looks as if all disbelief is about to blow and shuffles a little closer. We stand transfixed for a moment, trying to process what the newsreader is saying.

'Someone cut my hair last night, Jack. Right here.'

His face swings towards mine, eyes scurrying up and down my head. 'No, you often cut it. You must have forgotten.'

'I didn't cut it. *He* did.'

I feel the familiar shimmer of doubt, my stomach a ball of acid and I'm sinking into a hole, falling through the dark, never reaching the bottom. Here's Jack, clearheaded, sensible, telling me not to worry. But what if Edward gets bolder next time? A finger sliced off? A slit throat?

I'm listening to his soft murmurs of assurance, how Derek is putting up the bedroom camera in half an hour and that he promises the police will catch Edward. They will. They really will. I shrink against the couch and my heart hurts because I know it won't do any good. There's no satisfaction to be had by a promise like that.

'I've got an appointment with Dr Meyer. I *need* to be with Dr Meyer.'

He nods slowly, eyes scanning the room as if he can see something I can't. I feel the adrenaline building, the fear.

Edward has crossed the last line.

———— ◦ ————

For Trisha, the job of tailing a subject is demanding. She has to monitor me and anyone who follows me, which doesn't include looking after herself. The major obstacle is we don't know our subject's address, at least not the one he provided to the police when he made his complaint.

I had spent some time flicking through Dad's notebook. Inconspicuous is the word. Neither of us has the tools such as digital scanners nor listening devices to call ourselves proficient. We have phones with cameras and hidden microphones, and GPS connects us.

I keep the black car in the periphery of my vision. I imagine it is Edward, his quiet amusement radiating through the heavily tinted windscreen. I'm tempted to give him the finger.

My heart spasms and I can't drive to Dr Meyer's fast enough. While Trisha is now two cars behind, I notice she parks on the road, allowing the black car to follow me up the drive. I'm ten minutes early and I study a red brick building with patios and balconies. The driver of the black car doesn't get out and the tiniest frisson of fear bubbles up inside me. The windows are tinted and since he's parked two cars away from mine, I can't see his face. Trisha has some visual access between the trees that border the property, and I call her.

'What's he doing?'

I hear the pop of chewing gum. 'Looking at his phone. Looks like Aidan Turner if he brushed his hair. Seriously? I can't see shit from here.'

'Why is he sitting in his car?'

'Same as you. Talking on the phone.'

A spurt of anger and I pop the seatbelt buckle and grab the

door. I'm sick of doubting myself and being under someone's scrutiny. I'm not hallucinating.

'I'm getting out, Trish.'

'Wait!' Her voice pulls me back. 'He's pulling out. I'll follow him.'

She hangs up and I hear the rattle of gravel and crunching gears. The sense of menace subsides as he disappears along the drive, brake lights swallowed behind the trees.

It occurs to me the root of my neurosis might be something more complex. Why would this man be following me? Isn't he simply another patient, waiting in his car as I am? Maybe he was checking his phone calendar and got the wrong day, the wrong time. I wrap my arms around myself to stop from trembling. It doesn't seem real. None of it does.

37

FREYA

WHILE I SIT IN the waiting room, I google Dr Meyer in case there are any unknowns. A stretch in prison, perhaps? A secret in his past where none of us would be likely to look?

There are three hits: Sean S. Meyer, Psychotherapist and Bachelor of Science in Psychology. Durham University is his alma mater, and there's an article about him in *Psychology Today*. A short piece about his services and no mention of a wife, which leaves all bets open. He has a personal webpage and a profile on LinkedIn, and further down the page, there are three images; two professionally taken with a stock grey background and one where he is sitting on a log with the hint of amusement in his eyes. Nothing illegal, unless I want to pay a monthly subscription to dig further.

He fluffs up saggy cushions and straightens the couch. We sit opposite one another and Sean holds my gaze.

'How are you, Freya?'

'Could be better.'

A raised eyebrow encourages me to continue. I tell him everything new, from the missing stalking log to the letters and photographs I'd received. I wag the recently cut strand of hair between two fingers. It needs no explanation.

'You should have gone to the police before coming here,' he says.

'But I need you. I need you to ground me. Tell me I'm not going mad.'

'You're not going mad.'

Our eyes lock and I keep my expression neutral. 'Sometimes I feel as if I am. I'm tempted to start smoking again.'

'Are you exercising?'

'Not as much as I'd like. Not when some creep's following me.' My mind jumps to a question. 'Why do people stalk?'

'Sometimes stalkers are the product of a macho environment. Unable to vent or cry otherwise they're seen as weak. They act out their suffering in different ways.'

'So you're saying I should be sorry for him?'

'No. I'm saying it may help you understand.'

'I have no empathy for Edward. He's dangerous. I keep having nightmares and I think he's following me.'

'You *think* or you *know*?'

'I know. A man followed me here. Waited in his car. Then he left.'

'Maybe he was a patient.'

'Do you have any patients called Edward Besant?'

'You know I can't discuss that.'

Sean goes over to a small cabinet by his desk. He reaches into a built-in fridge and pulls out two bottles of water, handing one to me. 'Let's go back to the nightmares. What triggers them?'

'Smells. Particularly wine.' I twist off the cap and take a swig. 'You asked me last time if I'd had an affair. The answer is yes. A short one. A weekend fling, if you must know.'

He nods as if we're simply discussing the temperature outside. 'Does Jack know?'

'I haven't told him. He accuses me of things I haven't done, cancels plans at short notice, often without an explanation, and whispers on the phone. When I look for airfields near me in my browser, I'm sure he's not been to any of them. So there is something.'

'Are you still seeing this guy?'

'No. I've told him about the stalker and he's worried for his safety too.'

'Hard to get a protection order against someone you don't know, but keeping him in the loop is the responsible thing to do. What if this stalker is female?' Sean takes a sip of water and wedges the bottle between his knees. 'Someone who's attracted to you or your ex-lover.'

'His name's Miles.'

'OK, so does Miles have a girlfriend?'

'Yes, a very serious one. I'm hardly a threat to her. Do you think I need to take pills?'

'No. I wouldn't medicate you. The letters tear down

everything you've worked so hard to build. They don't allow you to move on. There are always two sides to us. The one that doubts and is naturally suspicious. The other has faith despite what's happening. Try not to push away all the good things.'

'What good things?'

'Life is good. Jack is good. Your job is good. Now you have a stalker. That's why we're here, to work through the trauma. I don't believe you have complicated grief, either. You're able to keep up minor tasks, clean the house, work, even though you may cry while you're doing it.'

He's right. I'd been having therapy to cope with the trauma of Kate's death, but now there's Elisabeth's body and a stalker to add to the list.

'Is Jack supportive?' he asks.

'As far as he can be. I keep telling myself it's ridiculous to expect him to understand what I'm going through. We've lived separate lives for so long, anyone would think I'm single.'

'Would you prefer to be single?'

'Sometimes.'

Why is Sean still single? It seems almost ridiculous to me. Either he's been fighting it off for the past ten years, or he's married to his job. Perhaps he'd be one of those husbands with a wedding ring in his pocket and a condom in his wallet. He's a loner because women are more trouble than they're worth. Ask Jack.

Jack... There was a time when I thought Jack was everything, that he would always be enough. I loved him completely. Still do. But now I feel stifled, and it makes me want to run further than I ever have, beyond the beach, the roads, the woods, flying out into the blue where I can't be confined. Sean coughs, and I realise I've been staring at him for the past twelve seconds.

'You're going through a great deal of stress, Freya. Especially now, this stalker claims to have enough evidence to blow the lid on your affair.'

I feel hot and uncomfortable and the word *affair* brings a lump to my throat. I stare down at my hands wrapped tightly around the water bottle.

'Any dizzy spells? Fainting?' He fills in the silence.

I tell him the last time I'd experienced anything similar was yesterday. It was only a few seconds, but I'd got up from the sofa too fast, grabbed the door frame because it felt like there was a cyclone in the house. I could hear the drone of bees or voices chattering. I snapped out of it by standing still for a few seconds to let it pass.

Sean likens my anxiety to one of those lanterns you set alight and launch into the sky. I tune out his babbling about PTSD and what might cause my nightmares. My muscles are wound tighter than a rubber band, and I roll my shoulders. Does Sean honestly believe we can work through my obsession with a stalker as part of some rehabilitation programme?

My head is fit to bursting, and I almost cry out with the pain. While my mind is working through Sean's words, I know there's something more profound and unexpected here. Something only I can work on.

'Has Jack ever contacted you about me?' I ask.

Sean looks at his shoes. 'No.'

I don't like that pause. It shows something worse than what preceded it. 'So he hasn't asked you how I'm doing.'

'Jack asking me anything would be unethical. I don't discuss my patients.'

Then I tell him people can judge me for what I did. They can say how awful I am, how I should never have allowed another man to have come between my husband and me. But they don't know what losing a child is like unless it's happened to them. I felt the ground had fallen away, that my life was unravelling. Every time I closed my eyes, I saw her in every part of the house, leaning against the kitchen sink with her pink coffee mug, waving at me from the bus stop, hugging me when she came home from school.

I took Benadryl to make me sleep, and when that stopped working, I'd go over to Trisha and talk. Sometimes I'd run into some of Kate's friends and my PTSD would kick in. They say denial is like a parachute that slows your descent into things too terrible to experience. I suppose mine was too small, and I'd slammed into hell.

Every night, I'd lie with my face pressed against Snoo, rewinding the minutes and seconds before Kate died. Her last pinned location had been somewhere between Poole Harbour and Brownsea Island. I'd kept a screenshot on my phone, willing for it to move a little to the left or to the right, so I'd know she was OK.

When I hated myself a little less, I wanted to get as far away from the house and the pain and from Jack, who couldn't fix it. I bought a rose and parked where the booze cruise boat had moored. I dropped it into the water, watched it float away. I kept up the facade of a hard-working assistant, but I'd burned too many bridges to find anyone to confide in.

Sean hands me a tissue. 'The man you saw in the car park just now. Do you think you'd recognise him if you saw him again?'

'I... I don't think so. The windows were too dark.'

'The licence plate then?'

'Possibly.'

His eyes flick to the clock and my time is over. Shouldering my handbag, I'm tempted to say, 'it's been fun' or some such flippant comment, but I decide on thank you.

He's right, though. We all wade through life-changing events and phobias, and we all have to find a way of dealing with it. If he doesn't look too closely at the faint circles under my eyes, he won't see a woman who tosses and turns in her bed – a woman about to crack.

38

EDWARD

HE WRAPS THE DIGITAL tape recorder and the strand of hair with a brief message to Freya and ties it with an elastic band. Touching her hair reminds him why he wants her.

It was almost a year ago, Monday night at the pub, football on telly. It was the perfect occasion. He ordered several shots of vodka, enough to stun a farm animal, and took a seat by the bar.

A woman sat down beside him, sipping the foam off the top of her beer. She wore a lace crop top – a cami, she told him when he asked. The waistband of her jeans was so low, he could see the diamond piercing in her navel. It was the ring on her fourth finger that bothered him, made him wonder how easy it would be to cut her loose from the squaddie hubby she kept complaining about.

'I've got to get back,' she said later, buttoning up her jeans in the women's toilet. 'Do you want my number?'

He didn't, but he took it anyway. Inevitably, Edward wished

he could "get back" to some kind of normality, back far longer than an hour. Maybe earlier to childhood, before the bindweed took grip.

When the woman left, he realised he'd called her Nisha. He washed the filth from his body and tore up her card.

How young had Nisha been when she came to live with them? Eighteen, perhaps?

He was twelve.

She slept in the room downstairs and bathed every evening at 8.00 pm. She had a tiny scar under her left breast, quite faint, but easy to see through the crack in the door. He remembered the feeling he had when he thought of her, wishing she would touch him so he didn't have to touch himself. It wasn't lust – at least not *real* lust, as he knows now – but more a need to acknowledge his own worth, to understand how it truly felt to be loved.

That same night, he saw Jack Thorne sitting at the other end of the bar, gripping a pint of Guinness and head bobbing to some kind of synth-pop. He kept looking down at his phone, likely trawling through hundreds of pictures of his recently deceased daughter. A group of fisherman had found Kate Thorne's body on the beach. It was all over the news.

Edward took a seat beside him, tapped him on the shoulder. 'What's the score, mate?'

'Sorry. Not much of a football fan.'

'Yet here you are on Monday night in the pub.'

'Stupid really.'

He liked to talk about his life as a pilot, his wife's dream to be a reporter, and his eyes misted over when he mentioned his daughter.

'For a second, I thought I saw her, there on the bed, in the spot where she used to sit. I can't talk to my wife. It's like you're shouting across a vast chasm, one where you're both standing on the edge, the opposite edge, and there's no hope of a bridge.'

'That's very profound.'

'I've been thinking, maybe there's someone else,' he said. 'Someone she's met in the library, Waterstones, wherever. There's a Christmas party this Friday at the High something Hotel.'

'Highcliff Marriott?'

'That's the one. Only I'll be away and she'll be living it up on her own. Makes me... makes me want to cancel my trip.'

'Trust is an important thing, Jack. I mean, without trust, where would we be?' Then a suspended moment that caused Jack's eyes to meet Edward's with a new pleading. 'But inside, we know. We always *know*. Look at the statistics. What percentage of couples are unfaithful? Approximately?'

Jack shrugged. 'Twenty per cent?'

'Forty-five. Staggering, isn't it?'

'What does that tell you in terms of who's at fault?'

'It tells you women are just as likely to stray as men.'

Jack fumbled with the Friend Finder app and tapped the screen. There she was, a little smiling face in a circle hovering over their home. 'Same routine. Never changes.'

'Doesn't really tell you anything, does it? She could be leaving her phone at home.' Edward handed Jack a gold solidus and he could see the curiosity burning in his eyes.

'Where did you find this?' Jack turned the coin over in his hand.

'It was inherited,' Edward said. 'Amazing, isn't it? Let's toss it. Put your mind at rest. Heads, she's faithful. Tails, she's not. Of course, if you'd rather–'

Jack didn't hesitate. He flicked the coin and it spun for a second before rolling onto the floor. Edward stooped to retrieve it and slammed it on the counter.

Tails.

Jack thought the whole thing was a joke. They always think it's a joke, especially when they're too hammered to appreciate the risk. Not that it didn't ring true.

Not that he didn't wonder... is she or isn't she?

———◦———

Friday evening was cold, a frosting of snow on the ground. From the open door of the Highcliff Marriott, Edward could hear a string quartet playing Vivaldi. All he could think about was how badly he wanted to see her, and he was counting on the fact that she would be alone.

He followed the sign that said GARDENS. Bordered by a huddle of trees was a cathedral style marquee pegged out on the lawn like a science experiment. Odd at Christmas, but heated by a powerful generator, pumping hot air into the space.

He passed on a tray of mini tomates farcies and went for some kind of vegetarian egg thing. He said to the waitress it tasted like broccoli and cheese soup, and made a face. The waitress laughed.

A woman with bottle-blonde hair eyed him up from the bar, one arm entirely tattooed in flowers. She slipped off her chair and held out a hand. He didn't catch her name. She curled one arm over his shoulder and leaned heavily against him. The drift of the conversation alternated between cultured and sensual, and he twisted his body a fraction.

'So, who's your date?' she asked, eyes searching his face.

'I thought I'd find one here.'

She probably wanted to believe she was the only thing that mattered, but his eyes searched for Freya Thorne and he found her. The stubborn constellation of freckles, pale lipstick and a sweep of dark eyeliner under perfectly drawn brows. No matter how hard he tried to mute the image, he knew he'd never forget her.

'No offence, but she's already taken,' the woman said, eyes tracking his gaze. 'The wedding ring?'

'Since we're gossiping, not all women are happily married. Most of them are looking for something.'

'Like what? A home invasion?' A coldness entered her voice as though he'd said the wrong thing. 'Did you hear about the Coventry man who got caught in bed with another man's wife? Twenty-eight stab wounds. Ended up in a rubbish dump.'

Edward looked up at thinning clouds and shadows lengthening across the grass. It had been dark since late afternoon. That was his cue. He brushed bottle-blonde off his shoulder, and she staggered a little, wine slopping over the rim of her glass. He weaved between the guests, curious at what he might discover.

It was a beautiful dress. Not so much the colour against her skin, more the way it skimmed her body without disguising a single curve. Edward studied the curve of her cheekbone, the point of her chin, the way the light pooled along her collarbone. Little by little, her mouth widened and her companion basked in the attention she denied everyone else.

Her companion? Miles Saroyan. Fashionably messy hair, charming, intelligent, funny. An MSc in Media and Communications from the London School of Economics and interned with Saffron Mahajan at *The Guardian*. Edward was simply a shadow floating outside Freya's field of vision and he should have warned her against Miles. But the unfolding of truth was far more delicious to watch. He felt a stab of envy at the life Freya had carved out for herself until she told Miles how lonely she was. She didn't exactly put it like that, but she said her husband was away on another flying trip. It was easy for Miles to pick up on the rest.

She smiled up at him, told him how she enjoyed running when the sea was dark and wind-chopped, and he agreed dawn was the best time of day. Miles tried to convince Freya to let him drive her to the beach. It was more challenging than he thought. He changed tack and asked if her husband was the type to have affairs.

'Do you know something I don't?' she asked.

'I saw him with some blonde in Exeter. I'm sure it was nothing.'

Nice try, Edward thought. Of course, she wanted to know everything about this mystery woman who, doubtless, was her boss. At first, Miles was a little vague, which came off as wanting to deliver sad news in the most sensitive way. She said she didn't want to talk about it and that was that.

What she did next changed everything. She took his hand and led him into the car park and stood against his car for a delicious moment. She kissed him and Edward didn't have to wonder what her lips tasted like or how they felt, but he asked himself if she would have liked him as much?

He followed them to the beach. Miles wrapped her in his coat and they ran to the beach huts. Freya was nervous at first, breathless, a cloud of condensation covering them both. When she pressed her lips against his, nothing on this earth could have held her back. Edward doubted Miles knew what to expect, but he must have savoured that time more than she knew.

The following day, Edward followed them to a hotel, one with a seafront view, a king-size bed and a balcony. This was a special date which, of course, Freya couldn't share with anyone else. She must have thought what she was doing wouldn't hurt a soul. Justified it by saying it was only one night or two. After that, it wouldn't happen again. But deceptions like these come at a hefty price.

Where had she got the nerve for this reckless adventure? Everyone lies. She simply swept hers under the rug, thinking no one would see it. Didn't consider for one moment she was above suspicion, because that's another lie.

A door slams and Edward flinches at the interruption. The memory is gone. His lodger slams the mail on the countertop and rips open a letter.

'Didn't hear me come in, did you?' he asks. 'Were you floating in outer space again?'

'Floating?' Edward sneers. 'People don't float.'

'You do, well beyond the earth's atmosphere. What do you see up there?'

'Nothing that would interest you. Anything in the post for me?'

'Just bills. Feel like a walk?'

'No, but if you're going, you could take this.'

Edward hands his lodger the envelope and tells him to post it three houses down from Freya's. He knows the home owner will redirect it. No cameras. No proof.

Lodger-boy glances towards the window. 'You know the police are watching the house. They will find you.'

'They won't. I'm buried so deep inside, I can't even find myself.'

39

FREYA

IT'S HARD TO THINK of time passing outside the mystery of Elisabeth's death. I watch Jack's blank face as I tell him Trisha had followed a driver who was following me. Either he is a consummate actor, or what I'm saying doesn't surprise him. Next, he'll say if I'm up for running around after a stalker, I'm up for going back to work. Monday can't come soon enough.

He sighs, gives me a long parting look before picking up his phone and strolling towards the door. 'I've offered to take Theo for chemo. It's going to be a long day.'

'You're taking him?'

'He said I make him laugh. It's his last chance to feel alive.'

'Liv would want to be with him, Jack.'

'It's Theo's choice. We need to respect that.'

There's no *you're welcome to come too*. He leans down, lips warm against my forehead. Then he's gone. He's sick of my impulsiveness and my failure to follow rules. I feel sure that if our friends had to choose between us, they would side with sensible, articulate Jack. If I continue to follow Edward, the police will request my phone records and trace me from the nearest phone masts.

Today, the BBC shows the tragic imagery of the beach. Long shots of the beach huts and voice-overs recapping the facts of Elisabeth's last moments. There are sequences of family and the public leaving wreaths, teddy bears and single roses. An appeal from her father, asking for anyone who might have seen something to come forward. I watch the news day after day for the single distressing reason that any information makes it better than none.

I scroll through articles in the *Dorset Echo*.

Alum Chine Killer 'luring women on Tinder dates'
By Jessica Tremel
Senior Reporter

Emails found on Elisabeth Sanders' computer reveal that she had been talking on Tinder with a man called Edward, Dorset Police have revealed.

Police are keen to speak to any other female Tinder users who may have had contact with Edward in recent weeks.

> In other developments, a silver Volkswagen Golf spotted near Elisabeth Sanders' house on or around 30 September, two days before she went missing, was found abandoned in Turbary Common with the keys left in the ignition. The vehicle was reported stolen on 29 September.

I've never seen a silver Golf in our street, but Edward's name in print, so public, so real, brings a dizzying wave of nausea. I'm not proud of myself for being so helpless. I'm better than this.

For the past few nights, I've watched Trisha behind her window, blinds open. She's usually hunched over her laptop, while Derek and Arthur watch TV. When Arthur goes to bed at ten, and Derek slinks off around eleven, she's a willowy figure illuminated by the glow of her phone. She doesn't see me. I'm too far back on the bed and my blinds are angled so I can see out and no one can see in. Sometimes, she leans forward as if she sees something. When she does, I lean forward too, studying every shadow, every car, and every movement.

There's a knock on the door. Roger Daniels' dad is holding out a padded envelope, eyebrows raised, and mouth open. I must look a sight.

'Sorry to bother,' he says. 'I think this is meant for you.'

I thank him for bringing it and I notice he looks back at me several times while walking along the street. Inside the package is a rectangular object tied with a red bow, a button for PLAY and another for REC/PAUSE. If I'm lucky, I'll see someone rushing away or ducking behind a car.

Could the woman in the silk scarf be watching me? What about the bald man with a long beard outside the flats, covertly looking at his phone?

My hands are shaking as I remove the elastic band and piece of paper around the tape recorder. A lock of hair falls into my lap. My hair. It takes every scrap of self-control to keep from screaming. This is a different nightmare, one that can never be put right. It's taking all my mental effort to breathe through the horror, trying to grasp why *me*.

The note reads: *All you have to do is turn me on.* Some kind of software distorts the voice, but it is clear enough.

> 'Freya, when you deprive the brain of oxygen, unconsciousness occurs within seconds and death within minutes. As Trisha Miller's will too, if she continues to follow me. How far are you prepared to go to stop another woman from dying? Her life is in your hands. Your life is in mine. You know who this is.'

———◆———

Patti and Lucian arrive within twenty minutes. I slam the tape recorder onto the kitchen table.

'You knew, didn't you? You knew Edward was the same man who killed Elisabeth.'

She keeps looking at Lucian behind me, assessing something far deeper than I can understand.

'It's this I'm worried about.' She prods the strand of my hair with her pen. 'Any video footage?'

'It was hand delivered by a neighbour. Mr Daniels. Number 26.'

'When did you notice it had been cut?'

'Yesterday morning. I do cut my hair, yes, but this... this wasn't me.'

'You changed your locks?'

'Yes.' I'm thinking about keys and which ones work in which doors and where we keep spares. 'What about the fingerprints from our house?'

'There were multiple sets, which are still being analysed and processed. No evidence yet that could lead to a conviction. The DNA report was inconclusive. The cord he used to strangle Elisabeth had an abrasive edge, which showed a quantity of skin cells, both male and female DNA. But after amplifying the male portion, there wasn't enough to quantify it. We still haven't had the toxicology report. Contrary to Netflix, it can take several weeks.'

'Elisabeth's Tinder report?'

'There's no proof Elisabeth went out to meet Edward, only that she'd been talking to him online.' She taps the iPad and swivels it towards me. 'One of the twenty-four-hour Open Access Centres at BU called us regarding a stolen ID. They recorded a man using their computers on 10th and 11th October. He was wearing a hoodie and a cap. I've questioned the students who used the OAC and nobody spoke to him. He'd used the ID to gain access and created a burner Facebook profile. From there, he signed into Tinder and began talking to four women, including Elisabeth Sanders.'

I watch a brief video clip of a man sitting at a computer, where the back of his head is the focal point. It shows the instant of a chin and the curve of his cheek as he turns for a second. A beard. My heart lifts a little. It's good news, despite everything being so tortuously slow.

'Recognise him?' Patti asks.

'No. Not remotely familiar.'

'Let's talk about Trisha Miller. Because provoking a stalker is not what I had in mind.'

She looks over at Trisha's flat and while she gives me a good talking-to about death threats being a serious crime, I wonder why I'd phoned Trisha for help. It's not simply because she lives opposite or that she has down-and-dirty contacts. It's because she's got a history of breaking the law. I realise how irresponsible that is. How self-centred. I'm seeing a side of myself I don't like.

'Andi Wynter says you want to be a crime reporter,' Patti says. 'That true?'

'You spoke to her?'

'I've spoken to everyone. Aynur Kaplan says you rarely speak and Jessica Tremel thinks you don't like her. Is there anyone you do like, Freya? By the way, they're hardly viable suspects despite the detailed dossier you've no doubt built. I wish you trusted me enough to leave the investigating to me.'

Patti bags the tape recorder and my hair, and seeing it feels like grief, disgust and terror all over again. I can't even investigate without turning everything into a farce. The best I have is television news, national and local. I don't have the resources Patti has.

I want to turn my eyes from that hideous thing she's holding, the thing Edward had taken from me at night. Because it's proof. He was here. I know he was.

40

FREYA

THE HOUSE IS TOO quiet. I like being alone, but inevitably aloneness comes with a skewed sense of suspicion. After texting Jack about the police, most significantly, the threat to Trisha, I open and close the front door, checking all windows and locks.

I go through every cupboard and every drawer to see if anything is missing. Our recycle bin is full of envelopes and bills. Instead of emptying it the wheelie bin outside, I take it upstairs.

Dad's room is empty, and his old teddy bear sits on the quilt, the same bear dangling from Kate's cot in the bedside photograph. His camera is on the desk next to a box of empty film canisters and I can still hear him popping them open, sliding out a few millimetres of film and holding it up to the light.

I feed everything through the shredder. Edward might go to unbelievable lengths to retrieve every sliver of our lives.

Even unwanted flyers and envelopes. He won't get these. I yank open the filing cabinet drawer and sift through bank statements, tax returns, old résumés and bills, and something flutters on the floor. A tattered photo, creased down the middle, once saved in a wallet. Jack's old girlfriend, wearing a bikini and standing on the beach. I'd seen her once in the high street. A statuesque blonde with a beautiful smile. What bothers me is not that it's here and misfiled in the drawer, but that he'd kept it all this time.

As I slip it between the tax returns, my eyes shift to Dad's confidential drawer, files once labelled with numbers. He'd shredded all of them, except for random notes he'd made in a spiral notebook and tucked behind a bottle of malt whisky.

I flick through the pages... *Rent a nondescript car. Dark colours are unremarkable. Pick a place that lets you keep an eye on your players but don't leave your back vulnerable. People are intuitive. They can divine a stare in a crowded place. When you consider a person blinks anywhere between 14,000 and 19,000 times a day, there's only one blink that really matters. Don't let it be the one to give you away. A subject without a routine: Lure them into plain sight.*

If I can do this – set a trap for Edward – then I'll know exactly who he is.

I hear a noise and glance over the banisters. Kate's yellow sou'wester hangs on a hook and next to it my Puffa and Jack's mac. There appear to be muddy shoe prints on the tile, stubbornly positioned where I can easily see them. My heart pulses for a few seconds and I tell myself they're Jack's.

My phone chimes with a notification, and there's a DM on Twitter from someone called *BoMoJoe*. The same someone who'd left a message on Elisabeth Saunders' Insta post. I'd never forget a name like that.

There's no genuine profile, but he's sent a picture, the torso of what appears to be a man, wearing a sweatshirt and standing in front of a green litter bin. I zoom in and see a tear in the seam where the arm meets the shoulder, and three long scratches. There are essential things in the background; a brick wall and tall glass windows, suggesting the library. An invitation to meet him there?

Despite both Jack's and Patti's warnings, I decide on one last trick. Edward is getting drunk on the attention and each message is an invitation to respond. I decide to leave a note on my car, something to tempt him in plain view.

For the first time I realise Edward doesn't have the control, not if he's obsessed and can't stay away. If I have the upper hand, now is the time to make use of it.

The phone rings and it's Trisha. She must have seen the police leaving my house. I tell her about the tape and my hair and how frightened I am.

'He's just a scumbag getting off on scaring women,' she says. 'Doesn't scare me.'

'It should. He knows your name. He knows where you live.'

'And how's he supposed to get in? Shimmy up my wall like Spiderman? OK, I get it. I had a break-in too. But Derek stays over now. So good luck everybody else.'

I hear a deep sigh, then a commentary of what her camera has recorded. Seven blue cars or the same one cruising past my house seven times. I'm yawning at a dog scratching up a spray of grass against the tree and other trivial activities on Burnham Road. Then she launches into how she followed the car from Dr Meyer's.

'I got his number plates,' she says.

'And?'

'Hertz. I'd have called you earlier, only they don't give out names or addresses. Not even for a tenner. But this guy, the one on the front desk, said he'd call me back. Took him long enough. He was a right motor-mouth, said someone stole it from the person who hired it. He told me residential CCTV on Mountbatten Road picked up a man wearing a balaclava with two slits for eyes. I doubt it's his first rodeo. Whatever you do, don't go off like the cat who walks by himself.'

Easier said than done, of course, when my life is in tatters. But this thief might have something to do with the Robin Hood thefts in Westbourne.

'Trish, I need a huge favour.'

'Whatever it is, I can't love. They've cautioned me. I'm grounded.'

I take a deep breath. 'In that case, can I borrow your car?'

41

FREYA

A THREATENING WEDGE OF grey cloud blanks the sun and something shifts in the air. The anxiety I'd sense earlier now fading to a ripple. I'm driving to the library when I look up at my rearview mirror. Three cars behind, I see a black Audi bouncing in and out of its lane.

I race towards a junction, swerving to miss a row of traffic cones and burning through a red light. I'm hoping to get to the main road, but the car in front slows down and I have no choice but to slam on my brakes. Trisha's brakes. Trisha's car.

Slow down.

I check the petrol gauge – a quarter of a tank. I must have picked the worst day because there's a cop car two vehicles behind looking for the idiot who's not following the speed limit. When the light goes green, my mind registers the gap between the kerb and the car in front. I punch the gas and power through. I'm second in line with half a mile to go to the roundabout. A wide street. Plenty of room.

The rearview mirror shows the Audi has the same idea. His bumper dances behind me, closer than it appears. Traffic catches up, hemming me in from all sides. There's no point in using roundabout etiquette. When the car in front goes, I go.

Horns. A shaking fist through an open window. I slot between two cars and take the second exit. This street is narrower, with thick trees and high walls. I'm fumbling in my backpack for my phone and it tumbles under the passenger seat. That's when I see the Audi in my wing mirror, swerving in and out behind another car, tyres screeching.

I race downhill, looking for a way out and he's bobbing behind me, turning every way I turn. I pray for a thick overhang of honeysuckle, a rusted out old caravan, a straggle of trees, but there's nothing but narrow streets and cars parallel parked. I feel a rush of adrenaline as I ease between the words "Road" and "Closed."

The only way out is through the park. I clip a bollard as I slice across grass and gravel. My head screams with pain as a climbing frame rushes towards me and I veer to miss it, ploughing through bulrushes, a shallow pond and onto the pavement. My body rams into the seatbelt as the back end of the car flips up and crashes down with a crunch. The airbag warning flashes but doesn't deploy.

I turn a sharp left and swing back into traffic. The wind rushes and whistles through a gap in the window. The Audi is a ghost in my mirror, gaining with every second. I know this area. Several arteries lead to the main road and if I bluff at a turning, I'll lose him. God loves an optimist.

A flash of red and I overtake a car. A child stares out, face squashed against the back window. Then at last I see a turning.

Left. Left *here*, my mind shouts.

I swerve across the mouth, mounting the pavement before settling back onto the road. Past two more turns until I spot the one I want. This time, I don't hesitate. Hugging the corner, I gun it to the main road, hearing grinding brakes in the distance as the Audi misses it.

I drive in grateful silence to the library, thinking through the fog of a headache. It's clear from the driver's behaviour that what started out as a bit of fun has turned into something terrifying.

I park near the library entrance and lean back and close my eyes, exhausted at the thought of narrowly missing another accident. Worse, I could have run over a child and crashed Trisha's prize Ford Sierra. Bile burns the back of my throat and I open the remains of a bottle of water from the passenger seat.

I'll get a ticket. There are cameras at every one of those junctions, roundabouts and speed zones, but the good news is they will have a recording of the man who was following me.

I compose a sentence on a piece of paper. *How do I know you're not a petty swindler out for a trust fund?* Fold it in half and write his name in capitals. It's a long shot, probably won't work. But I'm game for anything right now.

I anchor it to the windscreen and walk to the library in a bubble of anticipation. I take the stairs to the second floor and look down through the window. It's quiet, except for an occasional cough and a mother shushing a child in the kid's zone. A man sits by the window, cap tilted forward, fingers flicking the pages of a book. He stares across the library floor with the fixed detachment of a reader pondering over the chapter he's read.

Standing at my observation post, I'm curious that Edward night have thought I was Trisha. The idea mushrooms into terror. What I have I got Trisha into?

I wait almost twenty minutes, and I'm about to give up when I see two small boys in matching shorts chase each other across the lawn towards a figure shaded by the trees. A dapple of sunlight obscures his face. He emerges from the crowd wearing a cap and glasses. What makes me curious are the gloves he's wearing, especially on a warm day.

He turns a half-circle and slaps a phone against his ear, eyes grazing over the street and the crowds on the pavement. I lift my phone to take a video and within those few seconds, he strides over to Trisha's Sierra, plucks the note from under the wiper, and slips it in his pocket.

Did he actually do that?

I resist the urge to follow him for a second or two, but it's my only chance. If this is Edward, I'll follow him home. If he is the delivery boy, he could lead me to Edward. I'm looking around for a black Audi, parked somewhere off by itself, but I don't see one.

Crowds stroll along the high street and a skateboarder

weaves between cars, dodging children with foil windmills. My target takes long strides up the hill, passing a run of shops and restaurants. I can already picture him living in a squalid bedsit surrounded by a horseshoe of beer cans and cigarettes. It's not like I can run up to him and tap him on the shoulder. Or shout "Hey!" at the top of my voice. There's a street wariness about him that makes me vulnerable.

I follow him into Boots. He stands between a shelf of Emergen C and the Prescriptions counter. As I get closer, I can see he's stocky and his hair is russet brown. I angle my phone to take a picture, but he stoops to reach something on a bottom shelf and I miss the shot. Then he slopes off past the half-price items at the entrance and out into the street. Diesel fumes belch from the buses, and doors hiss open to a belly-full of tourists. I'm rocking my head from side to side as I peer past heads and shoulders to a lone figure walking up the street.

He crosses the road about twenty metres ahead, sprinting through a break in the traffic and then stops outside the estate agent on the corner. As his head turns, I shoot down Norwich Road, a lane running along the back of the houses, where the cloying smell of rotting food rises. I peer around the corner and see him up ahead, walking this time towards an Italian restaurant bordered by a leafy terrace. I trail him as far as the trellis, which juts out enough to make me invisible. Let's be honest. I'm shit at this.

I have every right to approach him and ask why he took the note from my car. It's private property. I'd done everything right, driven to a public place with CCTV, the only thing I hadn't observed was Patti's advice on leaving the looking to her. It would be dangerous to approach this man.

He goes inside and sits at a table near the window and I follow a group to the back of the restaurant and try to look as if I fit in. I select a table for two close enough to watch. He doesn't look up. Doesn't see me. I study long fingers, which appears at odds with the paunch beneath his sweatshirt.

A shrill beeping takes me a few seconds to realise my phone is ringing. As he turns towards the sound, my sleeve catches on the phone and it slips off the table and clatters to the floor. I grapple for it, every fibre of my body tells me to stay down.

Seconds pass in silence.

Then I inch upright, my eyes latching onto his empty table.

42

FREYA

At home, Jack is waiting.

'Is it my birthday or something?' I say, seeing a large slab of lemon cake on the table.

'No, we're passed that.' He hands me a cup of tea. 'Where have you been in Trisha's car?'

We both turn our heads toward the flats. The car wash took away the mud and clods of grass on the front bumper, and thankfully revealed no scrapes. I'm trying not to look mentally unstable, but it's hard. I tell him about the car chase and the video I took from the second floor of the library. It shows the bill of the man's cap, and dark glasses obscure the upper half of his face. It's doing Jack's head in, as much as it is mine. I thought I'd used up every ounce of adrenaline, but his voice produces another surge.

'You can't keep following every stranger in the street, Freya.'

'He followed me. Nearly drove me off the road. Then he took the note I left on the car. Why would he take it if it's not him?'

Jack's silent for a moment. 'He didn't see you chasing him up the street?'

'No, of course he didn't.'

'Every day, I become more frightened that your name will be on the news. The Zhen girl's family won't have a body to grieve over because they'll never find her. They won't ever know what happened. Can you imagine how painful that must be?'

My mind lags. What was I thinking? That I could talk to Edward? Make him give me the videos, so all this will finally go away? I see in Jack's expression something frail, something hidden beneath the surface. I think I see my misery reflected there, but he takes my hands in his and it vanishes.

'You can't tangle your wits with this man, Freya. You don't know what you're getting into.'

A knock on the door makes us both flinch. This time, it's Rabbi Aviel with a letter. He says someone rang the bell and bolted. And no, he didn't see who'd left it.

Jack reads the letter first and then hands it to me.

Freya,

I get used to the people I stalk, and when I'm deprived of the privilege, who knows if I'll ever find anyone as sweet again? These letters are warnings. Not guilt letters or snippets of information you can hand to the cop. She isn't the one I'm trying to impress.

How attuned are you to the nightly rhythms of your house? Every creaking floorboard, every squeaky hinge? Your past is catching up with you. When it comes knocking at the door, it could be a meter reader or a salesperson, and one day you'll go to sleep and never wake up again. Unless you find me first – and how are you going to do that? The rules are about to change.

Edward.

I feel the injustice swell inside me, ready to tear me apart. Edward lives somewhere under the same sky, breathing the same air. It brings a rage I never knew I had.

The doorbell rings nearly forty minutes later: long, strident bursts, and we stand aside to let Patti pass.

'How much more is it going to cost to keep this psychotic scumbag out of our lives?' Jack asks.

'I'm worried about proxy stalking, using a neighbour to deliver things,' she says. 'We've been conducting geographical profiling, looking at where victims live and work and socialise. Searching for anchor points which could lead us to the stalker.'

Could not *would*, and so far, *haven't*. Danger stalks me everywhere, cramping my independence and stealing my peace. The only way to beat this creep is to play him at his own game.

'I want you to know... I want you *both* to know that we are watching someone.' She wags a finger. 'I can't say any more.'

'Why haven't we heard anything on the news?'

'This won't come as a shock, Freya, but the less reporting, the better our chances.'

True. But it means she's watching a person of interest. Max Lalonde? Except he was away on business when it happened. Does he have longish hair, a paunch and delicate fingers? If only Derek had installed the camera inside Trisha's flat earlier, it might have recorded him. The area around our house is looking like a crime hotspot.

'It might be a good idea if you stayed with friends,' she says.

I zone out, deliberating for how long? Days? Weeks? Months? There's no end to all this. It would be the perfect time to spill every tiny secret, tell her about the texts. I could say I wasn't in my right mind, a hurl of grief because of Kate's anniversary. Only this has nothing to do with Kate. My overriding fear is Jack's disappointment and the legal consequences. If I've learned anything from this barrage of police intrusion, it's that I mustn't underestimate them.

I notice Jack doesn't tell Patti about the car chase, nor does he say anything about the note I left at the library. He simply sits beside me, pulls me towards him, and kisses me on the forehead.

I feel the tears welling and my shoulders are shaking. There is only one course ahead, and that is to sweep it all under the carpet for now. Unless there's a better way.

Jack's words keep swilling about in my mind... *What if he kidnaps you?* If Edward attacked me, dragged me from my car, from the bank, from any public place, the first thing he'd take is my phone. There's a small body camera in the top drawer of my desk at work which will record between five and eight hours of footage, night vision included. It would be prudent to get it.

Through the kitchen window I see the glint of glass and Jack's at my side, seeing it too. There's a snapper crouch-walking behind the hedge, camera perched on his shoulder. I can't believe I'm now the subject of a "doorstep", a reporter wanting an interview without prior arrangement.

'Get away from the curtains, Freya. Or you'll be everyone's business.'

That's why it's so daunting because I am. 'Will you drive me to work? I just want to say hi to everyone.'

'I'll drive around the corner to the short alleyway behind the houses, while you run to the back fence and struggle over it.'

I do as he says. He ducks me down in the back seat and tells me to stay under the blanket until the roundabout. I keep looking through the wing mirror at every black car, but none appear to have hooded drivers. We arrive at the Art Deco building on Richmond Hill, where the word *Echo* hovers over a blue front door. Built in 1932 on the slope near the Square, it is a grade II listed building formed from Monk's Park and Purbeck stone. If Liv isn't having a drink at The Ink – the Echo's former printing room, now a brasserie and café – she'll be taking a power nap in her office with a newspaper tented over her face.

I wave my pass at security and smile at Aynur on reception. Instead of having her ears plugged with buds and head bobbing out a tune, she huddles in muted conversation with the content editor. For a moment, they turn to look at me before resuming their whispering.

When we get upstairs, the air is thick with the aroma of microwaved lasagna. I expect to find Andi doing check calls at her desk, but she's in the board room with Liv behind closed doors. I'm too late to see her.

Drew Martin beckons us into his office. 'Glad to see you looking so well.'

'We're much better, thanks,' Jack says. 'Except for a reporter hiding behind our hedge.'

'I'm sorry. I really am. We had a call from someone this morning, promising a video of poor Freya finding Elisabeth Saunders. He asked for six grand. I declined. Damn rubberneckers.'

I'm feeling a spike of nausea. What if Edward had sold that

video to another paper including personal details about me? My eyes drift to Drew's TV. There's a picture of Nian Zhen with a Crimestoppers logo and the words "Police need your help". Then the screen changes to a huddle of officers on the beach and that awful white tent. Elisabeth's smiling face one minute and the words "cause and manner of death" the next.

'There's been a few changes since you've been away,' Drew says to me. 'Jessica Tremel is working with Liv now. Award winning reporter. We're thrilled to have her.'

This is the move Jessica alluded to when she brought the hamper. Which means I'll be reporting to her too. I tell Jack and Drew I'd like to congratulate her.

As I walk through the office, the newsroom television blares with coastguard and a police helicopters scanning the cliffs. A cluster of people watch the scrolling headlines, followed by the inevitable prattle about whether Nian Zhen had gone to meet Tinder man Edward. Soon everyone will go back to working their leads, writing stories. Business as usual.

The first door I come to is Jessica's. She's wearing a Zara polka dot dress and a shit-load of makeup.

'Hey,' I say.

Her face reminds me of a dog listening to the whine of a mosquito. 'Freya. How lovely to see you.'

'I wanted to congratulate you.' I settle in the chair next to her. 'I had no idea.'

She gives me this weird knowing smile and says, 'Thank you. I'm excited too.'

'I see you're all glued to the Alum Chime killer. Anything new?'

'Look at this.' She gives her mouse a few taps, and we're in Tinder.

I lean forward a little to take in what I'm seeing. It's a picture of Elisabeth Sanders, smiling and looking sideways at the camera. Beneath her photo are the words: Coffeeholic, Lit Nerd. Don't swipe right unless you're a cat-lover.

'Any other social media?' I ask.

'Twitter, Insta and Snapchat. Mostly #caturday.'

'Nothing to say who she was hanging out with?'

'Not really.' Jessica scrolls through a range of selfies and frowns at one. 'She has the same eyes as you.'

'You mean Kate.'

'I mean you.'

Blood thrums in my ears and I suck in breath. Something cold slithers down my spine, and I'm trying to shoulder-barge the thought from my mind. Just because I have Elisabeth Sanders' eyes doesn't mean anything.

I hear a knock on the door frame and turn to see Miles. 'Hey Freya, You back at work?'

'Monday. Just thought I'd pop by and say hello.'

'She wanted to know about the Sanders case. Quite the little private investigator.' Jessica swings her chair around and her skirt rides up to the midpoint of her thigh. His eyes drop and there are tiny beads of sweat on his upper lip. 'Andi said the police interviewed two men Elisabeth Sanders had dated.

One used to work at Waterstones and the other worked at a newsagent. Maybe it's an academic thing. A mutual love of books.'

He glances at Jessica and I'm mentally calculating what he might say. 'If you're trying to build a profile, you can't base it on two possibilities unless there's any prior history of domestic violence. Which there isn't.'

'Are you assuming it was a random attack or planned?'

'Planned,' he says.

'Someone could have plucked her off the street and bundled her into a passing van. It happens all the time.'

'If you're looking at statistics, then yes. 56% of kidnaps involve a stranger, whether or not they're successful. Not all of those are women. Most are kids. This is someone Elisabeth trusted enough to be lured on a date. That means she knew him.' Miles tears his eyes away from the short skirt and gives me his full attention. 'Want to see your new desk?'

'I thought you'd never ask.'

We walk along a short corridor to Liv's "conservatory". It comprises a large office – three sides of glass – and a meeting room. There are pictures of her reportage on the wall and souvenirs on every shelf.

'How's she doing?' I ask.

'Tired. Yawns a lot. How are you?'

I tell him about the man who chased me in the car yesterday and the man I followed. The words pour out in a jumbled mess. It's all so cripplingly embarrassing.

'The police are monitoring our house, and I'm to call the acting DC the minute anything happens.'

'Promise me you'll stay away from this guy.'

'I promise.' I realise he's not just worried about me, he cares. 'How's everything here?'

'Apart from doing a piece on famous residents in coastal locations, nothing much. I was more interested in your Edward Besant. His social media appears to be deactivated. Google keeps profile pictures, but a goat's eye isn't much to go on. I called a police friend of mine. He said they have an e-fit of a suspect they took a week ago.'

'Why are they holding back? Don't the public have a right to know?'

'He said there were other lines of enquiry and they didn't want to risk scaremongering.'

'Did he show you the e-fit?'

Miles scrolls through his phone and hands it to me. I see the reason for the enormous sigh. The facial composite is almost Neanderthal, big teeth and a wide forehead. Certainly not the man I'd seen.

'This cop friend of mine was in the pub a few nights ago, overheard two guys talking about Max Lalonde, Elisabeth Sanders' boyfriend. He's the only one with a sexual motive. I say he's being careful, doing nothing that would dent Elisabeth's reputation.'

'It's not him,' I say. 'He was away on business.'

'So he says. But he doesn't exactly work for Kellogg's or

Deloitte. He's self-employed. There's no one to corroborate his story.'

A light patter rattles on the window and I look outside at puddles dimpled with rain. Miles drifts a few feet away from me at the sound of approaching feet. It's Jessica, wanting to know where Liv is.

'Board room,' we say in unison, waiting for her footsteps to die away. The footsteps come trotting back, and she tells us she's forgotten something. Takes a notebook from Liv's office and leaves.

Miles points to a desk next to Andi Wynters. 'Yours. Brand new.'

I look, not at the flimsy wooden excuse where a folded beer mat had been wedged between the leg and the floor, but an assembly of glass and steel and a computer monitor as slender as a credit card. My eyes flick to the new filing cabinets. Miles follows my gaze and obliges by opening one of the drawers. Instead of the squeal of runners and the crash of a broken divider, there's barely a whisper. He says he's opened and closed them several times, and the problem with that comment is I can see him doing it.

My heartbeat staccatos for a second, and while he's talking with his back to me, I open my desk drawer. I'm relieved to see a digital voice recorder nestled in a tray and I slip it into my handbag.

'How's it going with Jessica?' I ask.

He turns to face me, two trenches deepening in his forehead.

'It's going, although I don't know where.'

'She's beautiful.'

'So is the painting of Whistler's Mother.'

His infectious chuckle takes me along with it. His eyelashes make long shadows over his cheeks, and I'm flinching from the heat that burns and spreads, afraid to lose myself again.

'Next, you're going to tell me you're secretly engaged.'

He wipes a pair of wire-rim glasses on the hem of one sleeve. 'Jess says marriage is like being in prison with a bunk-mate you can barely tolerate.'

'That's a pretty warped view.'

'She also told me nearly half of all marriages end in divorce, and most have some kind of restraining order. It's far-fetched to believe in perfect mates, even if Internet sites use matching algorithms. But you need to understand what she's been through.'

'What has she been through?'

'Mother died when she was thirteen. Father didn't want her. So she went to live with an aunt. Did OK at school, but had an unfortunate marriage at eighteen. You get the picture.'

'She doesn't want to get hitched again, I take it.'

'Relationships aren't things she does well. Both of us working here is a little too close for comfort.'

A breeze soughs over my skin and I rub my arms as if to smooth the gooseflesh. The silence stretches and my heart aches. I want to say, 'I hate you,' and I want to hear him let out a sad sigh and say how sorry he is for dating someone better than me. Every nerve in my body buzzes because I know she is.

'I've been punishing myself,' I say.

'For what?'

'Us. It should never have happened.'

'I'm sure it's not the worst thing you've done in your life.'

His words jab me in the ribs, as if the whole thing was petty. 'No, the worst thing was lying to Jack. Trying to pretend we were OK, and we weren't and everything's shattered into tiny pieces ever since.'

'Freya—'

'You're right. I had a choice and I should have walked away when I had the chance.'

'Hear me out, OK? Go to Jack and tell him I asked you out. Nothing serious. Just a drink.'

'I've already thought of that. I can't possibly tell Jack. He'd come looking for you and then what? An assault charge? Don't be ridiculous, Miles.'

'I was only trying to help.'

The truth sends waves of horror over me. I remind him of Edward's video proof which would seriously contradict any lies we told Jack. I look at him and my stomach flips. I hear the rhythm of the sea that night, the way it surged and rattled, a tidal heartbeat, and I can't stop daydreaming about him.

'I have to go,' I stammer. 'But thanks for showing me around.'

A warm hand on my back and all the anxiety leaves me.

'You're very welcome.'

Then the long walk back to Drew's office. I wish it was nice and slow, but I stride ahead, much faster than I'd intended. Miles turns right at the end of the corridor and I turn left.

I stand by Drew's door, resting my cheek against the frame, listening to excessive chatter about his NATO security clearance and his work with successful women in business. Probably way more than Jack wants to know.

'What about you, Freya?' Drew asks, breaking into my thoughts. 'How are you feeling?'

'Like shit.' I cut him off, and see him wrinkle his face in surprise. I try again, this time a little kinder. 'I'd look better with paper bag over my head.'

'Don't be silly.' He laughs. 'You've both been through a lot this past week. Jack was telling me about the guy that smashed into you.'

'Then he probably told you they've had no luck finding him.'

Drew looks from Jack to me. 'What? No cameras on that road?'

'Apparently not.'

'All is not lost. Jack tells me there was a witness, only the police wouldn't give a name.'

'It didn't need police or cameras to find her,' I say. Jack swings his head around and raises both eyebrows. 'Nice lady, lives in a second floor apartment. She said she couldn't give a description. Way too dark.'

Drew smiles even wider. 'Nice one, Freya.'

On the way downstairs, I'm not sure Jack agrees. I settle in the passenger seat of the car, wishing I could tell him why we really came here. He's silent on the way home while I'm picking at the cuticle on my thumb, tearing at it, feeling a sharp nip of pain followed by the feeling I've been having all day. The knowledge that the decision I have finally reached is the right one. Not just for me. For both of us.

43

FREYA

THE NEXT DAY BRINGS more news. Police are following several leads, which means they are questioning more than one man. Frustration seems to insulate me now.

My patience is running out and Jack's sympathy is, too. I can feel his eyes on me, but I don't look up. My mind goes somewhere else and I can smell a fresh, aromatic scent mixed with cigarette smoke. It evokes a memory. I don't know what I'm seeing, feeling. I don't know why it comes to me now.

Then the scrape of a chair. Jack opens the front door and stands on the doorstep, listening. He stoops over the bench outside and brings in a small leather box.

'What is it?' I ask.

He places it on the table in front of me and leans on two balled fists. 'Let's skip the lies, shall we? Who is he?'

'Who's who?'

'This.' He opens it and inside is a signet ring engraved with the letter F. 'Don't say you've forgotten. Your forgetfulness is a little convenient, given the circumstances. Are you in love with him? Is that it? Or is he some thug you're scared of? Tell me. I'm genuinely interested. How did we get mixed up in all this?'

'How I can be in love with someone who breaks into our house, drugs our whisky and cuts my hair? Someone who might end up shafting us for everything we've got?'

'So now he's drugging us? How? How's he doing it?'

His gaze darts from the kitchen cupboard, to the fridge, to the sink, remembering I'd thrown all the drinks down the drain. It can't be easy to discover your wife's been telling the truth from the start. I can tell he's agitated, unable to adjust. It's funny how little details betray a person if you know where to look.

'Before you slag me off, Jack, and say it's all my fault, let's talk about the photograph. The one that used to be in your wallet and is now filed under taxes upstairs. Your ex.'

'You really want to know?'

'Maybe I don't, but go on – tell me.'

'I'd forgotten about it,' he says. 'I certainly don't have some yearning, burning desire to relive the past, or her. I haven't looked at her since I married you.'

'So you're saying you're not in love with her?'

'That's exactly what I'm saying.'

'Because if you were, I could understand why we've been receiving these gifts.'

'I'm not following,' he says.

'A jealous mistress, a husband wanting to end a marriage. It all makes sense to me now. There I was, thinking it was me.'

'She's dead, Freya. She died over ten years ago.'

My mouth sticks and won't close. I can already tell from the spots of red on his face that I've done it now, and it's no good bristling at the pain I've caused.

'Maybe it is time we talk.' I say.

'No.'

'No?'

'I don't think I can stomach what you're about to tell me.'

I can feel the anger vibrating off him as he trudges upstairs. I don't hear slamming drawers and a suitcase thumping along the corridor. But I do hear a muffled voice. He's talking to someone on the phone about taking down a creep whose name he doesn't know at an address he doesn't have.

I feel breathless and anxious and I curse myself for lying. If only my mind was straight... but it's dark and deadly. I don't know if what I'm feeling is real or not.

I sit down, facing the window, trying to pull myself together. It's different, this nightmare. I've done something so terrible that cannot be put right.

Jack hates me now, and he's probably told everyone we know how terrible I am. Even the neighbours look at me with contempt and none of them will let me tell them my side of the story.

I want the past back again, to reclaim some of my old life and start all over again. I decide to go back to the place that started it all.

It's late afternoon when I arrive at The Cricketer's Arms. A popular Victorian building with vaulted ceilings and beams. There is a banner outside introducing a new band. A female singer with a remarkable voice.

It's a melancholy number. She is beautiful, long hair and a child's face, standing in my old spot where I used to play the violin. Jack and Kate would attempt a jig or two, laughing and twirling until they fell into their seats. But it's the empty table in the front row where Miles used to watch. I imagine him tapping his hands on his thighs, head cocked sideways. Was he interested even then?

So many ghosts.

I order a local cask ale and watch the door swing open. The man with a pale shirt and a bag could be him. Same hair, different build. He sits at a table and takes out his phone. Doesn't look up. Doesn't order a drink. Keeps on tapping out a text and then waiting for a reply. He runs a hand through his hair and shakes his head. His shoulders seem to sag. He or she has stood him up.

I feel the familiar tug of pity, the need to talk to a friend. I send Jack a text and tell him I'm at the pub. But I delete it before sending, and call him instead. It goes through to voicemail; the voice of a happy man with a happy home. The voice of a man who smells of moss soap and Dior aftershave.

Not the man I'd left earlier who told me my life is a total disaster, but a picnic compared to his. I look at my phone, steeling myself for another hit, another *Freya, you're a failure, a nutcase, a foolish, lying bitch...* Only he's never used the B-word.

My mind is sluggish, trying to pull up all the good times, the intimate times. When he used to undress me, his eyes were like his hands, tender and doting. When we were quiet or simply reading books, he didn't need to fill the silence with chatter. I miss him, the old Jack, the comfortable Jack. The lived-in Jack.

Through the numbing sense of failure, I think of the signet ring as if there's some new meaning behind it. My theories scatter and spin. I'm starting to believe Patti has been tailing me, watching me as I watch my stalker. Perhaps that's why she hasn't asked for my phone, so she can monitor my texts remotely. It would kill two birds...

Light slips through the opening door and a whip-thin shadow moves towards me. Trisha. I should have guessed. It's quiz night. She's wearing a black lace-up bustier and a pair of white jeans. I can forgive her for a little skin. Derek is pretending not to gawp, but a full-wattage grin tells me he's enjoying what he sees.

She's steaming to give me an update and wants a quiet smoke. So we leave Derek at the bar, grab our coats and inch outside to the picnic tables. Already there's a low-lying cloud above her head and a half-smoked cigarette in the ashtray.

'The police were nosing around,' she says, shivering, 'on the pretext of being concerned about my break-in. But they looked at my camera, looked at each other, and I told them it's a reliable witness because it sees things the rest of us can't. They told me the police know everything that happens on every street. I told them they don't know what happens on this one. They said it looked like I was stalking you. I said, "Call it what you want, but it isn't stalking, not when my neighbour asked me to do it".'

'I'm sorry, Trish.'

'Don't be. In the spirit of good investigating, Arthur took a picture of a car in the street last night. Black Audi A4.'

Deep breath. 'Sounds like the same car that followed me two days ago.'

'It had been stolen. Used to belong to a dentist in Millionaire's Row. Derek bought a GPS transmitter,' she says, taking one of the ales Derek brings and passing it to me. 'When Arthur took the rubbish out, he pretended to drop something on the pavement, took his time scrabbling about before putting it under the car.' My eyes must have got wider because she laughs over the rim of her beer glass. 'About ten minutes later, the car pulls out and I follow it to Surrey Road. Then he turns down a few too many streets and bluffs me at the next corner, and I swerve like an idiot because I'm scared I'm gonna lose him again. Then he takes me along the scenic route, up and down a few cul-de-sacs like he's lost or something.'

'Did he see you?'

'Probably. Maybe. Better take notes, Frey. This is dynamite.'

She flicks the accumulated ash off the cigarette and takes a long, hard drag. 'He parked outside a house on Sandbourne Road. It's not like I ran after him and shouted, "Hey, matey, do me a favour and give me your address." I was stealthy like. The lights went on upstairs and I saw him moving around. Number 31. House with a skip in the drive.'

44

EDWARD

THE CLOCK ON THE dashboard tells him it's past midnight. On the way to Freya's, his mind tracks back to another night. Long-forgotten fragments appear in his mind. Mother pacing downstairs after he'd supposedly gone to bed, words peppered with sobs.

Why, Lionel, why?

The whys trailed off eventually and, through the banisters, he saw her crumpled on the living room floor. There was a torn-up photograph on the landing. When he looked closer, it was Nisha with her long, black hair and inquisitive eyes. Mother was so pale and auburn and frumpy.

When Mother was out, Edward saw Father and Nisha grunting in bed, using words he'd never heard before. Later, at dinner, he'd asked Father what they meant. Father said he needed counselling for some childish delusion or another. But it made Mother cry.

He shouldn't have been watching Father in the bath either,

swallowing pills and sobbing. He'd never seen a man cry before, and he wasn't sure he liked it. It was minutes before Father went quiet, head lolling to one side. Edward crept forward and poked him in the shoulder. He didn't wake up. Leaning over the bath, Edward finished what Father had started.

He applied his weight to the top of Father's head and one of his hands flailed against the side of the bath as a knee broke the surface. Edward kept pushing and pushing, mesmerised by the foam floating like tiny glaciers on the surface of the water, revealing patches of skin underneath.

The police found the empty pill canister on the bathmat and ruled it a suicide. At the burial, Edward remembered the raw hole in the earth and his mother's shoulders heaving with sobs. She squeezed his hand as the first shovel of earth hit wood, and rain fell, *tat, tat, tat* against the coffin. Then a deluge.

He still feels Father's breath in his mouth, accusing Edward of stealing his. Instead of the person he admired the most, Father became the perpetrator of all things filthy and vile, like his bones will be in years to come. A putrid soup of muscle and flesh.

Edward parks at the corner of Freya's street and pulls on a ski mask. He knows she's been asleep for nearly two hours and the after-image of her still hangs in his mind. He doesn't know why, but he can feel it as sure as the breeze against his skin.

He's slammed from his thoughts by a boy walking behind him towards the skip, bag bouncing against his heels. Edward hopes he doesn't stare at the car, but of course, he does. He's done it before. Edward ignores him, but the boy doesn't take the hint. Even when he drops a plastic bottle on the pavement, Edward doesn't look up. He hears the clunk of rubbish into the skip and watches the boy skulk back to his front door. It's the same thing every night.

When all goes quiet again, Edward glides down the alleyway at the back of Freya's house. A proliferation of moss and cigarette butts line the foot of the fence and someone has made shoddy work of nailing the planks.

They've repaired the back door windowpane, but during an earlier recon visit, he'd watched Parker and Thorne, two jokers tasked with rekeying the front door. Jack left a set of new keys dangling from the back lock. It gave Edward plenty of time to take a spare and replace it with a similar key. A key, he's amused to admit, that fits the locks in his own house.

The biggest snag upon entering now will be a new camera. He checks for cameras in the upper corners of each room and behind the ornaments on the bookshelves. Keeping Jack and Freya down is child's play. Rohypnol in their drinks and they're out like a light.

He takes out the bulb in the kitchen nightlight and drops it in the bin. The stairs creak on the second, fifth and sixth step, and he keeps to the edge where the carpet meets wood. Approaching the door to her bedroom, he spots the camera hooked to the ceiling. An odd angle and rather unwise, now he thinks about it. Owing to the backlight from the landing window, he will be a silhouette. As for the lens, a smiley sticker will provide a little humour.

He doesn't give a rat's arse about etiquette. All he cares about is putting an end to his loneliness, the aching sense of despair. Approaching the bedroom, the first thing he notices is that Jack's side of the bed is flat. He feels a sudden wave of alarm, saliva draining from his mouth. He remains stock-still, straining to hear something. He detects snores coming from the spare room and walks across the landing and pokes his head around the doorframe. Jack is a hunch of bedclothes, so drugged up, he wouldn't hear a sneeze even if it hit him.

This display of separation between husband and wife excites Edward. He returns Freya's stalking log to her top drawer and grins at the absurdity. A little give and take never hurt anyone. The curtain catches the wind and lifts for a few seconds before shrinking against the wall. It jerks him out of his thoughts. Tonight, he doesn't brim with exhilaration. He understands Freya will prove harder work than he expected and he bets she has drunk no alcohol tonight. He shudders because each precious inch of her is an inch he worships.

She lies on her side, mouth ajar, and he's tempted to touch her. He takes off his head covering and for a moment he remains poised over her. Exposing his face excites him. He doesn't move, doesn't blink, as if in a blinding trance. He blots the sweat from his forehead with the sleeve of his shirt and notices the underwear she has shucked off in haste. Her jeans are heaped on the floor and he searches each pocket for her phone. He needs to ensure the geofence feature on the spyware app is sending regular notifications for when she enters or leaves her house, or any watched zone. But he can't find the phone.

He's surprised by another sound. A distant ringtone, like the sonar of a submarine. She murmurs and turns on her side. He knows the phone is sending messages to her brain, urging her to wake. Retreating to the bathroom, he watches through the gap in the door. Her heart-shaped face is barely visible from a distance of only eight feet. Her eyes, however, seem to shine. She reaches between the mattress and the bedhead, and takes the call.

'Yes. OK. Thanks.'

Sweat glazes his face and stings his eyes. For the first time in years, a deep, insect-crawling fear surprises him. Thankfully, the bathroom is not her first port of call. Instead, she moves towards the landing and leans over the stair rail. It would be so easy to end his pain now. A slight push and she will barrel headfirst into hard tile. But another part of him remains hesitant. He is in love.

He smooths the hair from his brow, where it has fallen in damp licks, and he follows her downstairs. He is not far behind. He is never far behind.

She doesn't turn on any lights because it would only illuminate her to the outside world where she imagines he's watching. Then the clatter and swish of blinds. She leans over the kitchen sink, forehead almost pressed to the window, her face lifted to the moonlight which shines between torn clouds.

'Where are you?'

Her voice both fascinates and alarms him. He wants to tap her on the shoulder and say, *I'm right here.* But he knows there is a hairline crack in the floor that runs five feet from the kitchen sink, possibly a leak that has lifted the flooring. If he miscalculates, he will risk her hearing him. His approach is thwarted by a neon beam, streaking through the darkness, and followed by a shrill chime. She answers a second call.

'Any sign of him? Thank you so much.'

His teeth are clenched so hard the arteries throb in his temples and silver pinwheels of light flicker behind his eyelids. No good sedating her now and carrying her outside. Someone is watching the house.

He retreats into the sitting room and races for the back door. His joints ache and his muscles burn as he squeezes through the back fence and towards the back alley. But he's met with something he had never expected, an officer with his back to him, shining a torch inside Edward's car. Doesn't anyone sleep around here?

The muscles in his throat and stomach convulse, bringing a sensation of seasickness. He feels the last of any self-control slide from his grip. Had the officer seen him? Or is it simply the threat of an unfamiliar car? Then he realises who had alerted Freya to an unwanted visitor.

Replacing the hood over his head, he steps back into the shadows, the sole of his boot clipping a stone. The officer looks left and right, neck stretching like a turtle's from his collar. The echo sends a false reading as if it came from across the road, and that's where the officer goes.

Edward gets that feeling of lightness when he wakes up from a nightmare and wallows in its residue. If he could find a jagged flint, the officer's head would burst like a melon. But he's angry with himself. Raging that he hadn't heard the arrival of a police car.

Edward has that dizzying sense again as he waits in the shadows for ten long minutes. He cannot see the officer's car, which he assumes arrived soon after he had and must be parked outside the front of the house. Exiting the alleyway seems foolish, especially if there is more than one officer.

He has no choice but to abandon the car and retreat into the darkness. Between Freya's house and the next door property is a five-foot wall. He decides to take a gamble. Vaulting from property to property allows him an egress at Earle Road, and he jogs past a block of flats and into the woodland that will take him home.

He rails at his stupidity, at a lost opportunity. It was a close call. Too close. It must not happen again.

45

FREYA

IT's THE FOLLOWING DAY when the weather goes mad. Chalky white clouds and a greyish pallor to the sky. I hear loud drumming on the roof and hailstones pelt the windows. People gather in bus stops and doorways, and no sooner has it started than it stops.

I appreciate the police surveillance last night, triggered by Trisha reporting a strange car in the street. The same Audi, we suspect, that had been following me. The same Audi on which Arthur had left a tracker. I'm disappointed they didn't catch him.

I've googled Edward's address and filled a backpack in preparation. I've imagined Nian shackled to a bed, very much alive. I'm her only hope. How much my body-worn cam is likely to pick up is questionable, but it's the only option I have.

The doorbell rings, and two officers stand outside, droplets glistening on their sleeves. One introduces himself as DI Stokes, the other is Bryony, only I don't catch her last name.

'We're checking to see if you're OK,' Bryony says before I can offer tea. 'Your neighbour reported a car on the side street last night. It's been towed.'

She asks if the locks and windows are intact and warns us about door-to-door scams that may be people casing our house. As I look at her, my mind rushes back to an earlier time when the police came to tell me about Kate. I remember throwing up and splashing the carpet with tea-laced vomit. I can still taste the sourness in my mouth.

After they leave, Jack gestures for me to sit at the table. He remains standing, arms dangling at his sides, staring at a pot of coffee and two rashers of bacon curling on a plate.

'You said yesterday that maybe it was time to talk. I think now I'm ready.'

There's a prickle on my scalp and I'm squinting into a bar of light between the blinds. Jack places his hands on the back of a chair and I know it's time for me to begin.

'Edward sent me a text,' I begin. 'Several, actually. I replied to a few.' I unlock my phone and let him read them. The dates alone tell him how long I've been clutching these secrets to myself.

'And you're telling me this, why? So I can fix it? Do you know what I went through when Patti had me in for questioning? It was what she didn't say that frightened me the most. That I might have been gaslighting you.'

'I wanted to tell you. I wanted—'

'I can't help you. No one can. God, Freya, this is a

bloody disaster. You can't go on blaming everything on what happened to Kate. It's not her fault. It's not mine. You're not the only one suffering here.'

He moves the chair back and sits, bent over, head hanging. I reach for his hand, warm and large, and he doesn't snatch it away. He's waiting for me to offer him a crumb of hope, but I have none. I try to focus my mind on what he's about to say and dreading it.

'You understand what this means? What it means for us?'

My body goes stiff and I say, 'Yes, I know what it means. The police will ask to monitor my phone and when they do, they'll find Edward's texts and mine, and they'll come to the only plausible conclusion. That everything I've been telling them is lies.'

46

FREYA

WE CHECK THE VIDEO taken from the bedroom camera last night. So far, me alone in bed, duvet on, duvet off. Then a shadow on the landing and an arm stretching up towards the camera. Jack's eyebrows squish together, his gaze is clouding. We both look at each other, and then we rush upstairs to make sure. As ridiculous as it seems, a yellow smiley sticker covers the lens.

Jack tells me not to touch anything and I'm stammering and the words don't come. How long have we been sleeping to the rhythm of a killer's footsteps?

As Jack speed dials Patti and listens to her voicemail, I imagine lunging at the intruder, pushing him downstairs, hearing his skull crack against the tile. I check my news app for any updates on Nian Zhen and skim through the latest report.

...Dorset Police received a report at 4.45

pm raising concern for the welfare of 39-year-old Nian Zhen. She was last seen at her seafront workplace in Westbourne... Nian is described as five feet five inches tall and of medium build with long dark hair...

Chief Investigating Officer Joshua Petersen, of Dorset Police, said: "Due to the passage of time since Nian has last been seen, we are becoming concerned for her welfare."

I should have been prepared for this, should have known she hadn't come home. Her face is everywhere, smiling from every newsflash; beautiful, flirty, happy. I don't want to read anything bad. But somehow I'm expecting it.

Dragging my hair back in a ponytail, I search the dressing-table drawer for a hair tie, when my fingernail clips a hard object and I stare at it until the enormity registers. I'm holding the only tangible evidence my stalking log ever existed.

This is a dogfight that deserves a response. No longer a legal, play-it-by-the-rules battle, but as one equal to another. I've absorbed every trick he's pulled, and all the bullshit that flies with some victims has hit a brick wall with me. An idea for the notebook pulls me out of a loop of rage. If he wants all the evidence, let him have it.

My mind twists off onto a different track. I have Edward's

address. The proximity is concerning. Had he rented the property to be near me? It's no good telling Jack where I'm going, he'll only stop me. The police are being too cautious and reactive, and while they assemble watertight evidence and wait for search warrants, women are being murdered.

Jack is sitting on the top stair, stuffing Patti's voicemail with angry expletives. I check and double-check my backpack. Water, latex gloves, a screwdriver, and now the notebook. I attach the body-worn cam to my hoodie. Trespassing is illegal and probably carries some hell-awful punishment. Even now in the morning, I worry someone might be watching. I can't deny there's a part of me that finds the idea of locating Nian galvanising. Edward deserves everything he's about to get.

I tell Jack I won't be long and I've already slammed the front door before he responds. Arthur is standing under the tree, waving his phone. He shows me the image of a man sitting in a car at the corner of our street, his arm is hooked over the sill. The wing mirror reflects a face. Not the full moon of a face, not even a quarter moon. Two eyes, peering through some kind of balaclava.

'Is your mum upstairs?' I ask.

'Yeah, she's busy doing all that "merci" and "Je vous en prie" stuff.'

'Tell her to call me, will you?'

Arthur airdrops the photos to my phone and we walk to the bus stop. I once made tracks along this pavement with my little girl and my heart lingers in the thought. After the bus sweeps him away, I walk to the end of the road and glance down at the beach. There's something beautiful about a stormy sea and the bleakness of an out of season promenade. A police officer stands near the lifeguard station, serving as a protective presence.

Just to be sure, I look for Trisha on my GPS and she's exactly where she should be. Jack, on the other hand, is either in a dead zone where I can't get a lock, or he's turned off his location settings.

The rain has rinsed off the mugginess of yesterday and the sky is a perfect deep blue. I pull up my hood and run past Liv's house. Theo is often on the balcony, reading, but he's not there today. I study every car that passes, every dog walker, the man at the bus stop who takes off his coat in the sunshine and the man clipping an ornamental evergreen. I text Trisha and tell her what I'm doing. Someone needs to know.

As I turn onto Sandbourne Road, I count off all the houses until I get the right one. A tall privet hedge, well over the height limits set by Bournemouth Borough Council, masks a cream facade. The skip in the drive is full, chair legs and cardboard boxes peeking over the lip, and I can hear paper fluttering. I press the doorbell.

There are no cameras in the eaves, and the whole place radiates silence. I try the doorbell again, waiting for a voice to crackle through the two-way intercom, but the owner's phone doesn't appear to be connected remotely. The distant shriek of a child gives me a sense of routine more than any thought of danger and I'm singing a song by The Clash in my head, *Should I Stay or Should I Go*.

The sky darkens as a cloud covers the sun. I notice a narrow gap between the garage and the house. Streaking towards the back garden, my hip grazes a spade and the sound as it clatters to the ground startles me. Anger flushes my face. *Get a grip, Freya*!

The jangle of a dog's collar next door forces me to crouch for nearly a minute, my legs fizzing with pins and needles. I creep to the back corner of the house and peer out. An enormous umbrella shades a patio with sofas and chairs and, beyond it, a swimming pool. The lawn stretches fifty feet or more to the cliffs. As far as I can see, there are no cameras at the back of the house either.

I tiptoe towards the first of two bay windows and cup my hands around my face. Sunlight puddles onto a couch and there are no ornaments or family photographs to personalise the space. A tingling sensation spreads to my fingers, a feeling someone's watching me. I look up at the neighbour's house. The flick of a curtain. A small triangle of light. Then darkness. It may have been a draught inside the house, but the possibility of a face stealing its way into the corner of my mind is more likely.

I break loose of thorns and branches, and turn my attention to the sunroom door. The frame has warped a little and the handle is loose. Pulling my sleeve over my hands, I'm not surprised to find it unlocked. But I'm guessing the interconnecting door to the house is impenetrable. I shrug off my backpack and pull on latex gloves. I rise on the balls of my feet and run my hand along the upper edge of the frame, dislodging a coating of dust. There are no keys under the geraniums or in the blue tea caddy on the table. What did I expect?

I could leave the stalking log on the table, but there's one glaring problem with that. What if this is not Edward's house? I pause, listening to the waves on the beach and a groaning tree limb, and the rhythmic clinking of metal against metal.

I look down at the narrow flowerbed from which sprouts the gnarly trunk of a vine. African violets and hydrangeas are well tended, and a three foot jade tree basks in the sun. I hear the clinking again. Tracing the vine upward, something reflects between the leaves.

I'm baffled. Keys dangle from a shoot, almost invisible in the summer. But in the winter, when the vine returns to its skeletal silhouette, it is the answer to a burglar's prayer. That's not to say homeowners don't leave hidden keys on the property. Dad did.

Rattling the key in the slot, I hear the clunk as the door opens. A sense of calm greets me and the air hangs in stale clumps from the absence of activity.

'Hello?'

A sigh comes up from the gullet of the house and it makes me light-headed, the emptiness of it. I slip off my shoes and leave them on the mat, shrug off my backpack and turn on my body cam.

In the kitchen, a bottle of oxygen bleach sits on the draining board and there is barely enough food for one day in the fridge. Languishing on top of the bin is a scalp of synthetic brown hair. My mind swings back to the man who took the note from my car at the library, Patti's video of the man in the computer centre at BU. I catch something then, a suspended memory, but the neighbour's barking dog snatches away it.

I rummage through every drawer. No keys or letters or bills. I find two syringes without a glucose meter and two ampules with the word *Ketamine Hydrochloride*. I know every piece of evidence counts, but I pocket them, if only to stop him from injecting another woman. Hooked on the inside of a cupboard door are multiple sets of keys, one with a silver disk engraved with my name. My scalp prickles and I feel cold all over. They're the ones I'd lost in the crash.

Leave them! They are a crucial link for the police to find. I tell myself to focus, to move as fast as I dare.

I cast another glance around the bland, oppressive sanctuary someone calls a kitchen. On the countertop are the remains of a Tic-Tac box, a cigarette lighter and a blackened key. A piece of tape holds the transfer of char, where a credit card shows the impression. I can't bear to think how many houses he's broken into, how many women he'd fooled into believing he was half-decent.

A sweatshirt with a rip in the shoulder slouches over the back of a chair, and a familiar scent of bergamot and citrus makes my stomach roll. My mind streaks back to the picture from *BoMoJoe* on Twitter, where blood-red scratches provided a dash of colour against pale skin.

Was it an ominous tip-off from a stranger? Or was Edward merely teasing me closer to his lair? A man so mysterious, he has retreated behind these musty walls into a chaotic world of his choosing. I'm aware of a lurking instinct that I need to be quick.

The pantry door catches my eye, not only the heavy-duty hasp and padlock, but a red ribbon tied to the handle. It stirs up deep and irreparable memories, but I can't think about that now. Light slants through the keyhole, and I crouch to see a mattress on the floor half-covered by a tattered quilt. Reddish-brown smears claw the wall, and I try to swallow.

'Hello!'

Nothing moves inside the slit of a prison cell. Would Nian's voice have called back to me? Is she somewhere in the house? And what of the future if this monster remains uncaught? Does he intend to lock me in there? Could it be my voice weakly calling, in the vain hope someone will rescue me? I back away, taking jerky steps into the sitting room. I'm shaking now – shaking all over – and I know I can't give up.

Thick layers of dust coat the side tables and a Rizla packet balances on the arm of the couch. For a moment, I'm reminded of Trisha, and I look around for traces of her until I tell myself how ridiculous that is.

Dark patches on the walls suggest missing pictures, and

my mind races for an explanation. Had they outlived their emotional worth? It occurs to me that the owner, or tenant, is moving out. It would explain the skip outside.

I ease through the door into the hall, feeling eyes everywhere, sometimes on my back, sometimes in the corners of each room. I pass under a light at the foot of the stairs, a metal arm gripping a glass globe. The buzzing of a fly trapped inside startles me and I grip the railing a little harder.

In the first bedroom is a double bed and wardrobe, and in the alcoves flanking the chimney breast are two chests of drawers. A black-and-white photograph shows a couple smiling as a young boy sits on his mother's lap. To the left of the mother is a younger woman with the natural grace of a ballet dancer. As I study her, every nerve ending tingles, like spiders crawling down my spine. She has Kate's eyes.

I rifle through the drawers. The scent of mildew is intense, as if all the silk chemises and twin sets have soaked up every last century. In the wardrobe are dresses wrapped in dry cleaning bags and patent leather shoes hardly worn. A pair of white Converse, blackened by rain and mud, straddle the shoe rack, and my mind flashes to Elisabeth Sanders' bare feet. Could they be hers?

The second room is smaller, with the same bay window looking out to sea. A narrow bed dominates the room, quilt pulled back and pillow dented. A laptop perches on the bedside chair and hooked over the arm is a cap with the letters BU. On the bedside table is an ashtray. Inside are the remains of two stubby joints and a few buds of pot.

I unzip my backpack and take out my stalking log. The bedside drawer is open a crack and I place it inside. My attention moves to a pink phone lying between a penknife and a charging cord. There's a hairline crack across the screen and a hole where the SIM card should be. Numbness creeps over me. Nothing about the house suggests a female lodger. Could this phone belong to Elisabeth?

I'm tempted to make an anonymous call to the police hotline number. For a second I panic that I'm in the wrong place. But a small green jewelery box embossed with my mother's initials is proof. As are the earrings inside.

The screech of tyres outside paralyses me for a second. It takes all my courage to leave the earrings and I hook the laptop under my arm and hurtle downstairs. I'm slipping on the stair carpet, hand squealing along the banisters. Down, down, down, rushing to the sunroom to lock the inner door.

I replace the key on the vine at the same time as I hear the doorbell. I hook two fingers around the laces of my shoes and tear across the back garden. There's a jagged hole in the hedge between the properties and, snagging my socks on a twig, I gun it across the neighbour's lawn. The rapid barking of a dog, claws scraping against the glass, threatens to expose me. I step out on a layer of crushed gravel, wincing with every step.

I look back along the road and at the neck of the cul-de-sac, a man stands in the street, looking up at number 31. A dark grey suit, polished shoes. Plainclothes policeman?

He whistles to someone I can't see, finger drawing a circle in the air. His eyes seem to sweep the front facade as if looking for any signs of forced entry. Something must have caught his eye because he walks closer to the house, the hedge obscuring him from view.

By all standards, this is a reckless plan. Houses have cameras. They could have seen me. But the compulsion to be on the move overpowers me and I run away from the house, laptop concealed under my hoodie.

47

FREYA

I TEAR DOWN OUR street and ring Trisha's bell.

She's wearing rumpled pyjamas, feet bare. 'Are you OK?'

I switch off my body cam. 'Oh God, I did it. I broke into his house. I'm so scared, I'm shaking.'

'Quick, come in.' She unhooks my backpack and places it on the couch. 'Sit here. I'll get you some tea.'

'Is Derek here?'

I turn and there he is, big grin, same white teeth. I hand him the laptop in the hope he can bypass the passcode. He mutters something about safe mode and the computer's boot order. My expression must have changed from confusion to frustration and back to confusion, all in a split second. He says he'll work it out.

Then he points at the gloves I'd forgotten to remove and asks if he can borrow them. The police don't need my fingerprints and they certainly don't need his. I slump on the couch, shirt clinging to my skin. I tell Trisha about my keys and the notebook I left.

'You sent me a text about forty minutes ago,' she says. 'Where were you when you sent it?'

'Somewhere near Spyglass Point. Why?'

'It would have pinged the nearest tower, putting you in the general area of his house. General. Not precise.'

'I could have been out running.'

I tell her about the room off the kitchen. How Nian could have been drugged and kept there, and I show her the ampules I found.

'Ketamine,' she says, reading the label. 'It's a sedative.'

'The police were outside when I left. They didn't see me.'

Trisha pulls her iPad from the shelf under the coffee table and swipes through the night views her camera has caught. At the far left of the frame, a man appears near the tree beside the flats, before receding under the leafy canopy. Then she fast forwards to where he walks along Beaulieu Road and turns into the alley behind my house. I want to scream, but not before Derek strolls into the kitchen with the laptop, which he tells me is licensed to NQS. I'm googling the name; newly qualified jobs or venture capital solicitor in the southeast, both of which mean nothing to me.

'Put these back on,' Derek says, handing me the gloves and then the laptop. 'When we put the tracker on his car, it showed he was either parked on Crosby Street, or on Earle Road, or Mountbatten Road. Never at any fixed address. And then I remembered the car was stolen, so he wouldn't be driving to and from work, would he? We're not looking for someone who works for a hire company and has access to different cars. We're looking for an opportunist. Someone who nicks cars while the keys are in still in them. People loading or unloading shopping. There is something else. You might want to check your car for a tracker.'

I look out of Trisha's window and see our car is gone. I race back across the road and find a message from Jack on the kitchen blackboard.

Taking Theo to see the new James Bond. Be back this evening xxx

I slide the laptop under the sofa and peel off my gloves. Silence comes like a blanket and I worry about what comes next. First search the house for anything missing or moved. Then text Jack and tell him to check the car for any tracking devices. Make espresso, perhaps with a shot of whisky.

The doorbell rings. Patti Franchek, slapping a notepad against one thigh. While I'm planning what to say, she knuckles the door a little more urgently.

'Freya? You in there?'

She pushes past me into the kitchen, eyes doing a sweep of the room. Her posture is rigid, cords twanging in her neck.

'We were called out to a possible break-in this morning on Sandbourne Road. Like to tell me where you were between

8.00 a.m. and 10.30 a.m. today?'

'Running.'

'Phew! You must be training for the marathon. Talk me through what time you came home.' She crosses her arms, fists wedged under her armpits. 'Roughly.'

'Tenish?' I decide to leave out the part about seeing Trisha.

'You came straight home?'

'I made a detour.'

'Let me guess. Sandbourne Road?'

'There's a marvellous view of the sea from number 25.'

'We're not talking about number 25, Freya. We're talking about number 31. I happen to be interested in that particular house. The only sea view is from the back garden. An appalling risk and an act of lunacy.'

I swallow. I can't feel my feet.

'The neighbour in 29A reported seeing a woman of your description around the back of the house next door,' she says. 'He didn't know if it was a burglary in progress or an interested renter. He was kind enough to airdrop a few pictures.'

Shit!

Patti hands me her phone. The view is from an upper window, and there's no denying the woman hunched over a flowerbed and peering into the sitting-room window is me. The hoodie has fallen back against the crown of my head, exposing one side of my face.

'Do you know who lives in that house?' she asks.

'We have a mutual friend who lives on Surrey Road.'

'Come on, Freya. You can do better than this.'

'OK, so I don't know him.'

'And that makes it civil trespass.'

It's like a slap. Hard and fast. What if my foolish act of vigilantism sets me up for criminal charges, and, worse, the laptop would be admissible as evidence in court? She must see the commotion in my head, the vortex of a storm and all that flying, lying debris. Only, I've been lying for so long, I'm starting to convince myself. I see the entire episode as rational. Edward has been helping himself in my house. I am merely returning the favour.

'I'm sorry. I shouldn't have done it.'

'Look, I know you're desperate.' She takes a step towards me. 'But you can't go around stalking people when you're being stalked yourself. See the problem?'

'Yes, but the car in the papers, the one seen outside Elisabeth Sanders' house, was a rental. Correct?' I show her the photos Arthur sent me. 'Rabbi Aviel saw the same car.'

'That's why you knocked on this particular door?'

I feel so tired, I might collapse. She gives me a tight-lipped smile and motions me to sit.

'I spoke with Drew Martin at the *Daily Echo*. He said, while an excellent employee, you had demonstrated certain behaviour... unstable behaviour at a couple of parties last year. He mentioned one particular instance at Christmas where you drank a lot of wine.' She flips a few pages of her notebook. 'About seven glasses, in fact, and you attempted to break into his car.'

'That's a total exaggeration. I mistook Drew's car for ours. It doesn't mean I tried to steal it. I was tanked.'

'So, on this particular night, you – thoroughly tanked – insisted the car was yours? Bearing in mind, there are no physical similarities between a blue McLaren 720S and a white Dacia Sandero. You see my point?'

I do. 'Did you talk to him?'

'Who?'

'The owner of the house?'

'Don't ask me for names or descriptions. In case you were wondering, the neighbour hadn't been around long enough to get pally-pally over the wall. He can't help you either. What's this thing about an indoor camera?'

'It's in the bedroom.'

She's careful not to pull out a chair to stand on, I assume because Edward's fingerprints could be recovered from every shiny surface. 'How's he getting in?'

'We don't know.'

It's no good digging for information. Patti will safeguard it as ferociously as she seeks it. She tells me not to touch anything until she's finished dusting. My heart is beating so hard I'm afraid she can hear it.

I blink in the sunlight as we walk to her car. We're shoulder to shoulder when she stops, narrowing her eyes as if straining to remember something.

'Perhaps your therapist forgot to mention that deranged

killers keep a frenzy of emotions tightly reined in under that supernatural calm. Don't believe the picture I'm painting doesn't apply to your stalker. Trust me, Freya. If you trespass again, I will arrest you.'

I wait until she pulls away before rushing back into the house. I can't risk Jack finding the laptop, wondering why I have a secret computer he knows nothing about. Using the gloves, I slip it under the mattress in Dad's old room.

My phone rings – this time a number I recognise. 'Hi, my beautiful friend. I'm sorry for blocking. I love you with all my heart.'

God knows I don't deserve this. A call from Aynur. The friend I used to watch fireworks with on the pier on Fridays and play tennis in the Central Gardens. Whose daughter I cross-examined because she was there on the boat the night Kate disappeared. Emma – lucky, safe, beautiful – Emma, who will reach a maturity Kate will never see.

'I have no time for haters,' she says. 'May it be in the past.' Which in her Turkish way means she hopes all the pain is behind me now. 'I wanted you to know Patti Franchek came to see me at work. She told me you have letters and a stalker. You must be so afraid. Who is doing this?'

I try to tell her, but my breaths see-saw and sobs muffle my words. She tells me about the Christmas party last year. I can still hear the rattle of voices inside a cathedral tent and the heady scent of flowers. I'm wincing at a couple of waiters I crashed into. I was so drunk. So miserable. I must have been toxic, to say nothing of unkind.

'You are in my heart always,' she says.

I tell her she is always in mine.

I don't know why I blamed her daughter for something she couldn't help. It wasn't like Emma persuaded Kate to climb over the railings or that she pushed her. I'd probably put the fear of God into Emma when I should have been comforting her.

My phone rings again and I think it's Jack, but the rounded vowels and rolled Rs suggest his accent is local, and the flat tone gives me no indication of his mood.

'You've been such a bad girl, Freya.'

I hear the distant strains of music – female groans layered into every chorus. I shrink back from the window and, for a vacant second, I feel the run-up to dizziness. Had I come clean to Patti about his texts, she might be monitoring my phone right now, getting all the proof she needs. I'm a fool and I know it.

'Stroke of genius about the notebook,' he says. 'I've got a few other things of yours, soap, perfume, underwear. The police might get the wrong impression and think we've been shacking up together.'

Fear drives a spear through me and I'm hoping he can't hear my breath hitching. 'Where's Nian? Don't tell me you don't know.'

'Where's my laptop? Don't tell me you don't know.'

My fingers go numb and I glance out of the window at the

street, the windows, the doors, the cars. Where the hell is he? I'm turning circles in the house, walking from the front door to the back, looking up the stairwell and listening for sounds.

'Remember the steamy video of you and your lover? It's ready to upload to YouTube with a link to your friends at the *Daily Echo*. Or I can cut Nian's fingers off one by one and send them to you. Call Franchek and tell her to drop the case.'

'Screw you!'

I hang up, visualising a dark stain in the sand and the sickening stench of a rotting flesh. Not Elisabeth's body this time. Or Kate's.

Mine.

48

FREYA

THE DRONE OF VERTIGO quickly turns to nausea. Patti has already threatened me with arrest. I'm not here to fight my corner, but it would be prudent not to go into too much detail.

She picks up on the first ring and I take a deep breath. 'Edward wants you to drop the investigation. He said... he told me he'd cut off Nian Zhen's fingers if you don't.'

Her voice is calm. Not a hint of anger at my talking to Edward. 'Is Jack with you?'

'No.'

'Do not leave the house. I'm sending a car over now.'

'There's something else, Patti. He threatened to upload a video, an intimate video.'

'Of what?'

'Of me and some guy.'

'Well, there's a first. I wouldn't give it another thought, not with so many other naked bits and pieces online these days.'

'No, wait.'

She's dismissing the video in light of the horror of Nian's disappearance and Edward's subsequent threat. I get it. Finding Nian is far more important than a stupid video. But she knows I've been lying from the off. I tell her about my brief fling with Miles and I tell her about Edward's threatening texts, some of which I answered. I decline to tell her about entering his house. The fact that I was wearing gloves means it would be hard to place me inside. She knows how trapped I feel and she's measuring my stamina. I defend myself by saying the affair was the worst thing I'd ever done. When Kate died, it left me with no heart for anything.

'Trespassing carries a fine or a maximum of three months in prison,' she says. 'Depends on the judge. Or a conditional discharge if you don't repeat the offence. Might want to get a solicitor, Freya, before you say anything else.'

She hangs up. I wonder if the police can extract mobile data without permission, or a warrant, because there's no forgiveness now. I bite down on my lip to stop from crying. Still, that familiar sense of dread and the feeling the temperature has plummeted into winter without anyone telling me.

Jack calls to tell me Theo enjoyed the film, and yes, he found a magnetic box under the back bumper. He was tempted to tack it to a passing bus, but wised up and asked a nurse for a Ziploc bag. I tell him about Edward's call. No matter how many times he tells me not to answer the phone or the door until he gets back, the unsettling feeling persists.

Giving the laptop to the police would be the most sensible thing to do. It would be over for the owner of 31 Sandbourne Road. But I have to be sure. I have to know that Edward has actual video proof of my affair.

I remind myself to wear gloves. It takes a few seconds to power up. The user account on the sign-in screen belongs to Edward Besant. There are lists and lists of files and one catches my eye.

Sanders. A woman is sitting on a bench with one hand pressing a phone to her ear, the other gesturing in the air. Another shows her running back towards the cresting swell of the sea. The last shot shows her lying on a mattress with a cord around her neck. Her lips slightly open, as if drawing her final breath. I feel cold and weak and dizzy.

Zhen. A young woman drinking in wine bar, dancing with a friend, waiting at tables, chucking a rosy-cheeked baby under the chin, and then, lying between the roots of a tree, face bloody and battered, and resting on a mossy bed. I'm praying that somehow these pictures are fake, photo-shopped, even though I know they are real.

Thorne, with a picture quote:

Talking about love, I've watched all my girlfriends as I watch you now. You can call it an obsession – an insatiable animal-gripping-on-tightly-with-its-teeth – obsession. Every time I have a girlfriend, I feel guilty because she isn't you.

There are wide-angle shots of lonely streets and a crowded

beach. Pictures of me tracking the coastline, slogging through wet sand or standing in the frothy scum of the sea. These pictures don't possess the same intimacy as Elisabeth's or Nian's. Edward's obsession with me appears to be in the early stages, a schoolboy crush that allows him a keyhole view of my life. There are long shots taken in the park; Jack sitting on a picnic rug watching Kate doing cartwheels and whooping like a crazed football fan. I remember the day – a moment of joy before she died. How long has Edward been following us? The thought terrifies me and I'm poring through every file, hoping, no – praying – that he hadn't been stalking Kate.

There are stacks of photos of me and only a few of Miles. The ones of us together are innocent, two people sharing a laugh with friends at lunch. Which leads me to believe the videos he claims to have of me are false.

Miller. A close-up of a damp, clingy T-shirt, and tightly framed shots taken in a nightclub. Trisha's lips poised against the rim of a glass, posing, smiling. Long shots of the flats, revealing a naked woman through a slit in the upstairs blinds. Every piece of evidence points to the fact Edward was there. Watching.

My mind jumps and I'm back in the car with Jack that night, only minutes before the accident. I picture the tracking shot from a drone as it streaks a few feet above, hovering on a thermal as we park on Spyglass Point. It banks to the left as if searching for the same cloud of vapour I had seen in my wing mirror. It spots the car behind us and makes a sharp turn, hovering three metres shy of the back bumper. A flash of light. Grinding metal. Screams mar the aerial hunt, and I'm sliding along a bend in the road and sawing at the steering wheel as the car yaws to one side. Tyres screech for purchase and somewhere beyond the shattering of glass, a face bursts through the darkness.

There's something in the voice. Panic. Encouragement. I don't know which. There are stars behind him as if he and I float in the night sky. I wish I could quash my instincts, but for a second – a fleeting, terrifying second – I realise I've been looking in all the wrong places.

49

EDWARD

THIS ISN'T A GAME any longer, Edward thinks. His heart pounds and his skin is slimy with sweat. She has been in his house, stolen his laptop. Where did such a timid little mouse get all that courage?

Outside, a car drives by, the noise receding before a hush of silence. He's drifting and dreaming and something wrenches him into wakefulness. The snick of a latch? The blinds are open. He always closes them before coming to bed.

His bare soles bristle on the rush matting before settling on the hardwood floor. Without turning on the light, he waits, hears a familiar sound – the squeak of a hand against the railing and the dry ratcheting of a hinge. The silence drags on and on, and he tiptoes halfway down the stairs, one tread at a time.

Spangles of moonlight streak through the windows and shadows skulk in every corner. Edward shakes his head. It's his lodger, always locking himself out. It never dawned on him that he might have left the key on the vine for Freya to find.

'We can all lie,' he says. 'We can all pretend we're someone else, starring in a movie of our own making. Why do you think there are so many murders, bomb threats and bank robberies? Everyone wants to be a celebrity, enough to keep the reporters busy.'

Edward knows love and hate can live together. Same as genius and madness are two halves of a whole. The temptation is to fight against hate and the alternative is to allow love to win, but it's a risk. Like a dog straining at the leash will only relieve the pressure on its throat if it stops fighting. No one listens to his story, his truth, but they'll listen now. Make the familiar segue from surprise to shock, and wish they'd listened sooner.

Elisabeth Sanders loved dogs and children and Edgar Allan Poe. Edward danced around the idea of honouring her body as in *The Black Cat*. But the thought of cutting out one eye and hanging her from a tree seemed a little extreme. He hears her ghost wandering around the house, trying to find a way out. Quotes from *The Pit and The Pendulum* fill his mind, all melding into one. "I call to mind flatness and dampness; and then all is madness – the madness of a memory which busies itself among forbidden things."

He picks up his phone and dials the code for India and then the number. He doesn't understand what she's saying, but her voice is exactly as he remembers it.

'Nisha. It's Lionel's boy. Do you remember me?'

There's silence and then a hitch of breath. 'Oh my God, is it really you?'

'It's me.'

'I don't believe it. How are you?'

He tells her about his father's death. But he can't bring himself to tell her what he did to protect her, to save her. He sobs a little and he knows she can hear it. Her voice is still kind, a little hesitant, a little distant, and he knows she's scared to tell him what really happened. But somehow she does. It all comes in short bursts, interspersed with her own tears. How sad she was for Mother, her affair with Father, but mostly for Edward and what he'd seen.

Edward tells her he will always love her. Before she says anything, he says he won't call again. He knows in his bones this is the last time he will hear her voice.

When he hangs up, the lodger is standing in the doorway. Edward is aware of the disparity between them – naiveté seeping from every pore. The way to deal with him is to throw him off his game. Edward knows this from years of living together.

'Who were you talking to?' he asks.

'The county coroner.' Edward sidesteps. 'I was asking about the Sanders' autopsy report. She kept banging on about conjunctival petechiae and haematomas on the tongue, like I needed to know. No mention of any DNA. So then I called Officer Petersen about the Zhen girl. It wasn't like him to clam up, get all hard-nosed about it.'

'Maybe he can't tell you.'

'He's never avoided me before.'

Lodger-boy keeps saying *shit, shit, shit* and walking in circles. Banging his head with one hand and muttering, 'no wonder the cops won't talk. They *know* something.' He's trying to keep a lid on it. But Edward can see tiny droplets at his hairline.

He feels angry and detached. One moment he's here, and the next he's not, and sometimes he can't bring myself back. When did it all start? The moment he thinks of the word *darkroom*, he smells chlorine and iodine and feels a swoop of hopelessness. If he got Father's answers right, he was let out.

'What was the first photo ever taken, son?'

'*View from the Window at Le Gras*, Father.'

'What year?'

'1826. Joseph Nicéphore Niépce.'

'Too big for your own boots, eh? Nothing a good spanking won't put right.'

'Please, Father, no.'

Edward doesn't remember how long he sat in the darkness, only that he could decipher every daily scent from morning to night and know exactly what time of day it was. Rain was easy to smell, so was sunshine and dewy grass. It's the white days that were almost unreadable, and anything he couldn't read bothered him.

After Father went to work, Nisha let him out. Bathed him, fed him. Hugged him. She put him back before Father came home, pasted some of those glow-in-the-dark stars on the ceiling. Sometimes she'd hide a hot water bottle under the mattress and a blanket behind the door. It was their little secret.

Sometimes, he'd pretend he had a friend to talk to. Someone like lodger-boy. At school he was always the one with the frayed sleeves and Father's borrowed ties.

But the thing he remembers most is Nisha ripping off her clothes before a bath, buttons skittering across the floor. She was crying. He saw the wishbone of her pelvis and the upside down heart of her buttocks, streaked with scars. Father did it. Father did all of it.

There's a shiver in the air between them. Lodger-boy can see through the opening in his mind, a tiny slit through which he can glimpse the filth. But he's the only person who knows Edward's story, teases it out of him, thread by thread. A secret shared.

Again, that feeling of hopelessness and Edward wishes they could trade places, even for a day, to know what it feels like to be decent. So impeccable in his wit, beautiful, and melancholy, everything Edward lacks.

The air feels thin and there's a humming, a vibration that separates him from the room and then catapults him back to himself. The black noise in his head becomes a deafening roar, and he feels the sickness rising inside him.

He'd like to slam the lodger up against the wall. Crack his skull and a few other bones, only there'd be no sign of any dents or bruises in the morning. Or blood. Like he could have sworn he killed him. But it wasn't him at all.

Lodger-boy lights a joint, takes a hit and hands it to Edward. 'Do you ever think of the consequences? The Sanders woman and now the Zhen girl. No offence, but it's your DNA they'll find.'

Edward lets the smoke drift back into his mouth. He's tempted to provoke the lodger because when he yells, it's so much fun to watch. By fun, he means crazy.

'She looked like Nisha.'

'They all look like Nisha.'

For years he's been dreaming of Nisha. Sometimes he sees her in Waterstones, or running along the beach, and he promises he'll bring her home.

Edward closes his eyes, conscious of the network of cells and nerves in his body, all sparkling like tiny fireflies, millions of them, and not a spare inch of air. Something shifts in his head and when he opens his eyes, an unfamiliar landscape emerges. The colours are different, flatter.

'Where is the Zhen girl?' Lodger-boy asks.

'Canford Cliffs. Behind the swings. She hit her head against the car window. Can't keep a screaming bitch down.'

Edward knows keeping trophies is dangerous. Nian Zhen's driving license reminds him of her face, and he can relive the moment when he has the urge.

'Best if I take it from here.' Lodger-boy says. 'We don't want the house to smell like an abattoir.'

Edward feels lodger-boy's eyes on him. He feels the heat spreading to his neck and chest, and he's no longer sure why he feels so tense. There's something in those eyes Edward has never seen before.

No one has silver, humourless eyes, the type where any sudden movement would be fatal. No one has a sense of smell so acute they can smell blood through the darkroom door.

No one, except a psychotic killer.

50

FREYA

'WANT TO COME WITH me to the dentist?' Jack hovers, unsure.

My eyes graze past his to the blackboard. The appointment is written in black and white, an appointment I'd forgotten. 'I don't think a waiting room is the best place for a headache.'

'When did you take your pills?' he asks.

'Over an hour ago.'

He feels my forehead with the back of his hand. 'I hate to leave you on your own.'

'I'll be OK. Trisha'll come over if I ask her.'

His face is a twist of anguish and all I have is a lie, another bloody lie. But I have to get rid of the laptop and he mustn't be here when I do it.

The silence between us swells and he takes the keys from the peg and opens the door. The sunlight is briefly blinding, Jack standing there with his back to me. Then he turns.

'I love you, you know.' He says it matter-of-factly, which

means a question is coming next. 'Do you love me?'

'Yes. I do.'

'Because that's what matters...' He tails off and goes outside.

I'm back on autopilot, alone in the house, listening to the silence. I feel wretched. I want to let go of the lies trapped inside my head. Lies he feels, but can't know. Climbing the stairs, I feel as if I'm gliding. My feet make no sound as I move along the landing to Dad's room. To the laptop. My overriding feeling is one of fear. I can't go back to Edward's house, not now the police are watching it.

I call Trisha. I tell her about the pictures I found of her posing in a nightclub, what she was wearing, even down to the colour of her underwear. She goes quiet.

'Do you remember someone taking photos?' I ask.

'Shit, Freya, I don't know his name. I didn't even ask. He was just some guy hustling me for drugs. It was a Friday night in The Vault. I was stoned.' Her voice goes quiet and I know she's gone into her bedroom to keep Derek from hearing. 'I was so screwed up back then, OK? I'm straightening out. At least, I'm trying. Frey? You there?'

'Yes. I'm here.'

'I don't want you being charged for stealing the laptop. Let Derek find a way to get it to the police station.'

I suppose you could say this is our chain of messengers. After Derek takes it, I sprint upstairs to watch the street, keeping my face aligned with the frame. The rain starts again, a slanting assault at the windows, and as far as I can see, there's no black

Audi to worry about.

Shadows lengthen and the sun disappears behind a bank of dark clouds. I can't remember a longer day. After making my third cup of tea, I settle into the sitting room. While I'm watching my phone, my fingers encounter an envelope wedged between the cushions. Inside is a letter wrapped around a gold coin. It is not addressed to me. It's addressed to Jack.

I hate to be the bearer of bad news, but your wife fell for it. Couldn't keep her hands off him. Life always has a way of keeping a few surprises up its sleeve. I wish you all the best.

Edward.

SURVEILLANCE REPORT ON FREYA THORNE

Dear Mr Thorne,

I have completed the surveillance on your wife. As requested, please find attached video and photographic evidence of her extramarital affair with colleague, Miles Saroyan, and any correspondence and meetings that occurred during the past two weeks.

Regarding your question about discreet access, I can suggest several options. First, keys. Second, hidden cameras. I can enter the home and set up the equipment at your convenience and will send footage to the email you have provided. I suggest changing passwords to all your accounts, financial and social media. A detailed summary of her activities is as follows:

I read the detailed summary, which lists everything from when I got up to when I went to bed. Dates and times of when I met Miles. Addresses. Text conversations. I'm reminded that surveillance firms usually refer to themselves as 'we' rather than 'I' which means this is a private operative. No wonder Jack had changed his password. He didn't want me knowing he'd hired a PI.

I call Trisha and the relief I feel when I hear her voice is palpable. 'Jack's having me followed. I've got proof.'

'Now you're scaring me.'

I snap a photo of the letter and text it to her.

'Except there's no name or address on the surveillance report, Frey. It's a fake.'

I take a few seconds to realise what she's trying to tell me.
I'd neglected to check the letterhead or determine a postmark
on the envelope. How long has it been here? When was it
delivered?

'I got to thinking about that man I saw outside your house a
while back,' she says. 'Not saying it was odd, just something
you'd remember. The stones he was throwing... it was an
overarm throw, like the ones cricketers do.'

The word *cricketer* throws me for a second. Bats... whites...
bowling. Then my mind swings to the sweet smell of alcohol
on warm summer nights. The slurs and trebles of the Irish
songs I used to play on Saturday nights at The Cricketer's
Arms. I'm searching the crowd for a face, but I can't see one.
A third of the population played sports at school, including
cricket. Theo played cricket and so did Jack, and so did Drew
at work. Doesn't explain why any of them would bowl stone
after stone at our bedroom window at night.

'Arthur's got a list of all cars parked in the street since last
week,' Trisha says. 'Colours, model, plates. Relax, OK? Be
more Zen like Bruce Lee.'

To keep my mind off Trisha's lack of urgency, after I hang
up I do another search for Edward Besant, this time based
on everything I know about him. I find an article dated six
months ago about a coin, a Byzantine solidus, stolen from the
Russell-Cotes Art Gallery. When I refine the search, not only
do I find the name Besant refers to a culture of minters during
Anglo-Saxon times, but that a *bezant* is the heraldic symbol on

a gold coin.

My phone beeps, deafeningly loud this time. But it's not Trisha.

'Hello, Freya. Have you worked out who I am?'

I'm trying to match a name to the voice, but nothing comes. This nightmare represents a very intimate form of vengeance, and I pivot back to the window, casting a glance over the street. Nausea creeps through my stomach before the line goes dead.

The windows blur with rain, and the steady drumbeat on the roof tells me it's hail. The phone shakes in my hand, and my head screams.

Then a text from a name I recognise.

Elisabeth Sanders: Death is nothing at all.
It does not count.
I have only slipped into the next room.

The chill of dead air, a bare echo that blows me off course. While I'm trying to work out why a dead woman would call me using the words of Henry Scott-Holland, I see a smudge of black by the back door. A figure in the shadows.

I can't move. I stand, transfixed in sluggish shock. I think of the poker by the fireplace and how heavy the lamp is on the shelf. I think of my keys on the peg. Even if I managed to reach them, I'd never make it outside the house. There's nowhere to go.

'Don't move. I won't hurt you.'

The voice rattles in the empty house and I don't believe him. He steps closer, his body loose-jointed and smooth, like a cat ready to pounce. I try to commit his face and hands to memory, each part of him covered in black, and I search his eyes behind the mask, but they are unrecognisable, barely human.

Six foot. Slender. Broad shouldered. My gut knots with panic and I tell myself to stay calm, walk back towards the kitchen. Slowly. No sudden moves.

I press the panic button on my phone and slip it safely in my back pocket. A chill sprints down my spine, and I'm paralysed, urging myself to run. I'm screaming it in my head. But it's too horrifying to...

I lunge for the kitchen, my feet sliding on the floor, hand gripping the door handle. Something sharp, like an insect bite, stabs the side of my neck. Before I can turn, a hood covers my face and I try to grasp the drawstring, but he hooks my hands behind my back.

I'm dragged across the floor, muscles unresponsive. I can taste fresh air through the fabric, heels bouncing on gravel and concrete. My tongue feels thick and I'm trying to scream and shout, but every sound seems muffled. I'm lying on a firm surface, fingers grappling at seams and stitching and then a hard, square object. The button release of a seatbelt.

A door slams. The engine purrs and rattles and picks up speed and I roll backwards, only to be flung forward again as the car brakes. The overwhelming sense of failure washes over me and then dizziness. My muscles are like soup and I'm sucking in cloth, not air.

My skin prickles and bubbles, and I feel as if I'm spinning down, down... the last thing I remember is my body cam.

51

FREYA

THE FIRST SENSATION IS a burn at the back of my throat. I want to sit up, but the nausea keeps me down. I don't feel the bite of rope at my wrists and ankles and the hood is gone. Whatever he gave me is wearing off.

Moonlight slants over the windowsill and a breeze taps against the blinds. I roll onto my side, but my groan quavers across the room and my head's buzzing like a wasps' nest. Rasping floorboards tells me someone is coming. A man strides into the room, torso speckled with water. He wears jeans. Nothing else.

'You're awake. It's good seeing you again, Freya. It wasn't easy. I'm not going to lie.'

The room slides in and out of focus, and I try to tune into what he's saying. The West Country lilt is lukewarm, hardly there. Behind him, the street lamp provides a burnished glaze to the bedroom and his face is in shadow.

'I gave you a little shot to make you sleep.'

I flinch from him, but his arm is firm under me and he hauls me up, puts a glass of water to my lips. I want to run down the stairs and out into the street, but my limbs are slack, and my brain is woolly. I can fake it, pretend to be who he wants me to be. Or I can be tight-lipped and pay the price.

He pulls me to my feet. My legs aren't as heavy as I'd dreaded and I lean against him all the way downstairs. I want him to believe I'm weak.

'Now, tell me,' he says. 'What did you do with my laptop?'

'It's not... I don't know...'

The crack of his palm against the side of my face takes me by surprise. My ear is on fire.

'It upsets me to hit you,' he says. 'I'll do it again if I have to.'

I'm searching for the front door and glimpse a cloakroom. I try not to stare at it. He rams me up against the wall, one arm creeping around to the small of my back. My hands instinctively fly to his chest, and my mind is trying to replay Trisha's words.

The knee has power. It has a shorter distance to go.

Part of me craves to punch my way out, but he is stronger. Deadlier. The drugs in my system are making me dizzy. As I raise my hands to his jaw, he grabs my wrists and pins them above my head. The room tilts. The scream coming from the back of my throat is so loud, it takes a second to realise it's mine. He hooks a hand over my mouth and I can almost taste his skin.

A sound. The muffled ping of an incoming text. He swivels

me around and crushes my face against the wall. His fingers search my pockets for my phone, and he presses my thumb against the home button.

'What shall I tell them, Freya? That we're having so much fun? Are you having fun? I didn't think so.'

Time slows down, as if I'm weightless, free-falling from a bungee line. I'm nearly at the end of my cord's reach and time speeds up again. He can't take the SIM card out with one hand, especially a phone with a case.

What did Trisha tell me? Shift my weight, bend my elbow and strike. Hard as you can.

He sees me twitch and tugs me back, phone clattering to the floor. My back is now fused with his chest, one arm trapping me in a chokehold. He pushes me towards the kitchen and rams me into a chair. Something wet creeps down my cheek and there, on the back of my hand, is a dark smear. The winder on his watch must have sliced my cheek open.

He is closer to the door than I am, and running past him won't do me any good. A clammy coldness seeps across my shoulders, and I try not to let fear cloud my thinking.

'Do you understand loss?' he asks. 'Not the type where you get drunk and black out for a few hours. The type where you lose an entire childhood.'

His voice slips in and out of accents. I can't believe what I'm hearing and I want to scream at him to stop. When I take in the slope of his shoulders, it comes to me. Perhaps I had awoken once and seen the curve of a silhouette, sitting in the bedroom chair and hiding amid the shadows. He'd been right there. In my house. All the time.

For a long moment, he holds my gaze, setting off a low buzz of dread. *Is he going to hit me again?*

'I'm glad you're home,' he says. 'It's times like this, when it's good to have friends.'

'I'm not your friend. This isn't my home.'

The ground rolls, but he keeps talking, explaining how his texts and calls were meant to comfort me. His voice is so sickening I want him to stop.

'You were special, Freya. Do you have any idea how special? I watched you every day for months. Yes, months. I wanted you because you're strong. Unbreakable. That's what I like about a woman. This isn't about Jack. It was never about Jack. You being married, or not being married. How good it is to be married. Because it isn't. How did I do it? It doesn't take much. Even the man you tried to follow to the restaurant – a few extra sweaters, a wig – enough to make you curious. Sorry, you dropped your phone. It was me calling because I knew you were hiding. Silly Freya. Such an airhead.'

He strains to keep his voice level, eyes searching my face as if he can see every clenched muscle. I'm bracing myself for what he might do.

'Why don't we go outside and catch the breeze?' He turns sideways and I see the shadow of glasses; a dark lens above the curve of his cheek. 'You'd like that, wouldn't you?'

I nod. Maybe going outside is a good idea. I could make a run for it. But we don't go outside. Before I say his name, he turns on the light and I can't stop staring, can't stop wondering if it's pity I'm feeling or fear. I notice faint welts on his neck and shoulder. Any illusions of the police not finding him are gone. Nian Zhen has traces of his DNA under her fingernails.

He snaps a tea towel from a hook, runs it under the tap, and presses it against my cheek. I see the signet ring on his little finger, identical to the one he sent me. His hair is lacy with moisture and his black eyes flicker.

No matter how I look at it, Miles Saroyan has been the perfect gentleman. And the perfect liar.

52

FREYA

He pulls out a chair and sits, and I can see tanned flesh through the shreds in his jeans. I realise how stupid and weak I'd been to have an affair with a man I hardly knew. Despite those few snatched hours together, he was choosing the parts of his life he wanted me to know and editing out the rest, enough for me to unburden myself in return. I had risked everything and given him the upper hand.

I know if I keep my voice steady, find his level, summon the feelings I once had, he might separate from his vilest animal self. He might be Miles again.

'You want to know the truth, Freya? Jack is the one who needs help. We met in the Brewhouse two days before the Christmas party. He was hammered. Surprise, surprise. I opened his mind to the possibility of a bet. It was touching how he tried to defend you, but it intrigued him enough to toss a coin.'

'You're lying.'

'He lost. Fumbled around blindly for some kind of deliverance, but a bet's a bet, don't you agree? He's a little absent-minded. Went to the Mens and left his keys on the counter. Since Jack carries a spare house key, I took it and replaced it with a dud. After that, I used credit cards and Tic-Tac boxes to replicate any keys you left around the house.' He anchors my wrists with his hands. 'Jack said. "Here's to my faithful wife", and I told him I'd drink to that. I didn't tell him how many bets I'd made over the years, to how many husbands. Imagine the buzz, so shocking, so utterly newsworthy.'

There's a mocking tone to his voice that serves to enrage me more, and I try to wrench my wrists from his hands, but his grip confirms I'm a prisoner. I'm thinking of his laptop, which is with Patti now, but mostly the login screen. The words NQS are short form for NQ South – NewsQuest – where all our computers at work are licensed. It's all so clear now.

I look into his eyes, scanning the countertops behind him for a knife, but the surgical neatness makes me shudder.

'You wouldn't believe how easy it is. But easy gets boring after a while. Women get clingy, begging me for a way out. You... you were different.'

His words stick to me like sweat. I need to keep him talking, to smooth the prickling tension around him. 'How different?'

'Does it matter?'

'No.'

His face twisted in disgust. I know I'm the one to blame. I broke the most fundamental marital rule. *Forsaking all others*... Nothing should have taken Jack's place. Nothing should have come between us. It's clear that what started as a bit of drunken fun turned into something terrifying. The silence lies heavy on the room and my heart beats so loud I'm afraid he'll hear it.

'You have no idea what it's like to be shoved aside,' he says. 'It started with my parents... that's a long story.'

'What were they like?'

'There was so much shouting. I tried to sleep, but you can't sleep through all that. You can't think.' He pauses and smiles at me. 'Mother was an idiot and Father... I can still see the bubbles and I want to push them back into his mouth. A tiny bit of air. A tiny bit of life. Mother said he'd taken an overdose and fallen asleep in the bath. I say he had it coming.'

My eyes slide to the hall where my phone still lies. I won't ask what he will do to me. I'm still alive and it gives me a giddy sense of hope.

'Why Elisabeth?' I ask.

'Yes, well, she had a lot of questions. She was always asking questions. She wanted to know why I was so obsessed with you. I don't like jealous types.' He leans forward a little and taps his head. 'Big vacuum up here. It was only a few months and she was reading my letters, going through my things. Telling me she wanted more. More than I could give her. She knew she was a version of someone else.'

Somehow, given all that is happening, I smell fresh air. The window must still be open in the cloakroom, but I can't reach it with him sitting here. I curl and uncurl my toes, anything to keep the circulation going.

'I was working in London when the first one happened,' he says. 'Kitty Arnold. Damn good reporter. I followed her to a secluded park while she was walking her dog. It didn't surprise her to see me, said I was so possessive and pathetic it was something she expected of me. I told her to apologise, but she was unrepentant. I remember very little after that, except my hands around her neck. I knew if I did it again, the police would be smart enough to put it all together.

'Mariah and I were lovers for nine glorious months until the guilt got to her and she buckled. Went back to her old man and cited me for sexual harassment. I resigned before they could fire me.

'Then I moved back here. Met Elisabeth. When she started drilling me with questions about my exes, I knew we were on the downward slope. I hadn't decided on a course of action until she decided for me. I should have tied her to a rock and sent her to the bottom of the sea. The ribbon was just a little detail to get you worked up.'

An almost imperceptible flash in his eye and I'm afraid he is about to unravel, grab me by the throat and squeeze and squeeze until there's no air left to breathe. A second trips by. I will die if I don't get out of here.

'Then there was Jack. Jack in your bed. Jack in your life. Jack in your heart. I don't want to hear any more about Jack. You should be over him by now.'

I take stock of the smell of weed on Miles' breath, his expression. Two halves of himself emerging in the most frightening way. Icy adrenaline snakes through me and my vision swims with tears. My life is disposable. I can't reconcile this shattered facade with the man I thought I knew.

He leans back and crosses his arms. 'I know you took the sedatives.'

I don't answer. Getting refills can't be easy and I'm hoping they were all he had.

'Ironic, isn't it? You think you're going to die. Turns out I'm not so keen on the idea. I was thinking more about running away together.'

'If I say yes...' I swallow, trying to put words to what I'm thinking. 'What about Jessica?'

'There is no Jessica. There never really was. I told her I loved you, because unlike her, you don't need me.'

I double over and retch. My throat burns with bile – I've barely eaten since breakfast. The cold slap of a wet flannel against the back of my neck makes me shudder. I'll have to pretend I love him and I know I can't. Sweat prickles through my hair and I hear the hum of the fridge and a car in the street.

He won't coax me into drinking anything spiked, which tells me he can't keep a struggling woman down without it. While he sluices the flannel in the sink, I take three quiet breaths, knowing he will see my reflection in the kitchen window if I sprint for the back door. He'd sense me as sure as a fly feels the change of wind before you swat it.

For a moment he paces back and forth and I think he's going to sit down again, but he turns away at the last second and leans over the sink to study something outside the window. 'You shouldn't have kissed me, Freya.'

While he ruminates on that kiss, I look at the floor and the legs of my chair. How much noise will it make if I move it? How much space do I have between the chair and the table to slip out? Instead of weighing my chances, I make a break for the front door.

He traps me in the hall, yanks my arm and spins me around to face him. I'm teetering on one foot, and his fist slams into the side of my face. Impact with the wall knocks the wind out of me. My ear explodes with pain again, and my jaw feels as if it's hanging off my face.

'I underestimated you, Freya. Won't happen again.'

I slide down the wall, and he catches me before I touch the floor. I want to twist and punch, scrabble for his eyes or some other soft tissue, but my body refuses to respond. His words are a hoarse rasp against my throat, but I can only hear through one ear.

The kettle screeches and puffs out a cloud of steam. His head jerks at the noise. I try to walk, but it's not happening, my body slumps firmly against his. Too many thoughts chase through my head: Will he kill me? Will he assault me? Will he ever let me go? I resist a sudden urge to scream.

I expect him to take me back to the kitchen. But he doesn't. He takes me to the locked room beyond.

53

FREYA

How long has it been? One hour? Two? Jack's face keeps flashing through my mind and I'm thinking about what his life will be like when I'm dead. It fills me with a painful longing, because the future I'd always believed in will never come true.

I pound on the door, screaming at him to let me out. My jaw pounds and blood trickles down the side of my face.

'Say please,' he shouts. 'Small word, *huge* possibilities.'

'*Please.*'

But there is silence on the other side of the door. Saliva pools on my tongue and I swing between being afraid of him to feeling a sick kinship. Not because of what he'd done, but because of what *we* had done. So appealing in his naivety, his perfectly pressed clothes and his quick wit. But putrid inside.

Trisha's camera will have filmed Miles carrying me outside to his car. But when will she check the footage? Wouldn't Jack have called the police by now? Patti mentioned they were watching this house. If so, someone must have seen something.

My foot collides with the tufted corner of a mattress and a rotten stench leaches from the fabric. This is where he imprisoned Elisabeth, a slimmer, frailer version of me. While I think of her wasted body, stomach cramping with hunger, I know he sedated her. If she couldn't get out, what makes me think I can?

My hands shake and flutter and I'm gasping to control my breath. His tuneless humming, this cramped room. A ghost of a man, supernaturally sensitive, biding his time and enjoying my torture. It's all real.

I can make out a full-bellied sink and shelves in the corner. I pat every surface for a pen, scissors, anything sharp.

His voice breaks the silence. 'I'm making tea. Want to join me?'

'Yes,' I shout, as if this were a casual visit.

Yes, because he will open the door. Yes, because he'll sit me at the kitchen table and I'll throw the boiling water in his face and run. He said "join me," but what if he hands me the cup and makes me drink it in here?

My thoughts close off and I'm desperate for it to end. Is he watching me from a camera inside the smoke alarm? A tiny red light flashes every few seconds and my muscles twist even tighter. I hear the kettle scraping against the burner and the click and whump of gas. I want to cling to this act of kindness, but I'm guessing he'll infuse the tea with a sleeping drug and I'll never wake up.

How long will it take me to stop measuring time? Two days?

I know I won't last a third. Dusty air burns my lungs and I could breathe it all in and suffocate. I touch walls and shelves, sharp edges angling to straight lines. I feel plastic bottles and cold porcelain, and boards nailed across the window – so little air. My fingers meet cold metal. A flat top and a groove. A screw. I look around for something to remove it, but there's nothing but wooden crates and a pile of old suitcases.

I slide down the wall, hugging my knees under my chin. A neon glow seeps under the door. The light from my phone, perhaps? It's a crazy thought, but he could be accessing my social media and pretending to be me. Telling everyone I've gone off for a few days so no one will miss me. Telling Jack I've left him. Only the worst kind of monster could lock me up like this. I try to concentrate on my breathing rather than my crumbling hope.

I hear pattering rain getting louder and louder on the roof, like a resounding applause. I keep thinking, I keep remembering what he'd said to me when I went to the hotel with him that night. We stood in front of the window, drinking and laughing and watching a woodsmoke sky.

This is the calm before the storm.

When I received the first text, I hadn't made the connection, and it barely nudged at my subconscious. Recklessly drunk, I'd loved him for a couple of nights and hated him for all the rest. It's like barbed wire in my heart.

I hear the kettle shriek and I try to work out what to do. What if his body fills the doorframe and I can't get past? Specks of dust spiral in a draught and I can smell the bitter tang of oranges – Earl Grey tea. A teaspoon strikes up a tune, baiting me gently.

I notice the glint of glass against the door frame. Directly above me is a light fixture, which appears to be nothing but a naked bulb. It's shattered, one piece curling downwards like a canine tooth. A weapon like this is more lethal than boiling water. I reach up, but my arms aren't long enough. I remember the wooden crates. The first one is too heavy to lift and too loud to drag. The one beside it is open and by the feel of it, filled with four bottles of wine.

He's moving around the kitchen now and the clank of china tells me he's reaching in a cupboard for a cup. How long will it take him to invite me outside? Is he playing me?

I empty the crate, deciding on whether a heavy bottle would make for a better weapon. But he'd see it in my hand and there's not enough room to swing it. Turning the crate over, I place my feet on the outer edges and reach up to unscrew the bulb. Curling my fingers around the metal cap, I silently work it loose.

The blade is thicker and sturdier than I'd imagined and keeping it behind my back won't fool him for long. The padlock clatters, latch grinding open. I squint at the bright light. His eyes drill through me as if searching for any falseness. Despite his hatred, he tries to be civil.

He studies my swollen face. 'You'll need ice for that.'

I allow the corners of my mouth to rise slightly, but I don't speak. Only the thundering terror in my head remains.

'Still so beautiful. You must hate me for locking you up. But you went digging into things. You shouldn't have done that.' A breath of air leaves his lungs and his fingers trace my throat. 'You were my favourite girl.'

Were. Not *are.*

'Do you love me?' His lips brush over mine, but he doesn't kiss me.

'Yes.'

He's waiting for a reaction, a tiny flinch, a sigh. I try to delay the inevitable, but I swallow. He feels it beneath his fingers. He knows I'm lying.

But he doesn't see the glass in my hand or drops of blood on the kitchen floor.

54

FREYA

I COULD HAVE RAMMED him, but there's no telling how strong he is. He drags me to a chair and, without taking his hand from my shoulder, pulls open a drawer and takes out a syringe. Sweat runs down the side of my face, soaking into my shirt.

I'm breathing too fast, adrenaline buzzing in my veins. If there's ever a right time, it's now. Kicking the chair out from under me, I extend one hand towards his chin as the other plunges and stabs with all the strength I have left. It takes my brain a few seconds to realise he's batted the blade from my hand, but my eyes don't miss the syringe scooting across the floor.

He staggers, blood pouring from a slash below his collarbone. Widening. Oozing. One hand grabs a clump of my hair, the other fumbles for the kettle. It catches against the edge of the burner and lists to one side, water splashing to the floor. He yells and arches his body to avoid the puddle, letting go of my hair. I see the syringe wedged between the table leg and the wall, so close I can almost touch it. Falling to my knees, I reach for it, my fingers stretching until my knuckles pop.

A shift in the air, like a door suddenly opened. I turn to see his face only inches from mine, his mouth moving, teeth bared. In those few seconds, I realise the syringe is outside of his field of vision. Keeping my arms close to my body, I ram the needle into the side of his neck, pushing down on the plunger with my thumb. But it's not enough. He jerks backwards, hands grappling for the syringe and pulling it free. In those few seconds, I'm running and stumbling through the hall and rattling the front door handle for all it's worth.

'Freya!'

I turn to see his silhouette, hand holding up the key in mock amusement. I freeze, fooling him into thinking I have given up. But the cloakroom is only six feet away. I run for it, slamming the door and turning the key.

'You stupid, stupid bitch!'

I feel the vibrations through the door, his knee slamming into the lower panel. I try to gauge what he'll do next, but there is no frame of reference with the devil.

Street light shines through a three-by-five foot window over the sink. I push up the bottom sash as far as it will go. Clumsy with fear, I slam a foot on the toilet seat and ease my head through the gap. A narrow path cuts between the house and next door's hedge. I bet I'm faster than he is.

My right shoe slips on shiny porcelain, and I land hard on the bathroom floor. My ankle explodes with pain, and I cry out. I force myself to take deep, slow breaths. I can't fail now.

The repeated thumps tell me he is ramming the door with his shoulder. I stretch out my foot, but when I put weight on my ankle, the pain rebounds, shooting up my calf. I'm tamping down the scream, gritting my teeth and willing myself to be strong. If climbing hurts, running will be agony.

Silence. I hadn't accounted for the silence. The torch beam wobbles along the alleyway between the houses, and I know he's slinking towards the open window. The only consolation is I'm inside. He's not.

I shift my weight and haul myself up on my good leg. With a quick tug, the window is closed. Lock engaged. His face looms behind the textured glass, but he can't see me limping towards the bathroom door. Even if I open it, how would I get out of the house? He has the key.

I don't see the torch outside or any sign of light. I reckon on six seconds to slip out of the bathroom, three steps to the front door if my ankle will allow it. I can't tell if it's swollen, but sharp needles of pain tell me it's sprained.

My eyes squint as I try to penetrate the darkness. It seems as if the world has gone to sleep. Then a siren wails nearby and stops, like a scream swiftly choked.

He's outside somewhere, waiting for me to make the first move. A flash through the window and I duck again, waiting for shattering glass and a body worming through. But it's thunder rumbling in the distance, lightning glaring like a strobe.

The bar of light under the door reveals the shadow of two feet. 'Freya. I promise I won't hurt you, OK? Just open the door. *Please.*'

It goes quiet, save for the sound of my ragged breathing. There's no street sounds, no more sirens. Breathe, breathe, breathe...

He slams into the door and the shock sends me slamming into the sink, shampoo bottles totter and roll, and a jar of talcum powder spits out a white cloud of dust. My nostrils fill with it, and so do my lungs, and I'm coughing.

I smell gasoline and hear it slapping against the floor. Then the rasp of a lighter wheel. An emptiness swallows me and I feel deeply alone. Dad's face flashes though my thoughts.

'Stop gawking at the door, girl, and get your arse out.'

The persistent beep of the smoke alarm warns me not to delay. I grab all the towels I can find and place them under the door to stop the smoke. I've seen house fires fuelled by petrol cans burning persistently despite the hoses. Flames snaking up the curtains and charred rafters barely covering the bodies trapped below. As the bottom panel of the door glows and spits, I rush to the window and slide up the bottom sash.

My mind screams, *get out, get out, get out*.

I feel the sudden lightness of my body as I lift one leg, then the other, and haul myself over the sill. I hear something clatter to the floor behind me. My body cam. But there's no time to retrieve it.

55

FREYA

Rain bounces off a six-foot wall to my left, one I can't hope to scale. Beyond it is the drive. To my right is the garden. Pain leaches up from my ankle to my calf, but I no longer care. I've got to get out of here.

I hobble sixteen feet to the back corner of the house, rain soaking through my clothes. Then I drag myself as far as the swimming pool where steam rises off the surface and the return drains slosh and babble. An impenetrable boxwood borders one side, with no sign of the yawning hole I'd crawled through two days ago. I instinctively look over my shoulder at a black stretch of lawn, horror squeezing my lungs.

A shout stops me, but only for a second. I limp to the back wall and, using a rectangle of shadow as a blind; I slide back a fraction. Every movement is slow, like I'm running chest-deep in water and holding every breath. The bubble of fear in my chest expands into a balloon and my heart jackhammers. How much sedative had I given him?

After two long seconds of indecision, a beam lances through the darkness and stabs left and right. It seems to drift along the narrow passage between the wall and the garage. I stand and I raise my elbows vertically with the top of the wall. The cliff rolls down like an aeroplane escape slide and it feels as if someone has scooped the entrails from my body.

Kicking off with my good leg, I knee the summit and thud to the other side, landing in a spongy carpet of wet leaves. A flash of pain and I'm rubbing my ankle. Trees jolt in and out of my vision, and the cliffs bear down in front of me. Panic tells me I have to run, because crawling into a dark corner would be suicide.

I shuffle along a narrow trail that runs behind the houses, my ears ringing with cold. The ground ripples under me and I stumble over roots, my hair yanked back and forth and smelling of brine. Wind pummels the cliff edge, rain drilling into the top of my head. Fear drives me on, every muscle twitching and alert.

I risk a glance over my shoulder and the view along the cliff path gives a strange sensation of looking down a black tunnel. My feet skid off waxy pebbles and I try to grapple for the wall. Instead, I slide down on my backside into the mud, feet wedged against a boulder. I stay there, cradling my knees tightly.

A wash of torchlight arcs over my head and jabs the bushes in front. It circles back around and then downhill, as if there's a defined route I'd missed. No one is out walking or running at this time of night, and even if they were, they wouldn't hear my shouts over the wind.

I take my chance, shuffling my way past two more houses, walls higher this time and fortified with box hedges. The sky cracks with lightning and the earth tilts beneath my feet. I try to adjust my gait, but I fall face-down, feet tangled in wet grass. I shudder from the pain in my ankle, but more from frustration.

A whistle. I spin around. The stark lights of a house illuminate Miles on the path three houses away, torch jinking from side to side. A shout rips through the wind and the torch bobs and diminishes to a pinpoint.

The sea heaves and paws at the sand, throwing up a string of foam that coils around the groynes. As the shadows grow, so does my unease. I can't walk fast enough, blundering into thick shrubs, my shoes sliding downwards towards the cliff edge. Fractals of light flicker and curve through the twigs and I look up at buckling clouds. The shaggy crown of a nearby tree rattles in the wind, and somewhere in the distance, another siren.

I catch a glint of something in my peripheral vision and turn to chase it. Torchlight winks off the roof of a house and dips down the rear facade. He's less than twenty feet away.

Rain slants towards me, needling my face and neck, and before I can find cover, it becomes a thick curtain. The path ahead curls close to the boundary lines and there are six houses with walls of the same height. One wall juts out about four feet long at its length and not flush with the intersecting wall at its width. Enough for me to duck behind. Where the path narrows against the cliff edge, a slick mire of mud and water cascades towards the beach. It's my only chance to end this.

I look for a sturdy branch, but the darkness hides any such weapon. My body tenses as I hear Miles tramping towards me through the saturated shingle. He stops, places the torch on the summit of a wall. His face is buttery yellow in the cone of light. I'm hoping he's going to vault over, but he hoists himself up briefly, poised like a gymnast against a pommel horse. Through a window, he studies a couple on the couch, caught in the glare of their TV. If I run, any sound or sudden movement will expose me.

I'm less than fifteen feet ahead of him, yet he's searching over walls, expecting to find me hiding in the shadows. His torch isn't one of those heavy tactical types he could use as a weapon. Instead, it is a small pocket light with a powerful beam.

He drops back to the ground, feet hitting rock and creating a sequence of echoing cracks. One arm braced against the wall, his body appears depleted – as if the sedative is finally working.

I've never believed in much, despite Dad's entreaties to join him at church. But as the moon illuminates the straggle of a path leading down to the beach, I pray.

Please, God. Get him away from me.

The moon hangs above the horizon, its glower hidden behind the clouds. The only light that shudders along the narrow path beside me comes from his torch. I press my back into the shadows.

'Freya!' His shouts are getting louder.

But what he doesn't see is where the path has eroded, rainwater and mud sliding down towards the beach. The torrents have carved a wide channel which is bordered by a series of staggered boulders.

I take a breath. *Relax. Watch for shadows. Track your target.*

I bend my arm at the elbow and shift my weight forward. *Spread your feet. Breathe and hold.*

I jab my elbow into his stomach and he jerks backwards, gasping for breath, feet sliding for purchase. I lunge towards him, hand slamming up into his jaw. His head snaps backwards as my knee drives into his groin. I don't wait. I turn towards the rhythmic squeal of a police car and a baying fire engine, lights toggling on and off through the trees. I drag myself over a scrawny box hedge, shivering in the bracing sea air. A motion sensor cuts through the darkness as I tear through a tangle of branches towards the edge of the street.

Hands grapple, voices whisper. I'm shaking and suddenly cold. Someone winds a blanket around me and I start to cry, tears unspooling the past twenty-four hours out of me. I feel Jack's lips against my forehead, his hands cupping my head. I look up at him and he looks down at me, and I can see the softness in his face returning. He is here. I am safe.

There are two of us, exactly as we're supposed to be.

56

FREYA

A NURSE BUSTLES AROUND the bed and places a hand on my arm. It's 6.00 am and I can't believe I slept all night. There's nothing wrong with me, nor do I have any signs of smoke inhalation. The concussion puts me under their watchful scrutiny.

I look at Jack sleeping in the chair, and through the window, white clouds and a clear blue sky. The nurse tells me there's a police officer outside. She'd like to take a statement.

Jack asks her to give us a minute. By the tone of his voice, I'm expecting the worst.

'How are you feeling?'

'Better,' I say. 'Any news of Nian?'

I know by the way he stares down at his empty hands she didn't make it. He tells me the police found her behind the swings in a park at Canford Cliffs. She'd been strangled. The pain in my head is not as sharp as the one in my heart.

'I got a text from you saying you'd left me,' he says. 'I

panicked.'

'You mean Miles' text. He took my phone.'

Jack nods and tries to smile. 'When I got home, Trisha and Derek were standing outside our house with the police. Trisha's camera caught all of it.' He pauses and looks at the floor. 'I want to tell you something, something I should have told you months ago.'

'That you set me up.'

His head swings up and his eyes are sad. 'Please hear my side of the story. It was last October. I was sitting in the Brewhouse thinking of Kate, the last time I saw her. She twirled three times in that new dress you'd bought her and I told her how beautiful she looked. I kept wondering why I was so gutted after she left. I thought it was because she was a woman, not a girl any longer, all grown up and different. Now I realise what that feeling was. Premonition. So while I was in the pub, crying in my beer, Miles came over. We ordered another round and had a laugh or two. We got to talking about fidelity. I told him you and I had always been faithful and, in my arrogance, I agreed to toss a coin. I was drunk. Blind stupid drunk.'

The silence hangs there as if we've run out of words. My mind is a fug of horror and grime, and I shrink back into the pillows.

'The surveillance report,' I say. 'Were you having me followed?'

'No. I'd never seen it before.'

The enormity of Miles' deception spins around in my mind

as the silence lies thicker and thicker in the air. Jack's furrowed brow tells me how sorry he was not to have been there to protect me. Tears sting the back of my eyes because I've betrayed him ten times over.

For months, I assumed Miles had moved on. My fling with him had been a brief distraction from my grief, but it had also been a misnomer. He was the sickest part of my healing.

The thing that frightens me the most is that Miles went to work every day, smiled, laughed, dated Jessica, and somehow she and Elisabeth had overlapped. Yet there was nothing about him to show deceit or violence.

'I didn't tell you this because I didn't want to worry you. But Patti called me a few times. Kept pressing me for any information on Edward. I met her and a detective from the Major Crimes Investigation Team for lunch. Told them everything I knew, which was nothing. It's always the husband, isn't it?'

It was the day I'd followed him to Moose Kitchen. The only reason I didn't recognise the back of Patti was because her hair was loose and not tied up as it usually is.

A knock on the door and Patti walks in. I know the sequence of events leading up to Miles' death is hard to prove and the link between us is complex. The stalking notes I've accrued have helped me, as did evidence of my items in his house.

'Glad to see you looking better,' she says, approaching the bed.

'Thank you for everything.'

'Don't thank me, thank an anonymous witness who brought Edward Besant's laptop to the station. After the house burnt down, it was all we had.' She sucks in her bottom lip for a few seconds. 'I wanted you to know that Nian was killed soon after she was abducted. So his threat to you about cutting... was a moot point. According to Elisabeth Sanders' diary, there was guilting and stonewalling and threats on her life. The day before she went missing, her phone pinged a tower in Durley Chine. She'd made two calls to her mother and a WhatsApp message to a friend. After that, nothing. We know from the coroner, Elisabeth's body exhibited significant levels of sedatives. We suspect we'll find the same with Nian Zhen. I can't imagine what you went through. It must have been frightening.'

I swallow. Can't manage a nod.

'We found Saroyan's body at the bottom of the cliff. Perhaps you can tell me what happened?'

My throat goes dry and scratchy, and I feel a sob building in the back of my throat. I wish I could have given her my body camera, but it is all burned to ash. Even my stalking log and my mother's earrings, and Elisabeth's pink phone.

I tell Patti everything I can remember, from being drugged and dragged to his car to being locked up in the darkroom. The cliff path, the mudslide, the pelting rain. The rest is a blackout, a curtain stubbornly pulled closed. I detect the faintest flicker of sympathy. She races through a description of women who'd come into contact with Miles, many of whom he'd met on dating sites while posing as a celebrity journalist. Liv's trainee reporter, Sara Farouq, has now confirmed Miles was her stalker.

'Saroyan had been injecting black tar heroin since his teens,' she says. 'Should have fried his brain. I showed Trisha Miller a photo and she confirmed he was the man who broke into her flat. Trisha wasn't selling weed. She was selling fillers, herbs of some kind. It's dangerous, like giving an alcoholic more tonic than gin. Apparently she met him at The Vault one night. He bought her a few drinks, but that's all she can remember – her words, not mine.

'I'd also like to mention Arthur. He overheard his mother talking to a car rental company and how they wouldn't give her the information she needed. So he took a bus to the police station and showed an officer the photos he'd taken. Saroyan had been stealing cars for a few months and disposing of them before we could track him. He drives a Jeep Wrangler. It's been in his garage since the time of your accident.'

I remember the car now, sitting outside Liv and Theo's house. Two mellow headlights. Nothing unusual. Then suddenly, my wing mirror was ablaze from the glare of halogen lamps. He must have turned them on only seconds before we were rammed, causing me a flash of blindness from which I'd had no time to recover.

'I don't need to remind you about the stalking laws,' she says. 'Getting tangled up in a murder investigation doesn't give you the right to do my job or attempt to. Or involve a neighbour in some hare-brained scheme to find a killer. None of us should go after perpetrators vigilante-style. He could have killed you.

'When you leave the hospital, Freya, I advise the back door to avoid newspaper and television reporters. I hope you feel better soon.'

57

Seven Weeks Later

AUTUMN HAS SLIPPED INTO winter, and the leaves are crisp and brown. Dr Meyer says I'm making progress, smiling more, laughing a little louder. Getting through those first few days were not my biggest problem. It was the nights, long hours that brought it all back.

Even though I suspected Miles and I shared the same therapist, it's still a shock to find that we had. Dr Meyer has since provided me with insight about dissociative identity disorder without mentioning the name of his client. He said that two personalities may not be diametrically opposed and the fragmentation isn't always clear. In this particular case, the two personalities often merged and Dr Meyer had no idea to whom he was talking.

Patti Franchek told me to write everything down in a notebook, with special emphasis on how I escaped. Because I'm a survivor, and that part is the most crucial. I took everything that reminded me of Miles and burnt it. All that silent guilt burnt to ash.

The nightmares are less frequent now and I've stopped replaying it all in my head. I attend a small support group in Poole and we share a little more every week. Going deeper. Trusting.

Today, Jessica sits on my left. I study dark hair, once sleek and tied into a chignon, now short and fashionably shaggy. She crosses her legs, both hands clamped around one knee. She tells us how angry she is that she hadn't seen the signs. When I look back at the company parties, at Aynur's palpable hatred, shrugging Miles' hand from her shoulder when he tried to flirt, I'm angry too.

After Jess finishes speaking, there are a few seconds of silence. I hear a hairpin hitting the hardwood floor and I flinch. The scars of abuse never go away. You can trace them with a finger if you know where to look.

To my right sits Elisabeth Sanders' mother, Jayne. She whispers the word "courage" and I take my cue. Raising my hand, all faces turn to me. I want to tell them how I feel now that it's all over, but mostly I have good news.

'You asked me last week if I'd forgiven Jack. As ridiculous as it was to barter me up to another man, he had no idea it would end in kidnapping. His deleted calls were a cry for help to Liv, the one person who knew us well enough to give an impartial opinion – someone who loved me as much as Jack.

'Apparently, Miles Saroyan had another identity – someone called Edward. Where Miles looked up to Edward, Edward despised Miles, referring to him as "The Lodger". When I look back, I wonder if there was any moment where he gave himself away. The police found a bug under our couch and a video camera in the bathroom light switch. He was also monitoring my phone through a spyware app. Elisabeth's death had no connection to Kate's and I've accepted it. The DC told me they're re-opening his father's case, so there's some good in all of this. The best part is I'll be assisting our crime reporter now.'

A clap ripples through the room and then evolves into cheers. I find comfort in their support. I know my life has spiked between doubt and being doubted – but mostly, I have won through.

After Jack and I had given our statements at the police station, he reminded me of a death row inmate, a caved-in chest and sadness that underlies it. He reached for me and I paused for a second, then put my arms around him. I felt the pain swell inside me, ready to tear me open. There's a long road ahead and we're both taking one step at a time.

Arthur comes to stay every other weekend and Trisha says it's a bit like sharing custody with an ex. She and Derek have moved in together. I've said nothing about watching her drug deals or the photographs I took. One day, I'll tell her, when she's in a good mood. Maybe a little stoned.

She and I have formed a band. She plays the bodhrán while I attempt to slur into the beat on my violin. We've got a few gigs at The Cricketers Arms next month, and there'll be dancing and a fair bit of drinking.

In my quiet times, I try not to think about that night. My lungs taut behind a jutting wall and fingernails split from clawing wood and brick. When all that fear ebbed into rage, words cleaved through me like a hatchet: *I can do this, I can do this, I can do this.*

I could hear his footsteps, his shoes sliding in the mud and clipping against pebbles. He was better equipped than me. For all I knew, he could walk this route blindfold. My elbow swung parallel to the ground, and in those seconds before bone struck flesh, I wanted him to die. He teetered, hands grappling for me. It was not a sharp drop, an acute angle that required more propulsion than someone losing their footing. A run-up with all the strength I had in my body, a battering ram I'd nurtured from hours lifting weights and running on the beach. He slipped backwards in the mud where the land sheered away to cliffs, arms flailing at the sudden loss of gravity. I heard a grunt and then a gasp as he tried to capture every last drop of air. His eyes found mine, fingers clawing the air, reaching for me. Gravel clattered, then the gust of a scream.

A snap. *Branch or bone?*

I was scared he was half-hanging on to a tuft of grass or caught in the crook of a branch. When I looked over the edge, his moonlit face was pitched skyward, limbs stamped into the earth like a ghastly swastika. I don't know how long I stood before crumpling to the ground, giddy and light. I remember the sea blazed with moonlight, waves sweeping up the beach and coiling into shallow pools of glossy black seaweed.

The following day, an article in the *Daily Echo*:

Police investigating a man's death on Alum Chine Beach

By Andrew Martin

Editor

Police are investigating the unexplained death of Miles Edward Saroyan, a thirty-five-year-old reporter at *The Daily Echo*, in Bournemouth.

Officers were called to reports of a man's body seen at the foot of the cliffs on Alum Chine beach by the ambulance service shortly after 9 am on Saturday morning, 9 November. A police cordon has been put in place.

A Dorset Police spokesperson said: At this time the death is being treated as unexplained. Saroyan's next of kin are yet to be informed.

It took four more days before another report stated that while the Dorset Police did not respond to requests for comment, evidence links Miles Saroyan to the death of his father Lionel Edward Saroyan, formerly ruled a suicide in 1997, and to Elisabeth Sanders whose body was found on Alum Chine beach on Tuesday 15th October. The death of reporter Kitty Arnold in 2018 and Nian Zhen last month are pending further investigation.

———◦———

It's cool today, the world looks clean and shiny under a blue sky. Aynur and I carry a wreath between us of hydrangea and delphinium.

The falcon lifts from Kate's windowsill and circles above me as we walk along the street. When we reach the beach, there are hikers and dog-walkers. Not many. The sea gleams, a calm sheet of pale green glass and the air smells of Ambre Solaire. I sense a change of energy, the sensation that I'm rushing towards something new.

When I look at the beach huts, I don't think of Elisabeth there. She is the tern that plunges for sand eels or the oily cormorant that suns itself on a groyne. Kate is not underwater. She is the moonlight on empty streets or bright laugher in a room. Nian is not in a park. She is warm sunshine and ice cream.

At the water's edge, a woman, brave enough to strip down to

a one-piece swimsuit, stands in the surf, friends goading her to swim. Her dimpled thighs are pale, and around her short hair is a multi-coloured headband. She's brave.

We're standing at Elisabeth's memorial site, where flowers burst through the sand and her family is singing *Amazing Grace*. We set out wreath down with the others and stand back to admire the colours. Aynur threads her arm through mine and lays her head against my shoulder. An old dormant peace comes awake in my body and I feel safe again.

'It's a good day for a paddle, Aynur. Last one in the water's a sissy.' I take off my shoes and roll up my jeans.

We run down to the sea until we're ankle deep, our toes sinking in the sand and cursing the cold. A bird shrieks and we both look up at the same time. The falcon skims parallel to the surface of the sea, wingtip almost touching the water. Then it banks towards the pier until the shape becomes a small grey dot, and all we can hear is a distant cry.

Today's a good day, a healing day.

Tomorrow will be an adventure.

Acknowledgments

I can't believe this is my tenth novel. If you've read this far, thank you for being here. Many thanks, too, to reviewers, bloggers, librarians, bookstores, and bookstagrammers and the book world of authors. What an exciting and supportive community. I loved working with developmental editor David Imrie on our first book together. Thank you for helping me navigate it all. It's a pleasure working with you.

Extreme gratitude to Sandra Mangan, editor and journalist. Thank you for your insights. To former St Martin's Press editors Dana Isaacson and Holly Ingraham, including Brenda Copeland, for being a fabulous cheerleader. To Kathy and my friends in P2P for their incredible support and BETA reads. To my classmates at Curtis Brown Creative, Graham Bartlett, police advisor, and the amazing Eve Seymour, Jericho Writers. To my fellow authors who have guided me and inspired me. Heartfelt thanks to the famous five: USA Today and NY Times bestselling authors Kristin Gleeson, Jean Gill, Babs Morton and Jane Harlond. What a great team!

A special shout-out to Paula and Kent Wynne at PageTurner for selecting *No Good Lie* as the winner for the Writing Award for Fiction in 2021. To my father, who studied under CS Lewis and gave us the joy of books. To my twin brother Mark Stibbe, multi-award-winning and bestselling author for always being so upbeat in a crisis, and to big brother Giles Stibbe for telling me never to let the bastards grind me down. To my husband Jeff, the love of my life, whose support means the world to me. To my coffee buddy and son Jamie. The laughs we have are priceless. And to my darling Edward. You sweet, cuddly thing. If it's not your idea, then it doesn't happen.

Thank you for reading. I hope you enjoyed *No Good Lie*.

About the Author

Claire Stibbe is the winner of the 2021 Page Turner Award for Fiction and a prolific novelist. Today, she writes dark, domestic suspense novels that draw on her experiences as a survivor of domestic abuse. Her aim is not just to tell gripping stories but to inspire other survivors to find freedom and independence.

Claire worked as an Executive Assistant for twenty years in both London and the Far East, including working for a Prince, for chartered surveyors, ship brokers, marine consultants, and hotel and catering. She now devotes herself full-time to writing and her novels owe much to her years as a member of the Albuquerque Police Citizen's Academy where her main focus was the impact of violence towards women and their families.

Claire now lives in Utah with a pilot husband and a method actor son, and her cat, Edward, who sleeps on her desk while she writes. She is addicted to reading and sharing the crime fiction love.

Made in the USA
Coppell, TX
07 November 2024

39823058R00256